the things we don't see

531 886 58 4

ABOUT THE AUTHOR

Savannah Brown grew up in a small town in Ohio and currently lives in London, England. She's the author of a collection of poetry called *Graffiti*, which was a finalist in the Goodreads Choice Awards. When she isn't writing, she can usually be found watching conspiracy theory documentaries, making faces at her cat or worrying. *The Truth About Keeping Secrets*, her first novel, was published in 2019. *The Things We Don't See* is her second novel.

savannah brown

the things we don't see

PENGUIN BOOKS

PENGUIN BOOKS

UK | USA | Canada | Ireland | Australia
India | New Zealand | South Africa

Penguin Books is part of the Penguin Random House group of companies
whose addresses can be found at global.penguinrandomhouse.com.

www.penguin.co.uk
www.puffin.co.uk
www.ladybird.co.uk

First published 2021
001

Text copyright © Savannah Brown, 2021
The moral right of the author and illustrator has been asserted

Set in 10.5/15.5pt Sabon LT Std
Typeset by Jouve (UK), Milton Keynes
Printed and bound in Great Britain by Clays Ltd, Elcograf S.p.A.

The authorized representative in the EEA is Penguin Random House Ireland,
Morrison Chambers, 32 Nassau Street, Dublin D02 YH68

A CIP catalogue record for this book is available from the British Library

ISBN: 978-0-241-34632-7

All correspondence to:
Penguin Books
Penguin Random House Children's
One Embassy Gardens, 8 Viaduct Gardens,
London, SW11 7BW

PART ONE

Who is She if Not Everyone Else's?

PART ONE

Who's Sick Now: Diagnosed with...

HOW TO DISAPPEAR
Episode 21

Narrator: The year is 1986, and if my demographics are anything to go by, you're not there.

I'll set the scene: Reagan is president. DNA was just used for the first time in a criminal investigation. *Challenger* exploded over Cape Canaveral in January. Chernobyl, just after that. But, hey – the previous March, 'We Are The World' became the fastest-selling single in pop history.

The year is 1986 and the sleepy island of Sandown Bay is waking up.

To its nearly two hundred year-round residents, Sandown is its own self-contained world – to the rest of us, and to its seasonal visitors, it's a miniscule island situated two miles off the coast of the Delawarean mainland, just past the end of the estuary of Delaware Bay.

Sandown Bay began as a sailors' port, then, towards the turn of the twentieth century, became a food and drink tourism destination, known for an unmatched abundance of the Delaware Blue Crab; nowadays, Sandown is home to fifteen bars and pubs and no hospital. There's one school for twenty-one students aged six to eighteen. One grocery store. One bank. One funeral home. A ferry travels to and from the island year-round, trips running every two hours in the summer. In the past, you could drive a quad bike across the frozen Atlantic – granted the winter was cold enough, which it hasn't been for the past two decades.

To an outsider, the small population and eccentricities of life are cited with incredulity. Claustrophobia. How could anyone live this way? But the residents would tell you they find it the most natural thing in the world. Or, they might, once you got them to talk.

Brought together by their unique circumstances and love of Sandown, the sense of community on the island was – and remains – impenetrable. Which is why, given the mystery it would later become shrouded in, no one seems to have anything to say.

The year is 1986 and a young woman named Roxy Raines steps into the warm August night and is never seen again.

CHAPTER 1

FRIDAY 28 MAY

The morning ferry leaves at nine and I've been in the parking lot since six, watching the sun unfurl its first pinkish tendrils over the Atlantic, which is wide and vulnerable and, despite appearances, not actually blue.

Departure time's approaching now but I'm still the only one here. Directly to my left is a small booth with an unmanned window, like a drive-through, covered in peeling white paint and with an indigo awning that reads TICKETS; to my right, a larger information centre framed by rickety benches and yellow-tipped ferns; ahead, the empty dock. I know the place is quiet because it's still early, but the lack of noise feels more like abandonment than inactivity. I'm the ghost of the pier.

In the far distance, there's the illuminated strip of land pressed against the horizon, thin as a strand of hair. That's where I'm going.

This is what I'm saying about the ocean: it's blue because of what it reflects rather than what it absorbs, as in, water molecules absorb the red and orange and yellow waves of light and reflect the blue, as in, the ocean is blue because blue is the only colour it's not. This is true of everything. Not to mention the steps that occur in the brain to even perceive colour in the first place.

I'm simplifying things, of course, and anyway, I'm probably wrong.

There's a prickle on the back of my neck and I turn, but nothing stirs. Behind is a quiet trailer park, patchy grass like an afterthought on top of the bone-dry lot. I'm under-stimulated. I tune my ears on to the radio.

. . . and a high of ninety-one. Whew! Heard reports just today that hurricane season's comin' early this year, the first storm predicted possibly as soon as mid-June, and it's looking like a doozy, folks, so . . .

And then the speck of the ferry first appears along the curve of the earth, the natural spotlights casting across it like some inviolable holy direction.

I stare at the morsel for as long as I can without blinking and count. One minute seven. One minute fifty-four. My longest is two minutes thirty and by then the ferry's grown to the size of my fist, close enough to make out the details: it's shaped sort of like a heron's head, an elongated lower bill and raised skull with seating and a windowed cubicle for the captain. There are no other passengers, as far as I can see. A faded American flag sags heavily against its helm, wilted in the windless summer-cusp heat.

The ocean spreads beyond me, infinite, like I'm at the edge of everything.

My phone vibrates in the cup holder.

> **Dad:** I'm glad you're safe but I need to
> know where you are. I worry that
> there'd be no way of knowing if
> something were to happen.
> Text/call. – Dad

Him signing 'Dad' makes my stomach ache. Obviously unnecessary and sweet at once. Zaps some humanity into the words. Of course it's you, Dad, and of course you're right. I imagine him as he probably is, faintly reeling, which isn't difficult to do because I've seen it before, only once; the dark shadows of his trail-run face collapsed, heavy grey brow stitched, eyes split and searching. And truly, how *could* I do this to him? It's the reasonability of his request that bothers me. I know I'm wrong. But this is the only way to become a synapse-trace, a nowhere girl.

I said it all already.

> **Me:** I won't be back for at least a few
> weeks. I promise I'm safe, and that
> this isn't anything like Celeste,
> obviously. This is very important.
> I promise I wouldn't be doing it if it
> weren't.

And then the frenzy in the middle of the night, zooming down the Virginia turnpike: the phone ringing and ringing

7

and ringing without an answer or even a declining to show there was something alive on the other end. Declining would've made the choice too intentional. My justification was that I'd already said the kicker, which, to me, is all that matters. *This isn't anything like Celeste.*

Or maybe *I'm safe* isn't enough. How could he not feel my absence the same way? Both of us here one moment and gone the next.

My decision came from a combination of things. Less urgently, it was the desire to know how the leaving felt, to drive away, age seventeen, and savour the sting of the tether finally snapping against my back after years of pulling, pulling, pulling – a promise to myself that I'm captaining an autonomous vessel capable of vanishing into the night if only it could muster up the courage to floor the gas. More urgently, I knew I wouldn't get a chance like this again, a corrosive mixture of a lack of responsibility, obligation, achievement and peace. Maybe I'm overdue something good. I didn't lie: this is very important.

This isn't only not like Celeste, or *despite* Celeste – it's because of her. For her. She's due something good too. Dad would never understand this. To be honest, it's difficult to articulate, even to myself, why this whole endeavour is a running-towards, not away. Towards atonement. Towards peace.

Towards Roxy.

In a different way, towards Celeste.

I didn't even think Dad would realize I was gone so quickly. *Shit*. I press into the jelly of my eyes with my

8

middle fingers until my vision's lousy with stars, and jab in another reply.

> **Me:** I promise you. No danger. I just
> know that you would come and get
> me and that really can't happen yet.
> I love you! I'm sorry.

I shut my phone off. I realize I've been sucking on the same gutted sunflower seed for the past ten minutes, maybe, and my tongue is eroded and sore from salt. I open my car door a crack and spit the shell on to the pavement, then shut my eyes and listen to the sea.

Soon the lull of the waves is sliced by the blare of a foghorn, impossibly loud; for all I know the ferry's teleported here, up against the sharp of the dock. It lurches to a halt. A pair of deckhands rope the thing tight and the gate falls open.

An older man emerges from the captain's deck, says something to the deckhand, and makes his way off the boat and into the booth I'm parked next to. I roll down my window.

'You're raring and ready, eh?' he says with a voice about as gravelly as I anticipate.

'Pretty much.'

'Car ticket?' he asks, and up close I can see the texture of his face, rough with sun damage. He's got a wild head of white hair poking from beneath a red cap emblazoned with a Sandown patch. Dense and unruly beard to match.

Nose thick with cartilage, small eyes peeking from a hooded brow.

'Yeah, but I'm a Seasonal, so should be free.'

'Seasonal?' He performs a laboured pivot towards the back of the hut, where there's a crossed-to-date calendar hung on a nail. 'You're early.'

The past twelve hours flash before my eyes, of another plate-scraping dinner and packing and gone, driving away from Indiana like it's the easiest thing in the world. Blurry highway bokehs. Seventies classic radio. I'm not even tired. 'Just eager.'

'Mmph.' He drags a clipboard towards him that rattles against the counter. 'Name?'

'Mona Perry.'

'You got identification, Mona Perry?'

I fish my driver's licence out of my back pocket and slide it across.

There's a beat while he scrutinizes, and I worry he can tell it's a fake, but he's not looking at my birthday, the 2002 where there should be a 2004. The picture. His small eyes shrink. 'This ain't you.'

If he's only teasing, it's lost on me. 'It is.' And I smile like I'm smiling in the photo, baring teeth like an angry chimp, unmistakable because of the gaps between them and the way my canines sit elevated in my gums. Dad used to joke that he'd always be able to identify me by my teeth – makes more sense upon the discovery that he's a sick-minded state counsel – but then stopped once that joke was no longer funny. Less funny after we could only wish there was a Celeste to identify. Less funny after I started dodging the nannies and driving out into Indianapolis late at night aged fifteen-and-a-half with only my temporary licence, nowhere to go and nothing to do except make trouble. This was always enough to bring Dad home, at least for a bit.

Anyway, I never got my teeth fixed.

'Your hair's different.'

This is correct. My licence says it's blonde; in the photo it's down to my elbows. Now it's dark brown and barely brushes my chin, with bangs accidentally cut about an inch too short. The dye is so fresh it's still bleeding on to my clothes, and I keep reaching for phantom lengths to pick through. I shrug.

The ferry master, whose badge tells me his name is Frank, tires of the inspection and hands me a laminated ticket from his moneybox. 'Well, stick that on your dash and you're good to go, I guess. Still ain't leaving till nine.'

'I know. That's fine.'

'All right.' He gives my ID one last quizzical look then returns it. 'I like it better blonde.'

So did Dad, which was unusual, as he never expresses any opinion towards me about anything. 'You know what,' I say, 'I do too.'

I accelerate before he can respond, down the gentle slope and through the ferry's yawning gates. Forward until my bumper nearly dings the far railing. Park and stall my engine. Here, I have an uninterrupted view of the journey: two miles of sea that will take a little less than a half-hour to traverse, if the website is right – which it ought to be, given this same trip has been taken thousands and thousands of times.

It's a straight shot, direct to her.

I might as well be eye-locked with Pandora's box and the urge to dig my fingernails under the lid and *pull* is already unbearable.

I swear my phone buzzes again but there's nothing when I check, so I slide the pamphlet off my dash. The cover bears a group of grinning college-age kids in polos and bandanas and sunglasses, punctuated by a bubble-font title: 'Welcome, Seasonals!'

Page one contains the information about the employment programme that I already know. It's a mutualistic swapping of perks: simply for some easy labour, you and a bunch of other tanned and smiley people get free run of an island, a bed to sleep in and some pocket change. The applicant pool is largely made up of students in the tri-state area looking for a free vacation. I researched everything. Lurked on the forums. I made myself the perfect imaginary candidate on the application forms: over eighteen, retail and food service experience. Turns out there's nothing easier than lying. The best jobs are at the bars but I knew with my baby-face I'd never pass for twenty-one. This was the deal I'd formally signed up for. And I was fine doing the work, because it was necessary to achieve something else: full immersion. Not just a front-row seat, but my show.

The last page has an itinerary. There's a bonfire tomorrow night where the Seasonals are meant to mingle, more activities over the weekend to get settled, and then everyone starts work on Monday.

I plan to start work right away.

Without the car's air conditioning the heat is already settling thick on my skin; cold sweat pinches the back of my neck and the windscreen is angling the sunlight into my eyes, like a magnifying glass cooking an ant. I get out to avoid the glare, lock my car and traipse up to the top deck via a rickety spiral staircase. Up here, the whole thing opens out, and I move to the railing, grip its edge and lean over as far as I can bear before I worry about falling and let my gaze travel over the indigo water to the jagged brown sliver at the break in the sea. Even from miles out it's easy to see the way Sandown Bay is split in two: there's the flattened half of civilization where the tourists visit and the islanders live, and then it's the peaks of the trees, deep green and tall, and this goes up and up and up until the incline swells into a mass of rocky cliffs towards the north. Though it's split in two, it's not split in half; the woods win. They own fourteen of the island's fifteen square miles, a largely untouched remnant of the past that probably would have looked the same in the 1800s as it does now. Same trees. Same Atlantic Ocean lapping at their feet. No point developing your island's natural scenery when everyone comes to your island for the exclusive draw of cheap booze.

The foghorn blares again and I jolt. The ferry lurches forward.

The view had distracted me and only now do I notice the smattering of people who have joined me on the top deck. A twenty-something couple slathers sunscreen on to each other; a group of middle-aged women in floppy sunhats cackle at something, maybe already sloshed; a family with young kids sits within the shade of the canopy. No one that looks like a Seasonal, as far as I can see. This is good; there's power in being the first.

From above, the island of Sandown Bay looks a bit like a misshapen person. This designation is understandable if not hugely accurate, but if someone were to point it out to you, you might say, *Oh yes, that does look like a person, and Louisiana is a boot*, and maybe everything actually looks like something else. All of us in a constant state of forced pareidolia, where if you stare at a mass of rustling leaves for long enough you might find a face; where if you stare at a Sandown Bay pamphlet long enough with its sort of vague, saturated pleasantness, you might see yourself there too.

The main ferry dock is situated on the southern half – that's the part that looks like a head. Then there's this long isthmus that stretches off, which is why one might say 'misshapen' – it's a neck, sure, but ghoulish, but too long and thin to be human. Then two stout, branching cliffsides for arms, and around mid-torso is where the woods begin and stretch and stretch and stretch.

I need to know all this because there can't be a learning curve, because anything could be a clue; knowing anything could unlock a door. Anywhere could hide answers. Anyone could hide bones.

I lean forward again, let the fear of it burn my ears to red; there's something pleasurable about the thin line of pain digging underneath my ribs from the rail, about the beads of sweat prickling my forehead, born to steamed in barely a second.

Roxy's name tumbles around in my head. 'Glass Daughter' slips past my lips without my thinking about it; barely a hum, only the notes, sound overpowered by the whirr of the ferry but the song is there and living.

> Eyes stare
> Oh, when a million eyes stare
> Who is the woman they see there?
> What of the life spread on display?

I fish my headphones from my back pocket and jam them into my ears and play the rest of the song. It's Roxy's voice, so seductively rough and full-bodied, that makes her music. Iron-clad. So not-delicate, so everything-in-the-room that sometimes she barely sounds like a girl at all – but she's only nineteen in this recording, just two years older than me. It's almost impossible to believe. Even then she never called herself a girl. Rightfully so; she had the voice of a thousand lifetimes lived. I can't get enough. Neither can the rest of the cult following.

Neither could Celeste.

> She's lost
> Oh, when they all learn that she's lost
> They'll pick out the letters that she crossed
> out when she gave them her name

Though even Roxy's not enough to totally quell the crackle of nerves in my gut. Stimulus.

On my phone I navigate on to Twitter and I search the hashtag for *How to Disappear*.

The announcement of my hiatus dropped like a bomb. The podcast doesn't have the biggest following, but enough people listen to justify it as a semi-fruitful endeavour.

I'd posted a short screenshot-explanation before I left yesterday. Melodramatic, sure, and it was all very in the moment so I hadn't read it back, but it got the point across.

When I started creating these accounts, I was doing so in pursuit of truth. Now, looking back at the years of episodes – I'm not sure I've accomplished anything I set out to. What's the point of any of this if there aren't any answers? Any conclusions? Who am I even talking to? Who am I helping?

What is the point? . . . Is anyone there?

This summer I'm taking on my biggest story yet. Episodes will halt while I dedicate the next three months (maximum) to uprooting my life to reanimate the cold case of someone whose disappearance has interested me for a long time. I ask that you be patient with me until I'm back.

Basically: please know there's no universe where I come back with nothing. I'm going to find out what happened to her. An entirely new experience for us all. Isn't that something!

See you at the end of the summer.

Thanks, CAP

When I checked my phone at the first gas station in Ohio I hadn't expected the excitement online. People were buzzing. Unusual, I assumed, for a so-called amateur crime writer to go to a scene themselves; amidst all this false, detached and saccharine empathy, I was going to do something real and good.

I couldn't tell anyone why, though, of course. Why it was *this* case specifically. Too close. Too personal. I hoped no one would question it.

I scroll through the hashtag.

Maybe it's someone she's already covered?

this is LOW-KEY scary and real i hope she's gonna be OK

Anyone think she might be going to that island in Delaware, where that singer went missing? Seems accessible, and i think CAP mentioned her before.

My heart skips but I quickly see there aren't any replies.

Above me, the sun beats down like a promise, the ferry picking up speed now, my hacked hair whipping across my face. Sandown Bay grows and grows and grows until I can make out the pier, the boardwalk, each tree, each leaf.

Roxy, I say to the wind, the sea, the trees staring back in the distance. *All I want from you is Roxy.*

She is nothing but everyone else's
Who is she if not everyone else's?

HOW TO DISAPPEAR

Episode 21

Narrator: Your first need-to-know about Roxy Raines is that she was a musician. A singer-songwriter whose lyrics tended towards the narrative – very little I or ego, bounding with natural imagery. A Spotify cut of her first album, *Glass Daughter*, was re-released in the early 2010s and subsequently developed a cult following, thanks to her unusually modern sound.

['Glass Daughter' plays quietly in the background.]

Those who knew her say she hated being photographed; in the few images that exist, there's a certainty to her beauty almost too obvious to mention. And in every picture, there's her rose-painted guitar slung over her back, attached like a limb. Or maybe, because of her inability to connect with others, a cord that fastened her to the rest of the human race. Or, rather, something lodged – a wedge that only pushed her further away.

That same guitar would be found two days after her disappearance on the first of September 1986, waterlogged after being fished from the bay.

Roxy had planned to move to Nashville the week after she disappeared.

That night she'd been performing her last set at The Indigo Lounge, her favourite haunt on Sandown.

She was twenty.

And this is all anyone knows of the night. At least from information that can be taken from the internet. But of course there's someone who knows more – knew *her*. It's just a matter of finding them.

And I was there, in the thick of it, surrounded by the only people in the world with the knowledge to break the whole thing open.

CHAPTER 2

The ferry docks with a sickly lurch. A screaming mob of seagulls hail our arrival, hovering overhead with the floaty aimlessness of kites. Because I was the first to board I'm also the first off, and I start on to the island, the ferryman catching my eye from the harbour with an unreadable blankness as I do.

As a consequence of the hours spent digitally cataloguing the island, I'm struck by the celebrity of the place; this is the same dock I'd virtually walked along, the same oaks lining the run-up, the same covered queue, the same hill reaching up and on to the first main road. I drive underneath a sign hung on parallel lamp posts that reads WELCOME, SEASONALS!, draped with multicoloured bunting.

The pamphlet says to register at the bicycle and golf-cart rental desk so that's where I head; it takes all of ten seconds to find it, as it's the first thing there is to look at after traversing the hill. Most visitors leave their cars on the mainland and get around on the island via bike or golf cart so the placement makes sense.

I park in the lot surrounding the shed-like structure and get out, footsteps crunchy on the gravel. The air is an assaulting stink of gasoline and boiling leather seats and sunscreen.

There's movement from a shape behind the counter of the desk, but with the sun beating in my eyes, I can't make out from what; it's only when I'm five steps away that the shape becomes a boy. He hasn't heard me yet so I observe. Even though he's crouched with his back turned, fiddling with something in a box, the disproportions of his body are obvious: he's all limb, too long, too thin. When he turns, I realize this is probably due to a recent growth spurt – I don't think he's older than fifteen, full cheeks peeking from under tousled reddish hair. And especially not with the seemingly abject fear he projects when he sees me, like I'm an apparition. He springs backwards and nearly falls ass-first into the box, but anchors himself with a hand on the wall. I feel as if I've poked a worm that's promptly wound itself into an airtight pellet.

'Oh,' I say. 'Sorry. I didn't mean to scare you.'

The kid collects himself with a quick squeeze of his eyes but he's still hunching, either not realizing his own height or distinctly realizing and wishing he didn't take up so much space. The sharps of his shoulders are prevalent even through his blue polo shirt. 'I . . . It's OK,' he says in a voice that can't quite decide its pitch, peaky and only half-deepened. 'C-can I help you?'

Obviously he's nervous, but the way his words come out in pieces doesn't sound like strictly nerves. 'I'm a Seasonal. I need to check in.'

This inspires another bout of anxiety. 'M-Mom!' he yells, directing the call towards the barely open door that leads further inside the stand. He turns back to me and says, 'Registration doesn't start until t . . . t-tomorrow.'

I eye the pamphlet. 'Sorry, I must've got my days mixed up. Was hoping it wouldn't be too much of a problem.'

The boy's mouth is opening and shutting like a fish's blub, searching for something to say, when a woman emerges from the back door – same tawny hair and the same skin, pale and red-rimmed instead of tanned. She's wearing a T-shirt underneath a pair of loose olive green overalls and is pretty enough that she wouldn't look out of place in a lifestyle magazine. In a sort of classical way, too: face like a painting, high cheekbones and soft curves set off by a hard stoicism. Looks young to have a fifteen-year-old. Barely crow's feet. There's something familiar about her when she locks eyes with me. 'What's the ruckus?'

The boy and I both go to speak at the same time but I let him explain. 'She's a Seasonal. She w-wanted t-t-to check in.'

'Registration's not for another day,' the woman says to me with a sort of thoughtful, floaty inflection.

This riles the boy up again. 'I t-told her –'

'I know,' I say. 'He did tell me. I'm sorry – I think I got the dates wrong. I hoped it wouldn't be a problem.'

'Well,' the woman starts, 'it's not, really, it's just that the rooms still need to be cleaned.'

'I'm totally happy to wait,' I say. 'Or I can do it myself.'

The woman wrings a rag through her hands, inspecting me. 'You look tired, sweetie.'

I shift, uncomfortable that she's noticed, that I *look* like anything at all. 'Oh, no, I'm fine.' My eye's about to twitch. I blink hard.

'You're welcome to wait, then, but today's gonna be a cooker and I don't wanna leave you out in the heat. We're just helping out here at the moment but we run a little B and B on the island, rest of the time. How about I take you back there and you can lie down in one of the rooms, huh?'

The unbridled kindness of the offer rattles me and I don't know what to say. I shake my head, suddenly feeling a bit stupid, worried they can sense it.

'I'll show her,' the boy says.

'No,' his mom says, 'Ellis, you don't need to be –'

He grabs a jingly set of keys out from under the desk and pockets them. 'It's fine.'

I'm about to protest – I'd really rather start mapping out the island physically – but the promise of a bed has made me very aware of the heaviness of my body and maybe I am actually tired. My eyes seem to regress further in my head and my stomach churns sickly with nausea and hunger. I'm far from home. 'OK. That's – really nice of you. Thank you.'

Ellis lumbers away from the counter, towards the side door and out.

These people seem safe. I can't pinpoint why – maybe in the same way any regular floating scrap seems *safe* when one is lost at sea. 'Sorry,' I say, 'I wouldn't be able to get something to eat somewhere, would I?'

'Ellis can whip something up for you.'

Ellis shrugs. 'I m-make good eggs.'

The woman lowers her elbows on to the desk and holds her head in her hands. 'What's your name, sweetheart?'

'Mona.'

She extends a lithe hand to shake. 'Sylvia. I help with Seasonal affairs, accommodation and assignments and such, so I'm sure we'll be seeing a bit of each other.'

'Sure,' I say. Behind me, Ellis is already at my four-door. I thank her again and go.

Ellis and I pile into my car, him from the passenger's side, and I'm struck by a pang of embarrassment when he sees the mess of wrappers strewn across the seat – mints, mainly, and gum, to keep me awake, but also a few from some oatmeal cream pies I'd picked up at a gas station in Pennsylvania, as well as the half-full family-sized bag of sunflower seeds. I scatter the detritus across the floor in one mighty swipe. 'You didn't see this,' I say, as if re-concealing the man behind the curtain.

'Wow,' Ellis says, glancing at the back seat. 'You have a lot of bags.'

'Where are we headed?'

'Just up the road. It's b-barely a five m-m-m-m – gah. Short drive.' He glances back at his mom, who's still watching from inside the stand with a sort of warlike intensity.

'Cool. Thank you for doing this.'

'It's OK.'

I look to him and he's sullen, kind of, but there's a boyish good nature about it. I'm not even sure what he's actually upset about. 'I'm Mona,' I say.

'I heard.'

'You're Ellis.'

'Correct.'

'Are you all right?' I throw the car in gear and we inch out of the parking lot.

'Fine. Do you know where you're g-going?'

Yes. 'Sort of.'

'It's left up here. It's really easy to get the hang of since the whole island is b-basically one b-b-big road.' Ellis tells me more things I already know. The main road is called Sycamore and it connects the entire southern half of Sandown, the back of a millipede. If the island is a body then these are its tree-lined veins. 'There's a strip that connects the main part to the b-back and our place is just past it.'

'That's kind of nice for you guys, right? Out of the way of the main tourist stuff.'

'Yeah, it's pretty quiet. Not much back there b-besides the woods and some cabins.'

Early on, we pass the expanse of the island's airport, which is less an airport and more an expanse the size of two football fields with a couple of propeller planes parked in it.

'Have you lived here your whole life?' I ask.

'Kinda. I was b-born here – well, not on the island; the mainland, b-but you know – and we moved away when I was little. Then we came back when I was ten.'

'Interesting place to grow up.'

He slumps in his seat. 'Yeah. Interesting is a word for it.'

'Oh. Sore subject.'

'No, I like the p-place. I think it's p-pretty cool. Kinda small. I mean, really sm-small. Different, I guess. It's just the p-people.'

'Mm,' I say like I know what he means, and I want to say more to get him on side but am uncertain what the words might be.

'Their attitudes about stuff – it's like they're stuck twenty years in the p-past, you know?' He pivots to my backseat. 'Hey, can I have some of those sunflower seeds?'

'Knock yourself out.'

We reach the strip, barely big enough for the road it holds, the perimeter seeming to gradually break up the further it stretches to the sea – slate then rock then pebble. There isn't a cloud in the sky and the sun's reflection against each peak of the trembling ocean forces me to squint. There's something dizzying about the warm blue haze.

Ellis breaks the not-uncomfortable silence, punctuated only by the *thwip* of shell being spat out the window. 'My mom is really overprotective. That's why she was being weird. That's why I was annoyed. Sorry.'

'Do you have a habit of getting kidnapped by girls via Subaru?'

'N-no. I guess she just worries p-people will . . . judge me.'

'Why?'

'Probably b-because I'm so g-g-good-looking.'

I turn to him, eyebrows raised, but he breaks, a smile punctuated by teeth that look like they're fresh out of braces. Not often swayed by anything overly cheesy, I'm surprised to feel myself smiling back. 'Fine,' I say. 'You got me.'

'Sorry.'

'And do they? Judge you, I mean?'

'Sometimes.'

'I'm sorry that happens.'

He shrugs. 'Eh, it's whatever. Annoying. What can you do. Anyway. We're up on the left here.'

The white Colonial sits on what's probably an acre of land, well maintained – flower beds blotch the lot's boundaries; wilful little bursts of lavender and baby's breath and orchids. Above us, tidy rows of windows framed by black shutters and sycamore trees. Tinkle of a windchime. A dark wood sign at the entrance reads WILLOWWOOD INN.

'It's pretty,' I say. My car's the only one in the lot. 'No one staying?'

'Not right now. I mean, it's a B-B-B and B, so it's never actually that full anyway. There's only, like, five rooms. And tourist season's b-barely started.'

I follow him towards the entrance, up three stairs on to a patio that encircles the house. There are two rocking chairs framing either side of the door, which sit eerily still. Ellis unlocks the door. 'Come on in,' he says in a breathy, ironic way, and I do.

The lobby is shaped and furnished like a living room, with a sturdy red wood reception desk in the centre, a straightened row of pens and a heavy leather-bound book sitting on top beside a vase full of carnations that look one day away from becoming potpourri. Patterns everywhere: the walls are papered a dark forest green; the couches upholstered with sort of yellow tessellated bursts; a throw is draped over an armchair that is nauseatingly reminiscent of a seeing-eye puzzle. There's a lemony sweetness to the place that's pleasant if artificial. Mahogany too. A glossy black piano dominates the far corner.

'This place is like a time capsule,' I say, and it's an understatement. 'It's cute.'

'Yeah, I'm pretty sure it's looked like this forever. Anyway. You still hungry?'

'A bit,' I admit. 'But don't worry, you don't have to make anything.'

'For real, it's no b-biggie. Eggs and b-b-bacon?' Ellis moves beneath an archway into what looks like the kitchen.

My mouth waters. 'That's really nice of you,' I say, lowering myself on to one of the couches, and am swallowed by it in a way that threatens to put me to sleep. I think suddenly of home.

'Did you come from a long way away or something?' a disembodied Ellis calls, punctuated by the clattering of a pan.

'Why do you ask?'

'Well, my mom said you look tired. I didn't think you looked like anything.' He peeks his head back in. 'Not that you didn't look like *anything*, just not tired, I mean. I don't know. Mom notices that stuff. Anyway you also had enough food in your car to feed a sm-sm-small nation.'

'I left yesterday from Indiana.'

'Oh, wow. And you drove *all night*?'

'Mm.' There's a fireplace that's caught my attention, homey and intimate, adorned with framed photographs. An unsmiling woman cradles a baby in black and white. What looks like a toddler Sylvia, wearing only a diaper, waters the flowerbeds outside with a hose arching from her puffed belly.

'But you're early,' he says.

'You know what – I didn't want to be home any more. Couldn't wait.' It's honest.

'Oh.' Quiet. I worry I spoke too seriously, revealed something uncomfortable without saying the words. Then, 'That's cool, anyway. I can't wait until I can drive. I'll be able to get my temps in November. I wouldn't be able to here but you don't have to be as old in Michigan, so that's pretty cool.'

I toss my phone from hand to hand. 'Are you moving?'

'Yeah. End of the summer, pr-probably. Mom wants to sell this p-place.'

Ellis emerges from the kitchen with a plate of what was promised and sets it on the coffee table.

Having not eaten anything hot in probably more than twenty-four hours, I can barely express my thanks before I'm being drawn towards the plate by some sort of foodstuff magnetism. The eggs are silky and warm and practically dissolve in my mouth; the salt of the bacon makes my jaw clench, my mouth watering to the point of caution. It's hard to keep up the conversation while I eat, so mainly we don't, me gorging myself while Ellis cleans up in the kitchen.

The kindness of the whole situation has stirred something in me. Neither of them had any reason to do any of this. The thought soon becomes uncomfortable; I banish it.

After I eat, Ellis shows me to my room. There's a heavy pastoral quilt on the bed, a three-quarter-length set of windows, cracked, lace curtains floating in front of them. On the ceiling, a fan spinning too slowly to be generating any meaningful coolness. 'This is great,' I tell him. 'Thank you.'

'I'm gonna go back to help my mom, so just hang out here, sleep, whatever.'

I lower myself on to the bed, fighting the urge to burrow in immediately. 'Is it OK that I'm here by myself?'

He doesn't seem to understand. Blinks his round blue eyes. I want to live in his world, where everyone has the best of intentions. 'I mean, I can stay if you want. No one's gonna b-bother you or anything.'

'No, don't worry. Thanks for everything.'

After he leaves, I consider having an uninterrupted look around the hotel, but I'm unsure what kind of secrets there are to unearth in the Willowwood of all places; I decide the promise of time in a bed that isn't mine is too good to pass up on. I fish my earphones from my backpack and jam them in – play 'Kelly Green' by Roxy Raines – and bury myself under the stiff sheets, and I think of her. Dancing, blonde hair cascading up and around her as if moved by an intelligent wind. I imagine her in the bed with me. If she wrote this at nineteen, or even earlier, imagine what she could have done with more time. Sometimes I think I'm in love with her.

I'm out like a light.

This damn place has got her wondering
If you threw her in the sea,
Would she wash up in that same sweet kelly green?

HOW TO DISAPPEAR
Episode 21

Narrator: Besides Roxy's guitar found washed up on the shore, only two pieces of evidence remained: her car, a Chevy Camaro, left in the parking lot of The Indigo Lounge – and later, a so-called 'strange' note that hasn't been released to the public, which lays out some degree of intent, allegedly written by Roxy herself.

Though calling them 'pieces of evidence' isn't even quite correct.

Law enforcement never investigated her case with consideration for foul play. A suicide, or a runaway, or something more sinister – the truth of what had happened didn't seem to matter to anyone. Because she was so troubled, known for causing a ruckus, supposedly prone to disappearing spells anyway, nobody was concerned. Of course this happened to

Roxy, they might have said – the firecracker, the unpredictable loose cannon, the enigmatic spitfire.

A cool bolt of lightning as commanded by the universe, finally instructing a hot-blooded woman to sit.

Local apathy didn't do much to ward off the media circus that ensued – expected given the disappearance of someone talented and attractive and young – and although the spotlight on Sandown waned relatively quickly, the tourism industry never fully recovered and the eighties boom would eventually be regarded as its peak.

And perhaps the island's industry isn't the only thing that never recovered.

CHAPTER 3

When I wake up it's impossible to tell how much time has passed or if it's passed at all. Hot panic grips me, half because of the strange, harsh midday shadows from the restless trees, skittering in the breeze like quick beasts, and half because I've forgotten where on earth I really am. I recount the events from earlier in the day to make sure they have actually happened and I'm not watching a fake life flash before my eyes while I'm dashed across the Delawarean interstate.

It's warmer now. The thin sheets are saturated with sweat where I have lain unmoving and there's a gnat flying dizzy circles in the far corner. There's one word blinking in my mind: *untethered*. This settles the fear. I am no one, in an anywhere place. This is what I wanted.

I sense, now, two pairs of eyes on me: Celeste's and Roxy's at once.

I head back into the lobby, mildly delirious, and rub my eyes. A clock ticks. The carpet's scratchy against my bare feet. There's a set of French doors in the back past the lobby, open a crack in a gesturing way, like they'd been expecting me, and I move through them out into the daylight, severe and bleaching. Here, there's a small gazebo and then, further back, the woods.

This is it – the seam separating the civilization of the island from the wild. Rows and rows of sharp teeth-trees jut from the ground. The depth is impossible; a thousand shades of green and brown, specks of matter floating lazily in the sunbeams that manage to break the thick clusters of leaves. The demarcation between their backyard and the treeline is disconcerting, like something man-made masquerading as natural. Moving closer, I see the whole thing is wrapped with a barbed-wire fence, signs hung against it at regular intervals read: DANGER. TRESPASSING IS STRICTLY PROHIBITED. RISK OF INJURY. The signs are worn and rusted, shrivelling at the edges, some with holes decayed straight through like caterpillar-gnawed leaves. I feel sickly suddenly and I'm sure it's from a combination of exhaustion and a biological clock run entirely awry but there's something about the close proximity of the trees, unmoving but coursing with life all the same, that makes me want to lie down again. I've never liked the woods. Then I swear there are eyes on me.

'Mona?'

Whip round. It's Sylvia.

'Sorry,' I say, startled. 'I was just looking around.'

'Not much to see back there,' she says and chuckles a little to herself. She peels a pair of gardening gloves from her hands.

I press my palm flat against the side of my head, still disorientated. 'No kidding. Didn't mean to snoop.'

'Not at all. Your room was ready a while ago but I didn't want to wake you. Feel better?'

A breeze somersaults past: sea, earth, sun. Ought to be comforting. I realize I never actually admitted to my exhaustion; she just knew. 'Yeah, actually. Thanks for letting me crash.'

Sylvia reveals a key from her overall pocket and hands it to me. The building I'm staying in, she says, is called Seiburt House.

'Is this your first year here, then?'

I nod. 'Going to try and get my bearings today.'

'Are you from in-state?'

'No – Indiana.'

'Oh, gosh. What inspired the trek?'

'I guess I felt like I needed to . . . get away from things? For a bit, anyway.'

Sylvia laughs. 'You're not old enough yet to be so world-weary.' The statement's not derisive, or patronizing, I don't think; I get the sense she understands. 'Do you want me to show you where the dorms are? I don't mind taking you – they're just back past the neck.'

'Don't worry, I don't want to take up any more of your day.' The heat, I notice, almost makes my voice sound different from normal, heavy on the air with a blurred, dull lowness.

'Not at all. And days I give freely, anyway. Nights less so.'

'It's OK, really.' I think of the boy from earlier. I like him. I like him and I don't like anyone. Between breakfast, and his attentiveness and thorough lack of suspicion, there's something about him that strikes me as truly kind. In any case, it'd be useful to know someone near my age who's actually a resident and not just a Seasonal; maybe he'll have some insight. 'Is Ellis still around?' I ask.

'He's back working the bike desk for me.'

'Oh. Well, please tell him thanks again. He was really nice.'

Sylvia massages the back of her neck. 'He's a good boy. I'm sure you'll see him around.'

I thank her again and go.

I trek along the side of the house, back to my car in the parking lot, and focus my modestly topped-up energy on getting to the dorm in one piece, the black ooze of sleep and strangeness still not entirely dissipated. The drive takes me, as Sylvia instructed, back on to the main road and down the sea-swaddled isthmus, the early afternoon sun beginning its downward arch on my left.

Seiburt House is easy enough to find, less easy on the eyes. It's a protuberance of a building, square and brown and landlocked, no real view of the sea, and inside, the hallway is poorly lit and paved with a muddy carpet curling at the edges. There's a modest kitchen and a shared bathroom on the ground floor. My room is on the first floor, concealed only by a particle-board door so cheap and worn I'm sure I could crush it in my hands. Opened and there's a cell: carpet with mysterious stains and cracked white walls, and I'm not actually sure what state the room was in this morning if this is how it looks clean.

The main issue, however, is one of duplication: two beds. Two desks. I'll have a room-mate. All my research and I couldn't even bother to anticipate this?

Without any guarantee of privacy my plans of day-by-day documenting, recording are all but dashed. Of course I could record when they're not here, but they still might show up unannounced, or ask questions about the equipment. A sinking resignation settles in me.

Each of the desks is adorned with a packet of papers – one addressed to me, the other to someone called Peyton Reed. My packet says I'm assigned to The Island Spot, a nearby diner with a thrillingly imaginative name, and I need to report there for my orientation at six thirty on Monday morning. My mercifully morning-person brain doesn't flinch.

With a huff, I choose the bed beneath the window and toss my duffel bag on to it, on top of a blanket not dissimilar from the disposable hospital variety. It's even hotter in here than outside, the air itchy and restrictive and smelling of something acrid that I can't place. I haul the window open from the bottom up; underneath, the sill is black with dirt and gnat corpses. Beside, there's a door that leads out to a small balcony that offers a less-than-savoury view of a nearly identical building, more dorms. I open the door too to get some air circulating and return to my bags.

I'd packed relatively light. Five T-shirts and five pairs of shorts – two of them a mesh material, for running – and the offer of employment email had suggested I buy a pair of khakis. One denim jacket. Two pairs of jeans. Wrapped in the clothes is the precious cargo: my enormous, bulky headphones, a small handheld mic, and my bigger standing mic that I'd shelled out a fortune for. They're not going to get much use now, but I'm still glad to have them, just in case.

I've been writing and presenting the podcast since freshman year. Three years of half-hour segments, all fully committed to documenting someone else's life – and all the ways a life can pause. I'm definitely not the only one doing what I do, but I like to think that where some people are gimmicky, I'm respectful; where some people are careless, I'm thorough. I like to think this. I'm not a half-bad writer, and given my personal experience with missing people, do my best to marry anti-sensationalism with viscerality.

There is no brighter beacon in a dim world than truth.

But, sure, I guess it started because of Celeste.

Growing up with a single, attorney dad means I'm incredibly well adjusted and feel I received an adequate amount of attention growing up. That's a joke. He was never around. But Celeste was always there.

My eleventh birthday and all I wanted was a weekend of Dad's time. We went to Charlestown Park downstate, even though I'd never liked the woods, but it didn't matter because no one really thought about what I liked. A case came up urgently on the first day. *Take Mona out, Celeste*, Dad said. *Take her hiking round the cliffside.* I was eleven and Celeste was seventeen, months away from starting at Harvard. Everything good a person could be. Clever and amiable, twinkling with life and infinite promise.

She was supposed to take care of me.

What was I even looking at? The sky, maybe. I think I was looking at the sky. I must have been, I remember, because it was blue and full of those skeletal, wispy half-clouds. That's what I was looking at. When my attention returned to the trail, she was gone. The only trace of her was her phone resting on the ground.

And that's how she disappeared.

I wish there were more to the story. The search parties never found anything. She was there one second on the trail, overlooking a twenty-mile reach to the horizon, and then nowhere ever again. We looked and looked and looked, and sympathetic strangers formed search party upon search party, and news coverage, for weeks, and nothing. I don't remember that time all that well. I remember being thoroughly questioned but not what I was asked. I remember the terror of the blackout, the new learned power of disassociation from my own body and experiences: how could I not have seen what had happened?

One thing I do remember thinking is that they weren't going to find her. I didn't tell anyone this, of course.

And I was right. No body or suspects. Like she had evaporated, mid-step, into the wispy clouds.

If I've learned anything from my write-ups it's that people get lost in the woods all the time. Everyone thinks that *they* would never get lost, but when the forest is dense enough, and sometimes even when it isn't, it's near impossible to find your way back to a trail once you're off it, even from barely ten yards away. I did a write-up once of a graduate student named Meredith Santos who was hiking with her boyfriend, then left the trail to pee. Boyfriend waited and waited. Hours he was there and Meredith never came out. She was reported missing, search parties combed the place, couldn't find anything. Weeks later, hunters stumbled across the scene: a shoddy makeshift shelter, an attempted fire, and Meredith Santos in the early stages of decomposition, who had starved and succumbed to the elements after a month out in the wilderness. She'd simply gotten turned the wrong way, and when she realized she'd been walking for too long not to be back at the trail yet, she panicked, turned round again, and before you knew it she'd walked and walked so far that a deliberate search couldn't even find her.

I think that this must be what happened to Celeste.

I think she went into the woods for some reason, lost her bearings, and couldn't find her way back out.

The worst part about Meredith's case is that when they found her, she was only a mile from a different trail. This is especially gruesome for obvious reasons. Succumbing to the elements is one thing, miserable, but to lose your dual against nature when you're a twenty-minute walk away from the rest of your life . . . well, at least she didn't know. That's better, in a way.

Celeste must have known.

I think about that a lot. I think about her, furiously trying to find her way back, dread clenching every part of her, the realization that she's wandering in circles, that she was just on the trail, that there's no escape, that she might as well lie down there and die – or maybe there's something greater and cosmic flickering through the expanse of woods, something that just won't let her die, and she's still out there, toeing unbroken undergrowth for the rest of time. Maybe she's changed now. Made different. Maybe from all that searching and wanting and dread she's transformed into something else. How could she not be?

Yes. I think about that a lot.

A fat bumblebee smacks against the balcony door with a *crack* and I jump. The buzz peaks then moves away. Birdsong drifts in, pitchy and fevered. It's a pretty day – distant, bright blue sky melts smooth as foam into the horizon.

I hang my few clothes in the shared wardrobe, fold the shorts and underwear beneath them. There's a deep drawer in my desk that I use to store all the podcast equipment, and after I've tessellated everything into place, I collapse on to my bed.

Roxy's case is special because the most interesting thing about her isn't that she went missing, which one can't always say of missing people. I'd read the blogs, the forums, all her lyrics time and again, every lick of information available on Sandown, on Roxy, on the investigation – more so, the lack of investigation. It seemed the bulk of available effort was put towards satiating the media vultures as opposed to anyone at all trying to figure out where Roxy had gone. Then, suddenly, calm. It didn't make any sense. My gut had always suggested there was something everyone wasn't seeing.

Celeste loved Roxy's music. It was all she listened to, the year leading up to her disappearance. And Celeste is gone. I've come to terms with it, maybe. No leads. No clues. Vanished. But that's not true of Roxy. There's so much left behind. So many unexplored leads.

And no, finding Roxy isn't the same as finding Celeste. But it is, at last, something apart from replaying that same terrible image of the empty trail one more damn time, hoping to find a silhouette rustling through the undergrowth.

After one is hollowed out by suffering, one might expect something to rush in to fill the new, unoccupied parts of yourself – but that's not how it's been for me. Nothing rushed in. Instead, I sometimes look in the mirror and see not a different person, but no one at all. Not a canvas. A canvas has potentiality, a promise, an ability. Just nothing. I'm no one.

But the stories are always there. Celeste's lack is always there. Roxy Raines is always there. This is what's left of me. The ignition and flame and ash, all at once. I've decided the only way to make it all count and fill what's empty is to find her.

I close my eyes again, the birdsong distant and hysterical, the heat prickling in microscopic eruptions across the breadth of my skin. Inhale for eight seconds, exhale for ten.

I need to know what happened to Roxy Raines.

HOW TO DISAPPEAR
Episode 21

Narrator: Of course, the investigation having been open and shut in an official capacity means nothing to web sleuths. Multiple theories have been postulated regarding what happened to Roxy that night: brawl gone wrong; police cover-up; jealous competing musician.

I'm reminded of the case of Ken McElroy – a bully and repeat criminal who terrorized a small town in Missouri for years until, apprehended by a crowd, someone's shot hit him square in the chest and killed him.

When questioned, no one had anything to say.

To this day, nobody's said who shot the gun, nobody tried for his murder. Thirty pairs of eyes, at least, who watched every part of what happened but didn't see a thing.

Of course, McElroy was a violent criminal. A veritable villain, compared to Roxy Raines and her harmless if persistent verbal lashings. But his case proves people are more than capable of keeping quiet if they think it important enough; if they've got something to protect – a person, or a way of life; if they have enough of a reason to, above all else, believe what they're doing is right.

CHAPTER 4

Indiana feels so far gone. At home, with the same backgrounds and sights and ghosts, everything reminds me of the worst. Here, I'm already addicted to the new anonymity, the unfamiliarity, the view; any sense of the way things ought to be has been discarded entirely in favour of whatever this *is*. I am anything here. A vessel. I slip into this sense of anything with disarming ease, lying in the new bed, then leaning over the balcony, keeping an eye on the quiet treelined road, sweat beading on my lip. Mona is what I'm called but maybe I am something else.

Though it's not long before this becomes unnerving more than welcome and I decide to get to work.

I break in my new desk, writing down everything that's already happened – the drive here, the ferry, Ellis and Sylvia – and then consult my pre-written notes.

I've come with an eight-episode outline. I've already written and recorded the first episode, primed and ready to be posted at the end of all this, no matter what I find. All expository, more of a teaser than anything, comprising the information I could find online from forum-scouring and speculation. Of course I can't be sure what might happen or what I might find or how long any of this might actually take so it's mostly guesswork, which isn't ideal, but I wanted to give the series some structure.

Assumptions. There will be paperwork. Honestly, the rest is sort of contingent upon what I find. I need to differentiate rumours and exaggeration from fact. I'm particularly focused on one main piece of evidence – the 'goodbye' note allegedly left by Roxy in her car, detailing her intentions (suicide, supposedly). This is what everyone on the forums says is the missing piece; nobody has ever seen it and the consensus is, if someone could find out what she'd actually written, it'd crack everything open. This is my first lead: get the note.

Interviews by the second episode to start the momentum. Then, first break by the third. Connecting the dots, midpoint, fourth episode. New information that changes things. Maybe I've been looking at it all wrong. Who knows. More snooping, second break, all comes to a head – finale by the seventh or eighth. Then maybe a reflection episode to tie it all together.

It's eerie, being alone in the dorms. I decide I ought to start exploring.

Once the heat breaks at seven or so, I let the middle spit of the island lead me wherever it likes, the spine of the vague humanoid that comprises Sandown. Mainly interesting-looking side streets, dappled sunlight like splotches of translucent yellow paint spilled across the sidewalk, poplars swaying above me. The island is picturesque, sure, but

48

stifling. There's something about its size, its openness, being able to see the conclusion of it from wherever you are, that you'd think would be freeing, or comforting – a three-sixty view of a wide open ocean, of waves growing smaller and smaller until they're just a suggestion of dark-blue movement against the vastness. Somehow, it's the opposite. Everything is too small. Too nothing. There's almost something sad about it. Air here runs thick.

I pass the laundromat, the grocery store. The neighbourhood side streets are lightly populated; I can almost use the tourists' density as a tool to gauge how near I am to the boardwalk, which is effectively the epicentre of the place, like a beehive's approach.

Without really looking for it, I find the diner I'll be working at. A *full* diner, like a movie set, sloping curved lines instead of ninety degree angles, the outside a bright seafoam green. A paper sign hangs from the front window that reads CLOSED. The windows curve all the way round the exterior, the shape a perfect rectangle but with soft corners – the sort of place new diners hoping to capture a sort of retro vibe would seek to replicate. There's a familiarity to it – nostalgia for something I never experienced.

A woman and a man are locking up the front door. The woman is the one with the keys, maybe in her late fifties, wearing a white tank top and a long floral skirt, dark hair spilling over her shoulders. The man beside her looks around the same age and stands with a slight hunch.

After a moment the woman clocks me looking. 'If you stand there starin' any longer I'm gonna have to charge ya.'

She has a voice that strikes me as the opposite to Roxy's – too young for her, too high.

I blink. 'Sorry,' I call, 'it's just – I start working here on Monday.'

'No kidding. What's your name?'

I saunter up nearer to them, through the parking lot. 'I'm Mona Perry.'

'That's right,' she says, realizing. 'You're our new front girl.'

'I'm looking forward to it.'

'Oh, you don't have to butter me up,' she says with a deep chuckle.

Up close, the woman is sturdy-looking, strong but feminine features offset by the width of her shoulders, which are darkly tanned and mossed with sunspots. She smells faintly of smoke. 'It'll be the worst part of your summer, I'll tell ya now. I'm Mary Anne, anyways.' She doesn't offer a hand to shake so I don't offer my own. 'I own the joint.'

I glance at the man, maybe expecting him to say something in confirmation. Though gravity has been unkind he looks like he'd once been handsome; a sort of wide, Elvis-like face wracked with worry, two deep lines running between his eyebrows. His mouth turns downwards. Even just from the nervous, sideways glance he gives me, I catch his pale blue eyes. Mary Ann must notice me looking and says, 'Archie's my nearest and dearest. Helps out in the kitchen.'

I take the man's hand to shake and it's rough against mine, but he's not looking at me – he doesn't seem particularly to be looking anywhere. I can't place the emptiness. 'Archie,' he says, and that's all.

'Nice to meet you both,' I say.

'All right, well, enjoy –' she casts a glance around us – 'whatever it is you're up to and I'll see you bright-eyed and bushy-tailed Monday morning.'

'Will do. See you then.'

They're old enough to remember Roxy, of course. But that can come later. For now, I walk away as they drive off, wondering what they might know, wishing I could climb into their heads, desperate to see how this whole thing will play out.

The most interesting part of the island, by far, is the main street. Not interesting in a *good* way, necessarily. But compared to the rest of the developed land the main street is certainly the most stimulating to look at and exemplifies what Sandown is. Shops full of souvenirs and tack, painted seashells and shot glasses and cheap, sweatshop hoodies hanging in the windows. Intermittent clusters of people buzz in and out of the shops that are open, which is probably only every third one. There's some quiet chatter from the patio of a bar further up the road. Without a meaningful crowd here, though, it all feels a bit pointless. Like a movie set, like none of it's real, like you could swing open any one of these doors and there'd be nothing but a grey void to fall into. It isn't pretty, really. The buildings are A-frames, blue and grey and red, hollow, seaside Americana. What did Roxy think walking down these streets? Looking at this every day might make anyone hate humanity. Living in a place that's meant for everyone except you, and not just that – a visiting place, a nothing place, cultureless and created to please only the passers-by, boarded up for two-thirds of the year. A cardboard house with curbside appeal. A bubble in the world. It must have looked not unlike this when Roxy was here. I don't envy her.

The carnival pier stretches down maybe the length of a football field; there's an empty carousel, a couple of boardwalk games, a tall Ferris wheel perched at its culmination. Though access is blocked by a wooden barrier as it doesn't open officially until next weekend.

Rules are important, sure. Signs too. Some are more important than others.

I hop the barrier and traipse along the boardwalk. Certainly something eerie about it. Empty carnival games, milk jugs and balloon darts and basketball hoops, all rigged, no doubt, some boarded, some not, rows of prizes left out in the open, thoroughly unconcerned by theft.

Further up, there're stone steps leading down to the shoreline.

I tread on to the stretch of rocky beach punctuated by an unlit firepit, pebbles clicking under my feet, clumps of seagrass bursting from below every few paces. Seagulls yap above me. A gust of wind ricochets over the surface of the ocean and envelops me, makes me aware of the sweat trickling down the canyon that marks the direct middle of my chest. I breathe in, out, salt, brine.

Beside me, there's the lighthouse, a colossal thing, maybe the tallest point on the island even given the island's ascent to the north. Floating towards it happens naturally, moth drawn to flame, and I want to go in. This is something else I'm not sure is a decision truly made by me.

I'm not sure any decision is made only by me.

No, trauma never goes.

There's a lobe of my brain that's staked and ravaged and it's Celeste, I'm sure of it, ripping squishy me-matter off and replacing it with something foreign, unrecognizable, decidedly not me. Am I impulsive? Am I about to swing open the grey, windowless door to the lighthouse just because I want to, because maybe I want to be caught, because I want someone to regard me, shake their head sadly and say, *That poor girl, so impulsive, drawn to danger, she never recovered, she'll forever be a problem because of what the universe decided to do and not do to her?* Am I pathetic? Am I Mona?

The door screams as it opens.

Must. My eyes water when it hits, spores and dust and tangy sea.

Why can't I go anywhere on this island without the sense I'm being watched?

Not from inside. From behind me.

A car's engine stalls.

I slink backwards and peek from the entrance. A quake sidles through me.

There's a man watching. Police officer. When I notice the badge I don't know whether to be relieved or more unsettled. By now the sun's nearly set and the sky is cloudless except at the horizon, strips of purple sky clinging to the edges, lighting the man from the back. He stands like he's young, straight and cocky, but his face places him around fifty or so. A salt-and-pepper beard, thick but well groomed. 'Ah,' he calls, the sound devastating in the quiet, 'lighthouse inspector. So happy to see you.'

His face cracks into a smile. It's a joke. 'Sorry,' I say, 'I was just exploring.'

'Are you a Seasonal?'

'Yeah.'

'Is this your first year?'

I nod.

'I don't think I need to tell you not to go sneaking around in lighthouses that don't belong to you. Unless you've just made an extravagant purchase, in which case, apologies.'

'Honestly I just wanted to see if it would open. I didn't realize it was –'

'What's your name, miss?'

'I'm Mona.'

'Pleasure, Miss Mona. I'm the chief of the island's police force. Booker.'

I fight the urge to ask if he isn't a little old to be a chief – and if by *chief* he doesn't mean *sole member*. 'So probably the worst person to catch me.'

'Eh, might be the best one to, actually. I've grown soft in my old age.' He chuckles a little to himself. 'You're not in trouble.'

'Thanks.'

'But – and this is important advice here – it might do you well to endeavour to steer clear of it. Sandown isn't a good place to seek it out.' His disposition strikes me as belonging more to a good-natured park ranger than a police chief. I glance at his hip; he's not carrying a gun.

I don't mean to shuffle my feet but I do anyway. 'Yes, sir.'

'Where are you staying?'

'Seiburt.'

'Happy to give you a lift back.'

'I'm all right.'

'You sure? Gonna be dark soon and the road back to Seiburt ain't as lit as you might like it to be.'

'Really, I'm fine.'

'All right, kid.' He ducks back into his cruiser. 'Enjoy your summer. Hope I don't bump into you again,' he says through the open window, 'unless you get in a scrap, in which case – call.'

I smile in return and he drives off.

I cut my losses, leave the lighthouse to glare over Sandown, and start back towards the dorms.

Booker was right; I can't see shit.

Without much open, the grid of side streets back to the dorm is lit mainly by porch lights, a spooky trek, all things considered, and when I get back to my room I collapse in bed, bury my face in the unfamiliar smell of the sheets and stay there.

As noted by the 2020 census, Sandown Bay has a full-time population of one hundred and eighty-two. I've met six, who have already given me more than enough to think about. Sylvia and Ellis, the ferryman, the police chief, Mary Anne, Archie. People I never would have known existed if I hadn't come prodding – spores leaping from a disturbed fungus. I'm overwhelmed, suddenly, by a planet that facilitates the living of so many lives in tandem, so much so that it makes my head pound even beginning to conceive of every story playing out at this moment.

I breathe in through my nose, out through my mouth. The nose is mine and the mouth is mine and the channel leading between the two is mine.

Now, having seen Sandown in person, I know these are the things I need to figure out: I need a snapshot of the time – of Roxy's relationships, of the sort of things she did on a day-to-day basis, all culminating in the actual *day*. I need to know what happened that night. Those pieces seem so far away, so elusive, but finding them is the only way I can time-travel thirty-five years back and see what needs seeing.

Some of the information was known because, at the time, there had been a bit of an uproar – Roxy wasn't just some unknown getting thrust into stardom by a record label. She'd been growing an audience steadily over the previous five years. People knew her name – in-state, at least. But that was enough. That was enough for word to spread, barbed with rumours and assumptions and fantasy, and that's what I'm left with now. Information that might be true. Might not be. Roxy Raines' mythology more than her personhood.

Anxiety rocks my belly and suddenly I feel very alone.

I think of my dad.

I pull up the texts between him and me, read the last one. *I just need to know where you are.*

I drag a finger across the screen.

Me: I'm sorry for not telling you but it's really important. I'm in Sandown Bay, in Delaware. Long story.

Just give me some time. I can show you I'm worth something if you just give me some time.

It's obvious that the island is harbouring something terrible. I know just from today. It permeates everything, the never-healing wound. I can't explain it. The people here are heavy. The island itself a pair of bloodshot eyes.

Meanwhile, truth is curative and unchangeable. God, it's the easiest thing in the world. It doesn't pull tricks.

The whole of Sandown is collapsing under the weight of what happened and I'm going to be the one to save it.

An unexpected wave of comfort rolls from the back of my neck down through my feet. The temperature is cooler now and I'm covered by the thin sheet and again comes the endorphin rush of the leaving, the room quiet, cicadas chirping nearby. The knowing will get all of us out of this.

I need to know what happened that night.

I need that note.

CHAPTER 5

SATURDAY 29 MAY

I'm awoken by an expletive.

'Shit!' someone says, and I shoot up out of a dreamless sleep to see her, a dark-haired girl frozen in ostensive horror in the doorframe – horror, I realize, which is directed towards me. 'Hello!'

My brain and stomach lurch in time – and it comes to my attention that I'm not wearing clothes. I tug the duvet up to my neck and wonder if my eye sockets can expand wide enough for their contents to evacuate. I speak the truth – 'I'm naked.'

The girl averts her gaze. 'Yep. Got that. OK. Have a second. More, even. Many, many seconds.'

The door shuts.

I scramble out of bed, sheets clinging on for half a second too long, glued by sweat. Shirt. Shorts. Thank God all the podcast stuff is shut away. Outside, there's a general commotion and clamour: everyone must be arriving now, laughter and clattering and doors opening and shutting.

Morning sunshine spills across the floor. I swear I had a T-shirt on when I went to bed; the heat must have made me remove it in my sleep. I'm compelled to check my hair for a yet unknown reason but there's no mirror in here so finally I just loudly and too angrily say, 'OK,' and an eye peeks through the wedge of an opening between room and hall, hesitant.

'All good?'

'Yeah, whatever, fine.'

She – Peyton, I assume – emerges fully, wielding her suitcase in a way that can be described as no less than violent. 'Apologies, friend.' Her hair's folded in a massive braid that slumps over her left shoulder, and a slim ribcage peeks from underneath a floaty white crop top. All her clothes fit her in that sort of intentionally-too-small way.

'It's OK.' I smooth down the T-shirt I'm now wearing, which, based on the unfamiliar itch of the collar, I realize is on backwards. My face burns red.

'I should probably say, though, that I think I saw your tit. And I just want you to know that.'

I wince. 'You *think* you saw? What else could it have been?'

She blinks. I wonder, briefly, if her eyelashes are full enough to create a draft. 'Well, Occam's razor is admittedly not working in your favour.'

I drop back on to my bed and resist the urge to tunnel within it. The ceiling is the most interesting thing in the world to me right now and I may continue to look at it until I die. 'I will invoice you later.'

'So *warm*, you. Welcoming. What an unforgettable summer we're going to have. What do I call you? Pout? Sulk?'

Never mind the ceiling. I roll over in bed and smash my pillow on to my head. 'Mona,' I say into the mattress.

Peyton laughs, a high pierce. Then, realizing: 'Oh. You're serious.'

I roll round to look at her, eyes narrowed. This is why I don't talk to people. My main concern with having a room-mate was privacy as it related to the podcast but just knowing I'm going to have to cohabitate with *her* regardless of anything else is enough to send me spiralling. Also, I wish I *had* come with a fake name after all.

'Would you like to know who *I* am?' she asks.

'Unfortunately, I already do,' I say, and gesture absently towards her packet.

'Ah,' she says. 'A sleuth.'

I stiffen. And what if I am? I want, suddenly, to match her energy, but don't want to give her the satisfaction of the matching.

'Anyway, lucky you. I would have picked that bed.'

'If I let you have it, will you stop talking so loud?'

'Almost definitely not.'

'I didn't even know I'd have a room-mate.'

'Uh, I could have *deduced* from your *tone* and also *nudity*.' She looks up and tilts her head in a way that is annoying to like. 'What'd you think it'd be, Caesar's fucking Palace?'

'That's *my* room!' a boy calls from the hallway, followed by a chorus of snickers. 'Caesar's *fucking palace*,' someone else mutters.

Peyton leans out into the hall. 'Ha-ha, cool cool cool.'

A boy peeks into the room and looks me up and down. 'Oh,' he says to Peyton, 'this'll be good.'

'Loves me already, obviously.'

I groan a little into my hands, more to myself, and something whacks me over the side of the head. It's a croissant wrapped in plastic.

'There,' she says. 'Sustenance. Up. Join the rest of the human race.'

I'm so hungry but I don't want to eat it because it's from her.

She nods towards it. '*Eat.* For peace.'

Fine. I sit up and take a bite. Peyton laughs to herself.

'Yeah, OK,' I say, mouth full, 'what is it?'

'You know that video of the raccoon who grabs a whole handful of cat food, and he's kind of cradling the pellets to his chest and runs away on two legs?' She's going to say I look like him. 'You look like him.'

An impossibly long summer.

'This is your first year,' she says. 'Obviously.'

'Is that a question?'

'No. How'd you find out about this place?'

I chew for a good and silent five seconds at least before replying. This is when I begin to lie. 'Visited a lot when I was little.'

'You from in-state?'

'No.' I try to swallow a bite of croissant but my mouth is dry and for a terrible moment it's stuck at the back of my throat. 'Indiana.'

'College?'

'Harvard,' I say.

'Oh,' Peyton says, and recoils. She leans back out into the hall. '*Liam, she goes to Harvard!*'

I assume it's Liam who cackles. 'And you're the dumbest bitch alive!'

Peyton cackles. 'I *know*!'

I smile a little. It's absolute mania.

'You?' I ask.

'U Del.' That's the University of Delaware. It's a public Ivy; she's clever. Book smart, anyway. 'Let me guess. Sophomore?'

'No, freshman.'

'Aw. Baby. You didn't want to stay for your last summer in the nest?' Peyton nonchalantly shoves a handful of underwear into her dresser drawer.

I shrug. 'I didn't have many friends or anything. not much keeping me there.'

'No? Why? What's wrong with you? Apart from the obvious.'

I think about this for longer than I should, and even my answer is a non-answer. 'I was just always busy with other stuff, I guess. Working.'

'Well, that's how you get to Harvard, right?'

'That's exactly how you get to Harvard.' It's not. But I don't mind slipping into this skin of distant workaholic or high-achieving recluse. Maybe that's who I can be, or who I already am.

'Well, make friends, don't make friends – I don't care either way. But honestly, as far as room-mates go, you should be happy to have me.'

'Should I?'

'I'm pretty normal – no, really,' she says when I scoff. 'This kind of job – the sort of thing where you board, work for the experience – sometimes it attracts weirdos with nothing to lose. Which doesn't always mean much. But sometimes people with nothing to lose think everyone else has nothing to lose either and drag everyone down with 'em. What about you?'

'What?'

'Is that why you're here? Nothing to lose?'

I think of the space behind my dad's eyes, empty rooms in a big house. 'Probably.'

Peyton chews the corner of her lip, biting back a smile that seems like it'd take over her whole face if released. 'Do some soul-searching and get back to me.'

'Will do.' I worry, suddenly, that she's seen right through me. I let myself recline against the windowsill, the glass of the window unexpectedly warm against the back of my neck. Peyton moves towards the drawer containing all the podcast equipment and I leap. '*No*,' I say, then try to reel it back in. 'Not there.'

Peyton blinks. 'Jeez, all right. That's where she keeps her *stash* of – whatever her poison is. We can talk about that later.' I look down, embarrassed. 'Oh. You coming tonight?'

'The bonfire?'

'You should go. It's fun, kind of ceremonious. And you can meet everyone.'

'Seasonals?'

She furrows her brow and says, 'Well, not the *locals*,' and I worry I've outed myself. 'If that's who you're after, you should go to church on Sunday and hang around Waite and Sons for a couple of hours.'

'What's Waite and Sons?'

Peyton discovers a box of crackers in her bag and devours an entire handful. 'The *funeral home*,' she manages through her full mouth.

'They're not *that* old, are they?' This is fun. I like asking questions I already know the answers to – fifty-three per cent of Sandown Bay's year-long population are over sixty, eighty per cent over forty-five – because I win either way, since it's not really about answers, but more about the person doing the answering.

'I mean, kinda. I guess it wasn't always that way. There were families once. Most of them grew up here and then just never left, and their kids moved away, and no one else moved in. And excuse me if I'm not the most complimentary towards them as most of them don't even *like* the Seasonals, which is very *whatever*. You think they'd be a little nicer given their whole island enterprise would fall apart without us, but what do I know?'

'I met Sylvia yesterday. And Ellis, I think? They were nice.'

Peyton's face bursts open like a solar flare. I was right about her smile – straight to her eyes. 'Oh, my God. You met Ellis? Isn't he the greatest?'

'You know him?'

'I've been bugging him for two years straight! I normally work at the B and B.' She scrapes her welcome packet off her desk and flicks open to the first page. 'And again!'

'Yeah, he was unbelievably nice.'

'He's the best. He's sort of the official Seasonal adoptee. Little shy at first but the sweetest once you get to know him. But –' she leans in – 'between you and me . . . I wouldn't have come back if I didn't truly like it here – OK, I love it here, but Ellis is the embodiment of how shitty this place can be.'

'He mentioned people treating him badly – because of his stutter, I guess.'

Peyton shakes her head. 'That's only the cherry on top. It has to do with their whole family.'

I leave a space for her to continue.

'It's just a – weird history. I don't wanna get into it. As eager as Ellis is to *share*, I don't even know the full extent of it, to be honest. People around here think they're cursed or something.'

'Cursed?'

'Well, OK, maybe that's stretching it. They keep their distance, anyway.'

'Ellis was concerned,' I say, 'about his mom being overprotective. He wanted to take me to the hotel and his mom almost wouldn't let him.'

She shakes her head sadly. 'This is the thing – because he does get it. He's not blind to it. He knows how people are but still wants to give them a chance to hurt him anyway.'

'He mentioned they're moving?'

'What? He did?'

'Yeah. Apparently Sylvia's selling the hotel.'

Deer in the headlights. 'I . . . didn't hear about that. When?'

'End of the summer.'

Peyton palms her face. 'Well, that's a bummer, I guess. But it makes sense. They deserve to be happy. At least, Ellis does.'

'Not his mom?'

'No, sorry, it's not that she doesn't – it's just always seemed like she enabled some of it. She hides him away and he doesn't know how to stand up for himself. I don't know. Not my place.' I'm quiet, and even Peyton, who had been ravaging the box of crackers, stops and chews with the slow, deliberate contemplation of a last meal. 'Sorry. This is dark stuff for the first day. I don't really even know what I'm talking about, to be honest.'

I shrug. 'I like the dark stuff.'

A knock on the door. Sylvia pokes her head in. 'Morning, girls.'

Peyton tenses and shoots me a furtive glance. I smile despite myself. 'Morning,' I say for the both of us.

'Nice to see you, sweetheart,' Sylvia says to Peyton. 'How was the trip over?'

Peyton says, 'Not bad,' stiffly.

'And Mona? How was your exploration?'

'Informative.'

'Hey, Sylvia, can I get a new room-mate?' Peyton asks. 'This one's a dud.'

'Don't mind her,' Sylvia says to me, faux-exasperated. 'All bark.'

'I *beg* you mind me!'

We say bye to Sylvia and, once she's left, Peyton shuts the door with a quiet click, turns to me slowly and puffs her lips. 'There's no way she heard me say that stuff. Right?'

I shake my head with a furrowed brow. 'Not with your sensible volume.'

'Ah, well.'

Peyton regards the pile of clothes in her suitcase, then looks me up and down. There's a practical sensation from the ripple of her gaze that shocks me the rest of the way awake, if I wasn't already before and it makes me want to say, 'You can have the bed. If you want. I don't mind.'

Peyton withdraws in what seems like surprise. I might be imagining it but I swear she blushes. 'No, I – sorry. It's fine. I was just giving you a hard time.'

'No kidding.'

She laughs a little. It's not *at* me this time. Shakes her head. She's glowing a bit, there in the morning sun, skin dewy and ripe, like something newly grown. 'Come on, Harvard girl,' she finally says, 'help me unpack.'

CHAPTER 6

I had planned to go to the police station today. I have no interest in telling this to Peyton, who will, if her past reactions towards me doing literally anything are to go by, lose her mind with ridicule and delight.

Instead I leave in a sort of faux-disinterested way around one – the latest I can leave it, because the station's website says they close for public enquiries at two on Saturdays.

When I try to weasel away, Peyton predictably asks too many questions – where, how long, if I want her to come. She has told me more about herself – she's studying social work; she's 'casually' seeing that kid from earlier, Liam. (I'd asked, in that case, why they didn't just share a room together, and she'd said, 'God, I'm seeing him – that doesn't mean I like him.')

Despite her overinterest, I decide that as far as obligatory room-mates go, she'll be tolerable.

According to the address online, the station is near to where I first docked yesterday, which means it's an easy dash down Sycamore and a left on Reimer, I remember without needing to confirm. I drive a golf cart there for novelty's sake.

The station is small, the shape of a shed and maybe the size of three pushed together, light blue and unassuming. Flower baskets hang from the awning above the entrance. I assume there isn't much crime to catch for most of the year – two hundred residents and flower baskets will do that – and, during the tourist season, probably just breaking up the occasional bar fight.

How unprepared they must have been for Roxy Raines.

The door opens with a chime and, to my left, there's a desk framed by glass panels. Closer and it's Booker behind the glass, who beams when he sees me and pushes the panel aside. 'Miss Mona! The lighthouse inspector. Pleasure to run into you again so soon. Why did I have a feeling I would?'

'Does . . . the chief work the front desk?' I ask, scanning the place. There's an utterly casual and unconcerned air about it, seemingly empty besides the two of us. Not just of people, but of anything – there's a small kitchenette with a coffee machine and a small basket of tea. Further in, a wall of filing cabinets.

'They do when they're as close to retirement as me,' Booker says with a wet chuckle, his brow polished in sweat. 'It's a quiet town when we're off-peak. Quiet town when we're *on*-peak. I'm sure you've noticed. Only two of us on patrol during off-season and then we get about a dozen mainland officers on during the summer. Anyway. How can I help you?'

'I want to make a formal request for access to public records.'

There's something fun about watching people's faces change when they realize I'm about to be more trouble than they'd anticipated. Booker shifts then links his hands together atop the counter. 'Ah,' he says. 'I see. Which records are you after, then?'

'Files relating to the disappearance of Roxy Raines.'

He stares at me as if I'd said nothing, then smiles, huge, not really in a happy or jovial way. 'Well. Damn.'

I don't say anything.

'And why might you be requesting something like that?'

'It's legally within my rights not to disclose a reason for my request.'

'All right, all right, I wasn't asking you *legally*. Just trying to make conversation.' Booker breaks my gaze, wiggles his mouse, bored. 'And unfortunately, I'm afraid it's likely that this station will have to uphold its legal right to deny such a request.'

My stomach drops. 'What? Why? What do you mean?'

'Those files have been exempt from disclosure for years.'

Well, that wasn't on the website, I think dumbly. Without that information – probably without that damn *note* – I might as well just go home. I should have known. I was so distracted by the newness of the island, the excitement, I assumed this would work simply; I should have double-checked.

'That's just a hunch, though,' Booker says in a laboured sort of way while leaning back in his chair and lifting his

70

hands to support his head. 'You're more than welcome to put forward your request anyways.' He nods to the notepad on the counter, runs his thumb and forefinger over his beard. 'Written, please.'

There's a beat and then I'm reaching for the notepad and pen, my insides deflated. I feel vaguely like I'm falling for something. 'All right.'

While I'm writing, Booker says, 'You do realize that – I don't know why you know about this, or why you're really asking – this situation was never investigated for foul play? Meaning, I don't know what you're looking to find, but there's not much. I don't even think the paperwork we have amounts to files, as such – more like *a* file, and even then –'

'That's fine. Whatever there is,' I say and slap the pen on to the counter, then rip off the top sheet and slide it to him. *Mona Perry formally requests all documentation related to the disappearance of Roxy Raines.* Signed. Dated. 'How long does it normally take for requests to be processed?'

'Depends. In this case, could probably have a response with you in – eh, three weeks? Early July, at the latest.'

July? 'Why would it take so long?'

He nods to the wall of cabinets. 'It's not as easy as just cracking one of those open. Gets sent to the mainland office, appropriate bodies need to sign off. A month is actually not that long a wait, all things considered – might be a speedier process considering someone else logged the same request recently.'

'Someone else? Who? Was it denied or accepted?'

'It wasn't *denied*, but –'

'Then why would you . . . People's requests are public record too. Who?'

Booker takes the paper I slipped him, scrutinizes it, and sets it to the side. 'To find that out, I'm afraid you'll have to *file a request*,' he says with a wry smile that implies nothing will come of the request.

I roll my bottom lip between my teeth and tap my fingernail four times on the counter. 'You know, I'm all right.'

'Anything else you need?'

'I – no. Thanks.' It's not Booker's fault, but I have no one else to be angry with, and I can tell he's being flippant.

There's a sort of amusement flickering in his hooded eyes. 'Remember what we said about trouble.'

I puff my cheeks. 'Yep.'

'Enjoy your summer.'

The finality of the statement irks me. Once I'm back outside into the stifling wash of heat, I take a long look at the door, turn the doorknob once, twice and go.

CHAPTER 7

I agree to go to the bonfire with Peyton. I have things to do.

Firstly: get along with the Seasonals. They're a valuable resource. And secondly, without a way of lawfully getting to that report in the required timeframe, I'm going to have to take drastic measures. I had intended to do the whole thing by the book – I was even going to suck it up and play nicely with the law enforcement – but without that report, there's nothing for me to do here besides knocking on doors one by one.

Peyton and I are fashionably late. We've taken a golf cart down from the dorms and I'm driving, the warm breeze on my face refreshing. Peyton's leather jacket sleeve keeps brushing against my bare arm because she's sitting so close to me. She's got her hair scrunched in a bun on her head, little wispy tendrils curling downwards around her face. I am apparently driving too quickly for her liking and this is all she wants to talk about.

It's a pretty night – the heat has cracked and there's a wash of lulling pink still clinging to the edges of the sunset.

Something hypnotizing, too, about the glow of the street: little round bulbs tethered like ship lines to all the lamp posts; a warm orange blaze from inside the bars; moonbeams bouncing off the sea, dancing erratically, a billion hands motioning *Come hither* underneath. I'm struck by all the ways light can reflect when one is surrounded by sea. I want, for some reason, to remember it, and look a little longer.

Firelight comes from the beach, and we follow it.

I park at a gravel lot just off the high street. Salt and smoke burn my nostrils and reach into the back of my throat. Maybe forty Seasonals are already scattered across the shoreline – as far as I know, everyone. I already recognize some of them from the hallways at Seiburt.

The beach faces the mainland, the arrival dock and lighthouse to our left and the jagged peaks of the north side of the island to our right. Then there's the bonfire, tall as me, a couple of guys absently tending it, tossing things into the fire that ought not to be burned – my inhalations are laced with a distinctly metallic tinge.

Everything makes me think of Roxy. The electricity in the air, the rhythm of the music, some thudding beat from a song I can't place, the people, wired and alive.

Peyton recognizes someone at the fringes and drags me over by my hand. I struggle to get my footing on the pebbles and worry about spraining my ankle.

The boy we're headed towards glances to the police cruiser on the street to the side where Booker and another officer are parked, chatting, and takes a lightning-fast swig from a steel flask he retrieves from his coat pocket.

'*Excuse me, sir, can I see some ID?*' Peyton shouts, and the kid looks like he might've imploded, but relaxes when he sees her. Still, casts a glance over his shoulder to see if anyone heard. 'Naughty.'

'Idiot,' he says, as Peyton nicks the flask and takes a swig herself. He nods towards me with a grimace, still reeling from the sip. 'Oh. It's your torture victim.'

Peyton introduces me properly – this is Liam, the boy from before, the one she's not-seeing. He's of average height with a square face and dark eyes, and has a cool, easy lilt to his voice that most girls would find attractive.

'Welcome, fresh meat,' he says.

I smirk. 'For who?'

'Me,' Peyton says under her breath, and snickers.

I'm not the only new kid, but everyone else has confidently settled into the roles of the island and I'm here, straining against the thing – the tide, literally, the foamed edge of the sea not quite swelling around my feet but close enough for me to be aware of it. A small and unexpected part of me wonders what this experience would have been like if I hadn't come with a motive.

Peyton introduces me to a slew of people, all of them returning Seasonals. She explains that Seasonals tend to lump themselves into two categories. Everyone older than twenty-one typically works as a bartender, easy jobs where nights are spent mixing cocktails in outdoor establishments where you walk on sand instead of a floor and get big tips without much effort. Otherwise you're running tours at the winery. The rest of us – there are nineteen under-twenty-ones in total, including Liam, Peyton and me – usually get stuck cleaning Sylvia's B and B, or flipping burgers. I meet a pretty girl named Maria, with long buttery hair and a lip ring, who's friendly enough; the second she's out of earshot Peyton turns to me and says, 'She gets to run the butterfly house tours, that floaty blonde *bitch*.'

Liam is seemingly pleased with his second placement as the boardwalk merry-go-round button pusher – before six at night for children, which isn't so bad, he says, and then after six at night, for adults acting like children. 'It's really not bad, most of the time,' he says. 'Boring as hell but at least you're outside. Rather be doing that than stuck at Mary Anne's all day, to be honest.'

'No kidding?' I ask.

He shrugs. 'We go to The Island Spot sometimes, hangover breakfasts, mainly, and she's always, like, mad as hell to see us. Just cranky. Anyway, at least it's hardly ever busy. Probably gonna be even quieter this year.'

'What makes you so sure?' Peyton asks, firelight dancing across her cheeks.

'All that crazy weather stuff they're talking about.'

'Well, today was already hot as the devil's *asshole* so I don't see how it can get much worse.'

'No,' Liam says, mid-sip, 'didn't you see? Hurricane season. It's supposed to hit here, apparently. And soon. Rain, all summer.'

'*Ooh*, but that'd be fun, though, don't you think?' Peyton drapes herself across his shoulders like a ballerina on a bar. 'Quiet island, rained in, nowhere to go . . .'

Liam grimaces. 'Off.'

'Hey, Mona,' Peyton says, still hanging from Liam. 'Do you know about the No-Names?'

'No. Is that Sandown lore?'

Peyton smirks, a new mischievous air to her tone. 'Deep lore.' She shifts forward, like she's going to tell me a secret. 'They're the woods on the north half of the island. They weren't called anything; we just started calling them the No-Names. Well, we didn't. Kids before us.'

My heartbeat quickens. 'Sure.' I remember the backyard of the Willowwood, staring into the seemingly infinite rows of trees. 'I've seen them, yeah. What about them?'

'Rumour has it they're haunted.'

I smile despite myself. 'Haunted?'

'Yeah, haunted. Like, oogly-booglies, *ooo*.'

'I know what haunted means.'

'No one ever goes deep into them, because it's, like, physically impossible. I guess the trees are super dense and there're drops and people kept getting hurt and that's why they just closed 'em off. But there're tons of stories about all sorts of weird stuff in them at night. Electromagnetic shit. And tons of stories from those weekender cabins on the edge, before they shut 'em all down – that the people who stayed in them kept losing their stuff, or saw it moved around, or saw people in the woods.'

'No kidding?'

'It's not just the woods, either,' she says. 'Weird stuff happens all the time around here. There were a bunch of fires a couple of years ago, like, some local buildings just set ablaze out of nowhere. It had to have been arson because, what a coincidence, you know, but they never caught who did it.' I think of the impression I got of Sandown my first day here: the fat red wound of it, perpetually gaping, putrefying. Peyton nudges me. 'Anyway, we can go check out the No-Names later,' she says, but I get the sense she's joking.

I bite my lip, watch the waves as they lick the shore. 'I don't believe in ghosts.'

Liam doesn't like this response, clearly. 'Nah, you should. I've had full supernatural experiences where –'

Peyton, unfazed, clocks something behind me. She erupts, flailing an arm above her head. 'Ellis! Buddy!'

I turn and there's the boy from the B and B, alone, hunched over, a few paces from the tide, face plastered with the alarm of a deer about to be flattened. There's something in his hands that he's carrying like an injured bird as he approaches, shuffling arduously across the stones. 'Hey, Peyton.'

She wraps him in a hug, saying, 'You're so *tall*!' over and over. 'Sylvia feeding you Miracle Grow? Holy shit.'

Liam says a cool *Hey, man*, which is perhaps too masculine for Ellis's comfort and he shifts, unsure how to volley it back, but then notices me and seems to relax, shoulders falling from his ears. 'H-hi, Mona.'

'Yeah, I heard you two *met*,' Peyton says with a mad grin, jiggling both of us by the shoulders.

'Potentially the best chef in Sandown,' I say. I look to his hands, the contents of which I still can't make out. There's a bunch of the things, round and partially reflective, even in the shadows of the gathering dark.

'What'cha got?' Peyton asks before I can.

Ellis seems to have forgotten he is holding them because he looks down, startled, remembering. 'Oh, they're just, uh, sea glass. Broken b-b-bottles or whatever else winds up in the ocean and the salt w-water erodes it into these –'

Of all the colours on the shore, you're the one she adored
Hadn't given second thought to tangerine –

Ellis presents a morsel – 'little stones. I collect them. P-p-polish them. Sometimes they're so clear you can see yourself in 'em.'

This damn place has got her wondering
If you tossed her in the sea,
Would she wash up in that same sweet kelly green?

That's a Roxy song. 'Kelly Green'. I'm struggling to focus, the combination of the strange shadows and the loud chatter weakened by the perpetual roar of the Atlantic making me dazed. 'Interesting hobby,' I say.

I'm staring at Ellis too intently now and I don't even know why. I can *tell* I am because he doesn't even shyly avert his gaze, the way he might if I'd just been *casually* staring at him, but there's an intensity to this that locks us both in the moment.

His mom was so familiar.

Then – 'Ellis!' It's Sylvia, behind us. She gestures him over to her.

'Whoops, sorry, I'll catch up with you g-g-guys in a sec,' Ellis says and shuffles off. I watch as he goes; Sylvia says something stern to him, a hand on his shoulder.

'Anyway,' Liam continues. 'So, yeah, I've had full supernatural experiences where –'

A boy comes up to Liam and smacks him on the back. He turns in surprise but they recognize each other and perform some sort of elaborate dude handshake-hug, pulling away from the two of us.

'Peyton,' I say, concerned I'm going to miss my chance to know, 'what did you say was the weird stuff with Ellis's family again?'

'Oh, gosh. I don't know if we should get into it now. Why are you asking?'

'I'm just curious.'

'Well, I guess it starts with: his *grandma* owned the Willowwood in the first place. I guess it's been standing for, like, a hundred years, but she got too sick to take care of it and that's why Ellis and his mom came back from wherever they were living. Right? To take care of her and run the place.'

'Sure,' I say, hoping to evoke a curiosity strong enough to justify my asking but casual enough to avoid raising alarm.

'Grandma just finally passed away. Like, a couple of months ago. April, I think? Super recently. And then some soap-opera developments: on her *deathbed*, Grandma drops that she's actually *Great*-grandma, and the person Ellis's mom thought was her sister – and didn't really know anything about – was actually her *mom*. Apparently the whole town knew but wouldn't say. Isn't that the craziest shit you've ever heard? They all kept it secret.'

'Wow,' I say.

Peyton continues, a conspiratorial air to her tone. 'Only thing is – Grandma Ellis *disappeared*. In the seventies, maybe? Eighties? People thought she killed herself but nobody ever found out for sure.'

My gut flips. 'Do you know her name?'

'Oh, it was Renee, maybe? Ra – R-something.'

I almost want to laugh. 'Roxy.'

With a snap of her fingers: 'Yes! Yeah, that's it.' Then her brow knits. 'How do you know that?'

'I think Ellis mentioned it. Or I saw something at the hotel. I don't know.'

Peyton softens, casting her gaze downward. The bonfire's heat licks my back. 'Well, that's all I know. All Ellis will tell me, anyway.'

Ellis is Roxy's grandson.

Roxy had a daughter.

Roxy left behind a *daughter*.

My brain is practically rioting; I need an exit plan. I double over. 'Shit.'

'What?'

'I'm just having really bad cramps, all of a sudden.'

'Oh. Shoot. Wanna sit down for a sec?'

'No, Liam's waiting for you.' He is, gesturing to us from beside the fire while joke-gagging himself with a marshmallow-stabbed poker. 'I'm totally fine. I might just golf-cart it back to the room.'

'Well, let me come with y—'

'*No*,' I snap, and she recoils. 'Sorry. No, it's fine, really.'

Peyton nods silently and I know I've scared her, maybe, but there's no time for pleasantries. I stumble from the group, clumsy and disoriented.

Behind me, a voice booms above the roar of it all — 'Hello, everyone!' The roar of the crowd softens to nothing, mellows to sea on shore. Sylvia standing in the light of the fire. 'Sorry, I know you're all having fun, and I don't want to keep you for too long, but . . .'

In the split second that I look, I swear Ellis catches my eye. Does he know that I know?

I speed-walk off the rocky shore and on to the sidewalk, down the main strip.

Roxy had a secret daughter. A daughter that nobody knew about — for a time, not even the daughter herself. I realize now that everything I thought I knew is useless in the face of what *is*.

How could nobody on the forums have known about this?

This information proves the most doubtful part of my suspicions – that people on Sandown know what happened to Roxy, but have kept quiet. If an entire town could keep the secret of Sylvia's parentage while she's living, breathing on the island, they could certainly keep quiet about the fate that befell a dead girl.

Roxy has a daughter. And a *grandson*.

My entire gait transforms step by step – each distracted stride further away from the fire and further into the dark sends another jolt of adrenaline zapping through me.

This is the person I am tonight. I am an outlaw. It does not matter what I was before this and will not matter who I am after. Here I am, now moving with a galloping, pounding rhythm that prophesies something wicked afoot, some new insanity, some freeing severance from reality that comes with leaving your footprints somewhere for the first time, where you may not leave them again. Solipsism makes the whole place hazy. Maybe I invented Sandown Bay. Maybe the whole place will fall into the sea when I go.

Now it's all blue. Darkness turns white indigo-grey; I look at my hands to discover that I, too, am blue. Everything looks blue, except for the water behind me, which, when I turn to see it, looks black. And it makes me think of sisters, too much of the same thing, an oversaturation of colour running the whole pool black –

Do it.

The station looks unfamiliar in the night. I approach cautiously, check the area, left and right – no one home.

Two officers, Booker had said, and as far as I could see, both of them were at the bonfire.

I learned how to pick a lock when I was nine.

Out of necessity. The first thing I learned was how to open a common door that's locked from the outside – all you need is to straighten a paperclip, hook it round the mechanism where the door meets the lock and pull it at the right angle. Eventually I was turned on to more advanced locks. I'd always known I was too small to ever obtain any means to an end through brute force. I'd be smart instead.

And this is why, tonight, I've come prepared.

The tools are daunting, vague torture devices, shaped like toothbrushes except the end where the bristles would normally be is shaped and sharpened in a variety of ways, depending on what lock one needs to fit. I've become so good at it that I can manage some old locks with just a hairpin, if given enough time – but tonight I'm committing a crime and I won't turn my nose up at a bit of extra haste just to prove how talented I am.

No dice from the first pick. A peal of laughter from far away makes me jump, but as far as I can see, no one even knows I exist. Second's no good either. I'm sweating a little now and my hands tremble in an unwelcome and inconvenient way. *Focus*.

The lock clicks with the eight-pin and then the door is open.

No alarm. I'm inside. I'm inside and alive and breaking the law and I don't let it bother me.

I dart behind the counter to the stacked filing cabinets, scaling nearly two feet taller than me. They're organized by year. I scan for 1986 and find it – there's a ring of keys on top of the cabinet and I have to jump three times to snag it, my wrist banging against the top and sending a hollow drum-hit all the way through, echoing impossibly loudly in my ears. I frown and turn to look behind me, but no one is there.

Ten keys on the ring. All the locks look the same; I assume one key is able to open each year. First and second jam. The jingling is barbed and too loud, but I now can't trade speed for stealth. The third I think is the right size and it fits but doesn't turn, and now my fingers are grease-slick against the metal, but the fourth slides in like it's meant to be and the cabinet opens with a click.

I swear I sense some flicker of an outline behind me, my line of sight dappled with vignettes, but I can't be sure. Did I leave the door open?

The cabinet reels open when I pull and I misjudge how fast and heavily it'll travel, so it slides out all the way with a deafening, echoic bang once it hits as far as it can go. I wince, but the place is still all silence apart from me, so I continue, thumb through the tabs – and Roxy's here.

But when I grab for the folder and flip it open, there's nothing inside.

That's when I become aware of the second presence in the room.

'What are you doing here?' Ellis whispers, shrouded in shadow.

CHAPTER 8

I nearly jump out of my skin.

Ellis doesn't seem to have clocked quite what's going on yet, his expression more a vague curiosity than suggestive of an impending confrontation – but I can't be sure. Curiosity alone doesn't will you to follow someone while they're breaking and entering. I close the folder as casually as I can manage and let it rest by my side. 'What are *you* doing here?' I volley back. 'You're gonna get us both in trouble.'

'What is that?' he asks, eyeing the folder in my hands, not taking a step forward but flinching like he wants to.

Let's do this, then. Maybe this is what the universe has dictated – that I wasn't to come to him, but he was to come to me. 'Ellis,' I say softly. 'Roxy Raines. You're related. Right?'

'I *knew* that's what this was,' he hisses, practically stomping as he does, like an agitated toddler. 'You looked at me funny on the beach. That song. I –'

A *yes*, then. Change the subject. 'Listen. We don't have much time. I need your help.' I waggle the folder around.

'This is Roxy's case file and it's empty. Do you know why it would be?' Something occurs to me. A conditional allowance for sharing information otherwise exempt from public disclosure . . . if the party requesting the information is *family*. He goes to answer, fumbling for the words, but before he can, I ask, 'Did you request the information?'

'I mean, yeah – a week ago, though, and I don't have it. Booker gave it to me for an afternoon and I had to give everything back. I took pictures. So I don't know why it would be empty.'

A sound cuts the quiet – the doorknob to the front entrance, jiggling from the outside. A ray of light slices through the station.

'Shit,' I hiss, and my body flutters as if dropped from a height. Everything happens in one fluid movement – the cabinet is slammed shut just as the front door crashes open and then my hand is wrapped tight round Ellis's arm and we're ducking behind the cabinets.

I have no idea if we were seen. My teeth are clenched so hard I worry they might shatter. But when there's no shouting I assume we weren't noticed and I ease up, but only enough to quell the hammering of my heart to a few beats per second. I glance at Ellis, whose face is cracked open with terror, whites visible even in the dark, and I will him to calm down with my eyes, narrowed and unblinking. 'Quiet,' I mouth.

A flashlight. The beam is from a flashlight and it plays along the wall over our heads but never falls on to us; when it goes in completely the wrong direction I get too brave and poke out an eye and it's Booker near the front desk. He's there for a perceived eternity. 'Anyone?' he calls into the dark. *No, no, no.* This could ruin everything. I'd be out before I was even able to get started. My brain runs black. *Please*, I beg silently, to no one in particular. *Please. Please. Let me do this.*

It's so quiet I can hear Booker's ragged breath.

I count the nine seconds more that pass before the light finally retreats and the door opens, then shuts.

A beat. The room settles.

'Are they gone?' Ellis whispers.

I give it another few seconds to confirm, and when nothing else starts I nod. 'Yeah.'

Ellis gulps air. 'Who was it?'

Outside, there's the sound of an engine revving and a car driving away.

'Booker.' I emerge from behind the cabinet and Ellis follows. He's rubbing the spot on his arm that I'd grabbed. 'Sorry,' I say.

'What a g-g-*grip*.'

'We should get out of here.'

'*What?*' Ellis hisses. 'But he just checked.'

'He might come back.' I unlock the cabinet again and return the empty folder.

I'm sure I heard Booker drive off, but as I'm dragging Ellis towards the front door there's a lit-up part of my cerebral cortex that is absolutely delighting in the possibility of getting caught. 'Ah,' Booker would say, 'I see you inspect lighthouses and stations.' How *fun.*

I'm almost disappointed when there's nobody outside – just the sizzle of the saltwater lapping against spheres of frosted cerulean glass, and residual laughter haunting the now-faraway bonfire.

The blanket of night trembles in time with the ocean.

'Do you see him anywhere?' Ellis asks.

'No. We should still get out of here, though. Are you going back to the bonfire?'

'N-no, let's just – I kind of want to go home.'

'Sure,' I say. 'I'll take you.'

'I have lots of questions, though.'

'You and me both, bud.'

'You picked the lock.'

'Astute observation.'

'How?'

I think of him the day I arrived, all stubborn action wanting to be taken seriously, but wanting to *help* – and not understanding when I asked if it was fine to be left at the hotel alone. With the apparent blind trust he has towards everyone else for no apparent reason, I decide now that letting him in won't hurt. I don't like the thought of having to lie to him – which is a new concern for me. Lying was always natural. But his wide eyes in the glow of torchlight make me want to tell him everything.

'I used – you wouldn't believe it – a lock pick,' I say, and pat him on the arm.

'What were you going to do with the stuff in the folder? Why were you looking in the first place? How did you know –'

'Let's walk and talk,' I say, directing our momentum out of the parking lot, away from exposure. We start on the trek, headed to the island's north, towards the neck.

Ellis, despite having a much longer stride then me, is scurrying at my side like a puppy, trying to keep up. 'What were you looking for?'

The decisions present themselves for choosing. I could say anything. I could tell the truth. I could say, *Yes, I've been obsessed with your grandma for maybe six years and her music gives me a strange inexplicable endorphin rush and I've come to right every wrong in the world, that is, to dig up her bones*. I don't think this would be wise. Small lies to obtain a bigger, universally beneficial truth.

'Before I came to Sandown,' I begin, 'I was doing some research about the island, just for kicks. Eventually Roxy's name came up. Her music, her disappearance.' I pause to make sure we're on the same page. Ellis is considering, it seems, eyes aimed at his feet as we walk. 'There wasn't much information online. I guess I got curious about it and thought I'd do a little snooping about the situation once I got here.'

He processes this, the news trickling down into him like a drink. 'And what do you think? About all of it?'

I know saying this is a chance but his eyes are glinting like they're full of hunger for the words, so I say it. 'Well, I don't think she disappeared.'

'What do you think happened?'

'I think she might have been murdered.'

And the words affect him about as much as a breath. 'I do too.'

I can't tell if my aura opens or clamps down; spreading open like a Venus flytrap after a meal – or having the meal. 'Why do you think that?'

'Did Peyton tell you about – so, I didn't actually know Roxy was my grandma . . .'

'You thought she was your aunt. Yeah, she said.'

'Right. And my mom's been really torn up about this whole thing. And knowing what we know now, I . . . can't believe Roxy would have done that to my m-mom. There's no way. But M-mom thinks she just . . . left her. And I want proof. I want her to kn-know that's not what happened. What about you?'

'Because it doesn't make much sense to me, based on what I read, that she killed herself. That's the accepted theory, right? That, or she ran away?'

Ellis nods.

'I think there's evidence to suggest otherwise. People say so online – there're rumours about a suspicious note that Roxy allegedly left. Or, at least, I was hoping there would be, but I just broke into a police station to read an empty file.'

Ellis perks up. 'I have pictures of what was inside. The note was there. Not much else, though.'

I do my best to mask my excitement. 'Can I see?'

Ellis fishes his phone out of his pocket and pulls up an image.

My eyes flicker over it, the pixels that read *Case Number 2041* and *Reporting Officer* with a space left blank and *Incident*:

Call received approx. 4 a.m. Sunday morning from resident who discovered property known to belong to Catherine O'Hare [alias Roxy Raines]. Later in day Mary Anne Miller called w/ regards to vehicle left on property, known also to belong to Roxy. Search of vehicle revealed note of intent [attached]. Witness testimony and general knowledge of victim conclusive of runaway. No further investigation required.

'Roxy Raines wasn't her real name?' I ask.

He shakes his head. 'Oh no. We're all O'Hares. She made it up.'

'Why'd she do that?'

'Nana always said she was so much her own person that no one could name her anyways. I don't think she meant it as a compliment. I think Roxy started going by Roxy when she was, like, eight.'

'Where she'd get it from?'

'I dunno. Nana thought she took it from the word moxie.'

'And Raines?'

He shrugs. 'She wrote a lot about nature and stuff. I think she probably just liked how it sounded.'

There's also a box for a *Suspect*, where someone's name should have gone; this, naturally, is blank. Not whited-out – I make sure.

'Isn't Mary Anne the one with the diner?' I ask. 'The woman I'm working for?'

'Yeah, that's her.'

'Well,' I say. 'That's lucky.'

'What do you mean?'

'Sometimes people insert themselves into an investigation when they're guilty. We'll need to talk to her.'

'You sound like you know what you're talking about.'

I turn poised to fight when my brain interprets it as an accusation, but it's not. It's a compliment.

'I – I don't know about Mary Anne, though,' Ellis says.

'Why not?'

'I mean, her and my mom have been close forever. And helped us out with stuff. Money when we needed it.'

All the more reason for her to be a suspect, really, but I do my best to assuage him. 'Well, sure. Not a suspect necessarily. But she might know something more than what's written here. Is this the only page in the report?'

'Yeah.'

Unless, of course, the rest of it was moved. Or hidden. And there was still the question of why none of this was even in the folder to begin with. 'We might also want to have a chat with our friend Booker and find out why the folder was empty. I don't know how we'd bring it up without it being obvious we'd snooped, but –'

'Wait, there's more,' Ellis says; 'the note that it talks about. In the car.'

I swipe over to the next image.

i am so sorry to all my Friends but I must Go
suddenly. please do Not come looking for me. by
the time you read this i am Long Gone. God bless

93

'Ellis,' I say. 'This is ridiculous.'

'Yeah, I thought so too.'

I read it again, again, and I love that it's the original – I can see all the minutiae of the pen marks, the swirls of letters where whoever wrote this had pressed too hard, where the pen ran out and they had to scribble again. I only wish I could have held it myself. The thought that this might have been Roxy thrills me – and the thought that it might not have been her thrills me equally.

But I, like the others, do not think Roxy wrote this.

'Do you have any idea why it'd be written like this? The weird capitalization and word choice.'

'No. I th-thought it was really weird too.'

'And the . . . *God bless*? Roxy wasn't religious, was she?'

'Definitely not.'

'How do you know?'

'My nana *was* really religious and, uh, no one really tells me m-much, but I got the sense that that was something they'd fight about a lot.'

My body lights up.

'Do you think that's enough proof to say th-that she didn't write it?' Ellis asks.

I want to say yes but I can't in good conscience. 'No,' I say, and Ellis deflates. 'People can say all sorts of weird stuff in the midst of a breakdown, things they normally wouldn't. Or, maybe far-fetched – could it be sort of tongue-in-cheek? Trying to be irreverent?'

'Yeah. You're r-right.'

'Your great-grandma would have been around during the investigation. Did she know anything about what happened? Or your mom?'

Ellis shakes his head. 'If my nana had known something then she never said. And Mom would've been way too young. Like not even a year old yet. Even if she hadn't been she definitely wouldn't help me out with anything.'

'Why not?'

'She doesn't want me looking into this stuff at all.'

'So that's why you needed Roxy's folder.'

He nods. 'And we're probably gonna be gone by the end of summer anyway, so . . .'

'You're running out of time.'

'It had to be now,' he says, then breathes, realizing. 'You're the only one who gets it.'

I muster up all the urgency and authenticity in my voice that I can manage. 'Ellis, you want to figure out what happened to your grandma? Let me help you.'

'I m-mean, sure . . . not to b-b-be rude, b-but why are you so interested?'

Now is as good a moment as ever. I normally wouldn't have told anyone this. But he's regarding me with such an honest and quiet curiosity, this boy who behaves like he's in pieces; and, yeah, I guess a part of me thinks this is a chess move – because everything, *everything* is a chess move – but I also want to tell him something for no good reason, just because we're two human beings in the middle of the night who both believe in the same omitted history. Why not, I wonder, tell him everything.

'My sister disappeared.'

This is a nothing-sentence, really; it's a string of words so meaningless that I don't understand how they can even exist on their own. I predict Ellis will stop and he does, so I halt too and face him, so he has to understand me.

'When I was eleven. She was seventeen and she disappeared off the face of the planet and they never found her. She loved Roxy. Her music. I thought in, yeah, maybe a fucked-up kind of way, this could bring me closer to her.'

Ellis offers a vague expression of surprise, his eyebrows leaping and falling, and then the rest of him falls, too, and he says sorry even though there is nothing at all to apologize for.

'It's OK. But what I'm saying is that she at least got a proper search, and Roxy didn't. I wanna give it to her.'

And then – I can't believe it – Ellis is crying. Unmistakably, the moonlight bouncing off the tracks on his face. I don't remember the last time I cried in front of someone. Anyone, let alone an outsider to my existence, let alone about something that didn't concern me, let alone out here, like this, utterly exposed. I don't remember the last time I cried. And here he is, flaying himself in front of a near stranger for no good reason, as if it doesn't come across as weakness.

'What was her name?' Ellis asks.

'Celeste.'

He nods. Something about her name has settled him. 'OK. Yeah. I'm in,' he says, and apologizes again.

'It's all right.'

'But how? Where do we even start?' he asks.

'Hopefully I can be a useful outsider; maybe you're too close and there's something you missed. We're gonna have to talk to people. Interviews. And if people don't want to talk, then we have to dig up dirt until they do. That's how these things work.'

'I don't know anything about how these things work.'

'You don't have to. I'll help. I'll tell you what to do. And at this point,' I say, 'you don't have anything to lose. Right? You're leaving any day now.'

Ellis scoffs. 'Mom's *temper* is what there is to lose.'

'Isn't the truth more important?'

'I guess I'm scared of getting in trouble. And I'm scared of making her m-m-mad at me when all I want to do is help.'

'A boy who's really scared of getting in trouble wouldn't have followed me into the police station.'

There's a glimmer in his eyes then; for a moment I think it's biological, bioluminescence, but it's actually only the reflection from the quivering sea; we've reached the isthmus. A smile. 'I guess.'

'Let me help you,' I say again, lower and terse.

Ellis shuffles his feet. 'Well, do we need to make a bl-blood pact, or something?'

I smirk, spit into my taut palm and offer it to him.

'Ugh, gross,' he says, giggling, but returns the favour and we slap our hands together and hold, and then we're one. 'What do we do first?'

'When can we meet up again?' I ask. 'If there is some of Roxy's stuff in the attic then it's really important that we take a look at it together.'

'There's no way you can come over when my mom's at home,' he says. 'She'd never let us go up there.'

'When isn't she home?' *Now,* I think, remembering she's at the bonfire, but I don't want to suggest it lest Ellis thinks me too eager.

'Well, she goes to the mainland to stock up on Saturday mornings.'

I shift. Saturday might as well be a veritable lifetime away.

'I'm just really worried about her being suspicious,' he says, having sensed my dissatisfaction with his answer. 'You said we have to be careful, right? Well, I don't want to risk anything. Next Saturday. That's the only day I'll do it.'

My impatience is unfounded, I figure; we have the whole summer. 'All right. I can try to poke around and finagle some answers out of Mary Anne in the meantime.'

I look up and realize we're here, the Willowwood looming in the moonlight.

'Sounds good,' he says.

We exchange numbers in case we need to get in touch.

I watch Ellis leave. Once he reaches the front door he waves, a smile stretching across the whole of his face despite the heaviness of everything that had just transpired, despite all of it. There he is, headed into the house full of secrets that'll save us. Him, me, Sandown, Roxy.

This has all gone so well so far that I feel an inexplicable sense of rightness – that I'm meant to be here, in this spot, doing this. My cells are utterly aligned. I am Mona and maybe the only thing I'm meant to do in this life is be here. Ellis – I can't explain it – doesn't seem real. He at once seems younger than he is but wiser than he lets on. So much hurt and still so gentle. Maybe even gentler than he would have been otherwise.

This gargantuan shadow of the investigation shrinks into something manageable. I'm light on my feet. Nothing like the police station break-in will happen again; everything will be under control from this moment on.

Celeste doesn't deserve anything less.

I turn and head back towards my dorm, my footsteps barely a suggestion over the sizzle of waves from every direction dying against the rocks.

PART TWO

Take the Bullet Out

CHAPTER 9

MONDAY 31 MAY

There's a shadow in me that doesn't waver.

The eternal tar-dripped facet of my personhood. I could make myself whatever I wanted to be, were it not for the trauma – a chameleon always outed by the shadow, marked by the same dark matter.

I fight my way out. If I'm locked in, I jemmy the lock. If I'm lost in the woods, I draw a map.

And when I first noticed Celeste was gone, vanished from the trail like an unlit firefly in the dark, I was sure she'd done it to scare me.

Vision whipped straight from the sky, wispy half-clouds and back – I was alone and the world was so big. Music, from somewhere. It was driving me crazy, the cacophony of the birdsong and the drone of the *music* from an unknown source.

This part of the trail wasn't commonly frequented, too big for anyone to come by too often. So I sat and didn't move. A quiet sort of fear, agony put on pause. Full body shut down. Sit here. Don't move. An older couple found me eventually, not before it was starting to get dark. Me, and Celeste's phone on the trail, a few yards from me. I hadn't even noticed it there.

By then, the music had stopped.

I felt their worry like a wave over me, and only then did I really start to register the fear. *Where do you think she could be? She left?* I wanted to save myself the embarrassment of having to explain that *Yes, that is like her*, and *Yes, she would do that.*

She must have got lost. Did she go off the trail? Yes, maybe.

Oh dear. Oh dear. She's lost.

They helped me back to the parking lot. Everything that followed is a blur.

Dad asked a million times if I saw anything and each time that answer was the same. That was when I learned that some things are so troubling that one's brain doesn't simply lock a memory away – it's possible that the memory isn't registered in the first place. One's body remains in the moment, fleshy and warm as the day one was born, unoccupied.

Everyone loved Celeste. She was going to Harvard. Beautiful and whip-smart. Teachers who had had the both of us would get to Perry on the register and there was always a look of disappointment. Mr Newhouse had chuckled a little under his breath and said, 'Oh, wasn't expecting that.'

After this, after the girl who was supposed to make good use of her life vanished, I decided I was to make good use of mine. Dad didn't even approve of the podcast – he saw it as some weird profane vestige of grief, a sign I hadn't grieved correctly. What he doesn't know is the podcast was born from the searching rather than the losing. I don't know why, but as we searched the woods I knew they'd never find her.

Maybe it's a secret I keep. I hope I'm wrong. I hope I'm just growing. But I can't shake the fear that when combined the stuff Dad and the woman who gave birth to me are made of can only combust. Or maybe we were rigged as a pair with premature time bombs and my countdown's shrinking. But the most pressing concern is that Celeste and I had never been separate terrors at all – that the two of us and our paths are inexorably bound to one another – and I'll find myself at the bottom of a ravine one day too, mind splintering as I'm taken back by the dark.

Maybe.

The podcast came from the buzz of a hunt without capture. The somehow comforting futility of a search with nothing left to find, the certainty that nothing was waiting behind the trees to catch you.

And I'm thinking all this on Monday morning, when I realize despite all the uncertainty, the disconnect, the unfamiliarity, that I am happier now than I have been in a long time.

Peyton and I spent Sunday driving around the island, her showing me all the relevant locales, which I already knew about but pretended like I didn't, in case she had any interesting insights – grocery store, laundromat, cheapest liquor store. ('Here is where you will *not* go because it is very illegal, and the dude that runs it does *not* forgo an ID check if you give him five bucks.' To be fair I didn't know that one.) I'm now entirely confident in my bearings; it would be next to impossible to get lost. We'd gone halfsies on a cheap fan and its low buzz is both comforting and useful, firstly for its intended purpose of recirculating the humid air in our room to create something resembling coolness, and secondly for droning out Peyton's intermittent snoring. Despite this, so far, I don't hate having a room-mate as much as I thought I would. Sure, the notion of sharing what had always been a private space with someone else is odd, and if aliens were to visit Earth and Peyton was the first one to greet them I'd say they were being thrown in at the deep end of humanity. But otherwise, I'm unusually comfortable.

But a lack of privacy still throws a wrench in the plans and I'm unsure if I can trust her. I'm minding myself, and still keep the podcast stuff in the locked drawer in my head.

It's six and I'm already awake; with a ten-minute walk to the diner, enough time for me to get ready. I pull on my khakis as quietly as I can manage, casting a sideways glance at sleeping Peyton, aware of my nakedness. Her bare leg hangs over the side of the bed, blanket twisted around her like a Grecian drape, the light filtering through the still-dirty balcony window in bits. After the comedown time from Saturday (the revelations about the island, my time here, Ellis) spending Sunday with her was easy and light.

But of course I'm thinking about the case. About Ellis, and Sylvia, and Roxy's empty folder in the police station. About the whole town concealing an unconcealable truth.

I'm about to leave when Peyton groans and sits up behind me.

'Are you alive?' I ask.

She moans, holding her hands to her lower back. 'Christ. Not for much longer if the mattress keeps doing *that* to my spine. I'm getting old. Whoa,' she says when she sees I'm dressed. 'What time is it?'

'Quarter past six.'

'*Yeesh.*' She props herself up on her elbows, one eye screwed shut. 'I like your khakis. Real prep school douchebag chic.'

'You should actually shut up because you have to wear them too.'

She shrugs. 'Sylvia lets us wear whatever we want. No khakis for me. Enjoy your day, Dead Poet Society.' Meanwhile, I'm watching her mouth, which turns up as she speaks, even when she's half-asleep.

'Did they even wear khakis in –'

'Leave this place.'

'*Gah.*'

I gather my things and shut the door behind me, smiling a little to myself. Suddenly I'm thinking about her lips and then I'm not thinking about her lips and the day goes on.

The walk is assisted in part by Google Maps and some cold water fished out of our mini-fridge. God, it's already hot. I curse the dress code – and myself, for choosing what now seems like a pair of unreasonably thick khaki pants.

The diner is off the main strip, sandwiched between two residential blocks – more of a local spot, which is why they only needed one extra hire to handle it, apparently.

Then the diner's in view and the seriousness of this all comes flooding back to me, to the bomb that was going to roll in and knock the whole thing off its hinges. I was going to learn this island and its one hundred and eighty-two inhabitants from the inside out. Over half of the island was over age sixty-five. I considered age ten in 1986 to be the cut-off of potentially knowing any useful information, so that meant around seventy per cent of the island would know.

And Mary Anne makes up half of the names on the police report. I decide not to ask Mary Anne or Archie pointedly about anything today – probably not even for the first week. I need to gauge everyone first, and their limits; who might have a motive for what. With the whole summer to pick them apart, barrelling head first into interrogation, I decide, wouldn't be wise.

The front door of the diner is locked, the only light from inside coming from the kitchen. Jiggling the doorknob a couple of times makes enough noise to make myself known, I figure, and before long, it's her – Mary Anne, apron and blue short-sleeve button-up, emerging from the kitchen. She unlocks the door without pleasantries and turns away; I assume I'm expected to follow her.

When she speaks, slightly crooked gradient teeth slip from beneath thin lips to say, 'Welcome back. You're late.'

'My packet said six thirty.'

'Six thirty means six fifteen.'

Of course it does. 'Right. Sorry. I'll be here at six fifteen tomorrow.'

Mary Anne grunts.

If nothing else, The Island Spot is clean; the black-and-white tiled floor shines and, as far as I can tell, the spongy sea-green booths look relatively unworn. Quiet, muffled clanking drifts through from the kitchen (not a Seasonal, I don't think; I met two others at the bonfire who were placed here but I don't think our shifts are going to overlap). There're only six booths in total – I count them – not including the small bar, which has five stools. A variety of ocean-themed tat adorns the walls, shells and buoys and what looks like pictures of Sandown taken from decades ago.

'You've got food-service experience,' she says, as I look around. It's not a question.

Food service. My application. 'Yes,' I lie. I am, however, a quick enough learner to make this not seem like a lie. I found a poorly designed website for the diner that included a menu, which I've already memorized. Not that this is even the sort of place where you had to do that, anyway; seems more like coffee, grits, smile, done.

'First year, you said?'

'Yep.'

Mary Anne wanders back into the kitchen and she hasn't told me to but I figure I should follow her. This is the source of the clanking from before – Archie. He's washing dishes in a substantial industrial sink. I say, 'Morning,' but Archie doesn't acknowledge me, either, and I wonder if I'm a ghost, which Mary Anne must notice because she explains, 'They say it's early-onset dementia,' like it's the least inflammatory piece of information in the world, as if she was merely providing the context of a photograph. Archie doesn't even flinch. I do.

'Oh, gosh.' I don't know what to say.

'Don't mind him. We used to run the place together but he just helps me out, cleaning and such, now. Though I don't know how much longer he can keep that up for, either.'

I'm uncomfortable that she's saying all this in front of him but I suppose I don't have a right to be. 'I'm sorry.'

'Eh. What can you do? Anyway. You won't be needing to come back here much, 'cept for the service counter, handing off tickets.'

She introduces me to Charlie, the other line cook, a short, friendly man, maybe in his forties, who's missing his left front tooth.

'So it's just me out front?'

'That all right?'

I blink. 'Definitely.'

'Small operation.'

Mary Anne gives me some basic training – waiting tables and hosting and how to write down the orders and how to use the register. Most of which she assumes I already know how to do, which I don't, necessarily, but it's not proving especially difficult. Mary Anne says I have a face for waitressing, which I guess is a compliment. I'm allowed to keep my tips and read when it's slow – no phones, though.

I shadow her in the morning, seeming vaguely bored the whole time, and I learn something useful, if intensely irritating – I can tell who is a local by how they react. One of the first groups is a mom, a dad and two little girls – suspected tourists by the bathing-suit straps that poke from under their T-shirts. They are perfectly pleasant and agreeable and Mary Anne speaks to them formally but they don't seem to mind.

When the locals sit down, they are perfectly happy to see Mary Anne, who calls them by name, who call *her* by name – but as soon as they catch sight of me, they turn in on themselves, quieten down, comment something about 'that time of the year'. My fanciful hope of becoming one with the locals is fizzling out by the second seeing how much disdain they have for outsiders. Not that I imagined they'd welcome me with open arms, but I'd hoped for better than active discomfort towards my existence.

Five groups of guests bring us nearly to noon and I decide this isn't going to be a particularly difficult job.

Over the eight-hour shift Mary Anne takes eleven smoke breaks. Smoke breaks, I come to understand, don't always mean that she smokes but she disappears into her office to do . . . I'm not quite sure what. The door to her office is kept locked and there's a faint beeping coming from inside that I can't place. On the fourth time I catch a glimpse – a full bookshelf, a cluttered desk with drawers, a safe, and what looks like a collection of radios and radio equipment hanging and displayed on the far wall. I decide that must have been what the beeping was from.

I'm not sure yet how I plan to bring up the subject of Roxy with Mary Anne. Her noticing the car could have been entirely innocent, of course. I'm trying to place Archie as well and am finding it difficult.

Before I came to Sandown, I'd hoped I would have been taken over by some sixth sense upon my arrival, that I would've felt *Yes, she was here*, but I don't. No premonitions. Nothing supernatural.

I was happy to rely on facts; it was the matter of *obtaining* them that would prove difficult.

When my shift finishes, a hot rush of panic tells me I'm in way over my head, that this is impossible, that who do I think I am, trying to turn an entire town, an entire island on its head? But then I think of small me climbing inside my guts to upturn anything that needed upturning. If that fixed me, if all it took was a bit of uncomfortable rooting?

Well, I'd say thank you very much.

CHAPTER 10

I'm surprised by my exhaustion when I get back to the dorm, despite it only being three in the afternoon. A combination, I assume, of the past few days of intensity – the fact that working at the diner, although not that busy, is still a bit more gruelling than I'd anticipated, what with the constant social performativity and being on my feet. Also, apart from the English muffin Charlie slung me for breakfast, I haven't eaten, and there's not anywhere near enough fluid in me to compensate for the heat. I grab a bottle of water from the mini-fridge and swallow it all in almost one gulp, then immediately crack open another. The icy shock of it trickles along the edges of my empty stomach.

I pull out the notebook from my podcast drawer and get to scribbling – catching up, logging every solitary, seemingly unimportant thing I can remember. These episodes, although obviously about Roxy, will hopefully serve to document every element of my time here. It's not only about Roxy, it's about Sandown – and it's not only about Sandown, it's about me, the messenger of it to the rest of the world.

Before I know it, two hours have passed and Peyton comes crashing into the room.

'*Phew!*' she says, falling on to her bed. She takes a loud, gurgling slurp from an iced coffee. '*Ah*. Hello, sport.'

I nonchalantly but quickly shut my things and shelve them away. 'Hey. Everything go OK?'

'Just as mind-numbing as I remember. Cleaned. Cleaned. Goofed off with Ellis. Arranged some flowers. Pulled some weeds. And, oh yeah, cleaned. How was ol' *Mary Anne*?'

'Definitely kind of intense.'

'A rock and a hard place, come to battle it out.'

'Which is which?'

Peyton looks me up and down. 'Hard place.'

I think of my notes. I'm tempted to ask about Ellis – I don't want her to suspect anything necessarily, but in the way that I don't want *anyone* to suspect anything, and Peyton, I've decided, isn't just anyone. My gut says she's harmless and potentially knowledgeable, which at this moment is a winning combination.

'Hey, so, remember what you told me about Ellis's grandma?' I ask. 'How she went missing?'

'Yeah, followed by you vanishing into the night like a weird and moody bat? How could I forget?'

'Do you know why Ellis would be looking into her disappearance?'

She recoils in a way I find exciting. Mystery afoot. 'What – what does that even mean? Is he?'

'Apparently he put a request in with the police chief for a copy of her case file.'

'Really? Ellis, he's not the sort to – *yeesh*. No, I don't know why he'd do that. Oh, poor kid, he's probably now all obsessed with his *real* grandma or something, I bet. How do you even know Ellis was looking into it?'

'Well, I was kinda curious about Roxy after I'd spoken to you, and I wanted to look at the report myself, but Booker wouldn't let me have it. He mentioned though that someone else had asked for it recently. I put two and two together and assumed it was Ellis.'

'Huh,' she says. 'Weird. Weird that he did that. Just – don't bother him about it, I guess. I don't think he really likes to talk about that stuff. He's processing a lot.'

I want to tell her that maybe she doesn't know him quite as well as she thinks she does.

Peyton falls back on to her bed, which sends the straps of her tank top splaying outwards, and I notice her tan lines, the thin strips of parallel pale skin tracing the curve of her shoulders. I think about touching them. 'Right.'

Then my phone buzzes beside me on the desk.

Dad.

It rings three times, no part of me wanting to react to the situation at hand, before Peyton says, 'Uh, you gonna get that?'

I hadn't wanted to answer, knowing Peyton would hear everything – but I'm feeling especially nihilistic for whatever reason. This might as well happen. 'Hi.'

'Mona.' The metallic twang of his voice burrows into me and expands into a longing to hear it in person. He's an absent father but he's still a father, the only remaining extension of myself, and a part of me wants to be close to him. I've never been further away. I move my free hand on top of the one holding the phone without thinking. Dad says my name again. I'm embarrassed by it, for some reason. 'What have you done?'

'I'm fine.'

'I don't care that you're fine. I care that you're gone.'

'Thanks.'

'I looked up Sandown – what on earth are you doing *there*? And so soon before college – when were you planning on coming back? You only have, what, two months before you move in?'

I needed to tell him eventually. 'It's not as big of a deal as you're making it.' Peyton doesn't understand and is still flashing me a wicked smile, a conspiratorial glance of *Oh, parents*, some response to my ardent teenage rebellion that understates what's about to come.

'Of course it is.'

He has to find out eventually. 'Dad, please, can I call you back? My room-mate is –'

'You need to come home.'

He has to find out. 'I need you to *listen* –'

'I mean, you're not there for *money*, obviously. So what is it? You're not . . . finding yourself, are you? *Finding yourself* is a lie perpetuated by –'

'I didn't get in.' The line crackles. Peyton cranes her neck up like a bird.

Dad breathes. 'You didn't get in *where?*'

'Harvard. I didn't get in.' Silence. I'm sorry I'm not Celeste. I'm sorry the one you loved is gone. I'm sorry I'm all that's left.

I'd wanted to apply to other schools but Dad said it'd hardly be necessary – legacy students have a forty-six per cent greater chance of getting admitted. He'd always encouraged that in me, a sort of ugly, bullheaded confidence, scoffing at fallbacks or contingencies (in Celeste, as well, but it suited her better). Celeste was accepted no problem, of course. My application was solid. I'd written a perfectly mawkish essay about Celeste and my 'journalism', but the night before it was due I'd removed every reference to my sister and satisfied the word count requirement by, at the end, writing 'o what a tangled web we weave' two hundred and fifty times. To be honest I don't remember doing this; I only realized what I'd done after checking a couple of days later to make sure the application had submitted. I didn't tell Dad.

'Maybe,' I say, 'I can reapply next year. Either way, right now I'm here and that's the way it is.'

A beat. 'I'm coming to get you.'

My gut drops. 'No, that's impossible. You know that's impossible. You're so busy.'

'What's today? The thirty-first?' The phone rustles. 'I have a case that we can't leave but I should have a spare day at the end of the week, next at the latest, and when I do, I'm *coming to get you*.'

It's always been complicated.

He's always been like that. Detached. Distant. Formal.

I fight the urge to comment on the ridiculousness of the lack of urgency my dad has towards even what he has deemed an emergency scenario. Not even urgent enough to come get me now. Not even after Celeste. I could be wandering through the woods myself and I wouldn't even be sure he'd drop what he was doing. Of course I don't *want* him to come. But, yes, maybe I want him to want to.

'Are you gonna drag me away kicking and screaming?'

'I won't have to. Surely they're not letting a seventeen-year-old work and board without parental permission.'

'Dad, please. This is really important to me.'

'Not important enough to do it honestly.'

It's for Celeste, I want to say. But Peyton's looking right at me, and I can't summon the words.

'Enjoy yourself while you can,' he says evenly. 'See you soon.'

The line dies against my ear.

He's not the type of parent to punish, but when he does it's because a rule has been broken, not because of the severity of the indiscretion or the act itself. I know inside Dad might be battling with the knowledge that nothing dangerous is happening, that perhaps I'm seventeen and alone, but really, what else is new? It doesn't matter that I'm safe. It matters that I've disobeyed the unspoken rule of not becoming a runaway, that I lied. And he would never say it, but it matters that I've scared him.

'Was that –' Peyton offers. 'Sorry. I'm confused.'

'It's sort of hard to explain. But I lied,' I say. 'To you. I don't actually go to Harvard. I don't go anywhere. Sorry.'

'Oh. Why'd you do that?'

The real answer is too complicated. 'I don't know. I tell lies sometimes.'

She sucks on the straw of her coffee for a moment, then says, 'I mean, you wanted to seem smart, right? New place. You can be whoever.' That sort of affirmation that comes at unexpected moments – that isn't the way anyone ought to react to anything – well, it stays with you, says *This is how the world is*. This is what others will tolerate. Act accordingly. Peyton doesn't know it but she's validating my brain as we speak. *It's OK to lie*, she says, and I understand. I'll carry it.

'I guess that's it. You're not mad?'

She shrugs. 'I don't even know you.'

I almost laugh. What a bizarre thing to say.

Peyton riffles through her dresser drawer and emerges with a deck of cards. 'You know how to play Egyptian Rat Screw?'

'*What* did you call me?'

We play until the early hours. It takes a few rounds for me to get the hang of it, but then I end up winning a couple hands, even though it's one of those fast, flailing sorts of card game I'm not usually good at. I like playing with her. I'm so close to her that I can smell her gum. Cinnamon. At one point we both go to slap the deck and I'm there first but she smacks down on my hand so hard, the sound absolutely piercing, that I see stars, the back of my head practically neon pink, and Peyton laughs so much that she topples over.

'I'm sorry! I'm sorry!' she screams through tears.

I roll over, laughing too, curling my arm into my chest. 'I need . . . medical attention . . .'

'Sorry, let me see, let me see,' she says, and holds my wrist firmly and smacks it again.

She lets me whack her hand in retaliation and it hurts me more than it hurts her, and that makes us crack up again.

'So she does smile,' Peyton finally says.

I like her.

Though I'm still thinking about my failures and my lies and if the latter are something I actually want to stop doing or just *feel* like I should stop doing. The worry fades quickly. Do I like Peyton? I don't know. Peyton is fine. She won't get in my way. Sunbeam down a well.

I wonder if that is something that comes with age – a desire for self-betterment, to change the parts of myself that are largely undesirable. For now, I'm enjoying them. Not enjoying, maybe. I understand them. They get me what I want.

A stem without thorns is lesser. A stem without thorns gets eaten.

Though I worry, as the night blackens, as Peyton hops from bed to bed like a maniac, as I keel over with laughter, curled in the knotted cradle of the dark even while all this joy sprawls around me: I worry that I'm only thorns, and nothing else.

CHAPTER 11

TUESDAY 1 JUNE

I turn between waking and sleep. Waking and sleep until each is the other and I can't tell the difference. Darkness, half-darkness, spinning . . .

> She traverses the brush in the light of the moon
> How does this all end, speak to her soon –

Celeste.

They found her. She's back – but she's wrong she's different the woods made her different made her different changed her and she's crawling up the foot of the bed and her hair's made of leaves and her hand gripping on my blanketed leg feels like fire have you ever felt yourself decay it's like

> For comfort in trouble she whispers her name,
> And Orion waves,
> Orion waves . . .

and there're spiders falling from empty hollows of her eyes and they're on me, me, they're in my mouth and my nose and everywhere every where ev ery   where

Up!

The year is 1986 and the sleepy town of Sandown Bay is –

Wake *up*!

Up.

Up.

The room is dark. I'm not in the woods. I am in a bed. My bed. Mine – does any of this belong to me? This bed. Peyton's asleep, breathing softly from across the room. I'm intact. I'm alive and breathing and beating.

I am Mona. I am Mona. I am Mona.

But I don't believe it. And the bed still feels gory and wet so I need to get out.

I rip my headphones from my ears; I'd fallen asleep with them in. Roxy had been playing. *Orion*. It's four-thirty in the morning.

I'm on edge, that's all. I'm exhausted after the weekend and yesterday, trying to keep my cool in front of Ellis, in front of Peyton – the awful call from my dad.

Originally I might have been thrilled by the ease of the leaving, my ability to be anywhere in the world at any given moment, as long as I had enough money and nerve. But now without any familiar sense of place or normality I'm tense. I broke into a police station a couple of nights ago to illegally look at the decades-old police report of a woman whose body was never found; of course I am.

Am I becoming myself or moving further from her?

Run. I need to run.

I slip on my tennis shoes. I'm going to circumnavigate the island, up past the isthmus to the edge of the forest and back down towards the pier. Twice, hopefully. Maybe three times. In high school, before a run, there'd be a compulsive itch in my feet, in all of me, the sort of itch that is only quelled by propelling yourself forward on your own volition, a reminder of what your body can do and where it can get you.

The going is fine at first. I'm seemingly the only one awake and the air is already hot. The rhythm of my feet scraping against the ground is slowly dulling every other sound; seagulls scream across the bay. The air smells hot and clear. I am seventeen and my name is Mona Perry and this is my body and I am running, running, and I could continue to run until I drop and no one would know the difference.

Two minutes in and my breath is already sputtering out in uneven gusts, my calves burning red. My whole body is prickling, almost, and then I realize I'm not imagining it and I peel a pair of mating mayflies from my arm. I wipe my forehead. A bead of sweat travels down my chest and I smooth down my shirt to eradicate it and all the while my legs are turning like cogs.

When I guess I've been running for twenty minutes, I check my phone. It's actually only been ten – and I've only gone half a mile.

I wipe a bit of spit from the corner of my mouth with so much force that my incisor cuts into my lip and a burst of copper sinks into my tongue. What's wrong with me? God, it's hot. My eyes water.

Now I'm through the cemetery and I stumble on a shallow hole in the ground. I nearly fall but catch myself. The burn is wonderful. The burn keeps me alive. I am boiling water and the burn is all that will keep me moving. I'm impossibly warm. Hell is not as hot as my flesh on Sandown Bay.

Faster.

I think of Ellis the night of the bonfire and his big pleading eyes shining wet in the moonlight. I think about lying to him, right to his face, want to throw myself into the sea. I don't want to lie to him, but I have to so I can help him.

Am I like my sister? Am I just here to hurt and lie and take? Am I worse than my sister? Can I not even wear the mask she wore?

Legs legs one foot in front of the other shick shick shick . . .

Will the thick deep green be the last thing I ever see when I wade out of this world and am given back to the dark?

Roxy, where are you? Roxy Raines and your poor lonely grandson. Show yourself so I can bring you home, so all of them can learn your real name, so I can dust off your bones.

Do I have anything to offer the world besides anger . . .

I've made Dad so unhappy. Celeste made him happy. Mom made him happy. It should have been me.

Anger and fear . . .

I'll make Dad happy. Bones will make him happy. I'll be worth something, then. Bones will bring me closer to Celeste.

Then, ahead of me, slinking through the oaks lining the road, I swear there's someone watching.

Suddenly, someone, watching me. Long hair spilling around them.

Celeste? My breath catches in my throat.

This is when I fall.

My legs are going too fast, fighting for ground one after the other and they tangle and lock and I fall, propelled forward, and I know my chin bashes against the ground based on the pressure but not yet the pain. But when I get back up and keep going, I know the wetness on my face isn't sweat, and this realization makes my legs buckle again.

It's so hot. *It's so hot.* And the last thing I see before I melt completely is the sharp drop of the pier and a man I recognize at the dock, the massive ferry, his confusion becoming alarm when the infiltrating grey becomes too obscene to endure and I fall again for the final time.

The water-smoothed pebbles press into my back and hold me there, suspended in the black. Like little hands. Little round eyes, watching, spread so wide that I'm compelled to open my own, flooded by the sizzling white-hot. Little clicking tongues. Or more than clicking. Voices. Say it isn't right for a girl to be so angry, to claw merrily at her own flesh, for the pain to remind her of coming home. No, it isn't right. But there's nothing else.

Blinking conjures a face. I recognize it. Handlebar moustache, small rodent eyes.

He says something that echoes and hurts my ears and I don't hear it because his shadowed face is swimming laps in the dark. Yes, all of him is swimming, but then he's offering a hand to me and I take it. The roughness of his palm, like a hand pressed to bark, is enough to shake me out of my daze. 'Hey. Girl. You all right?'

Frank. The ferryman. I let him haul me up and say I'm fine but in a trembling not-fine way.

'Ain't you that girl who looked nothing like her picture? Gave me lip on the dock?'

Salty sea air wafts past and I breathe it. In the distance, the lighthouse hangs from the sky as an omen, light like an explosion against the pinprick stars. 'Yes,' I say pathetically. 'I'm sorry.' I don't really mean to apologize.

'Well, s'all right,' he says. 'You gonna be OK?'

To my ringing ears the question seems incredibly profound and it makes me woozy again. *I might not be OK, sir. Help.* I brush my chin with my fingertips, which reemerge with enough blood to make my knees buckle. 'Uh,' is all I can say.

He looks behind like someone's expecting him and turns back, hurried. 'Come on, then. There's a first-aid kit in the dock station.'

'Thank you. I'm sorry – this is really nice of you.'

He grumbles in a way I suppose is a response as he leads me down the hill and towards the dock. Red seeps between the gaps in my fingers. The ocean wobbles.

'You not good with blood or something?'

I sway as though at sea.

'Whoa, all right, pull it together for a few more steps.'

I follow him down the dock, into the small shack labelled with a nautical sign reading TICKETS. This is where we'd docked, the first day. He's talking but I'm still thinking of the life spurting from my chin and I need to sit down. 'Where the hell are you from that you don't know not to work yourself that hard in the heat? And you're a skinny little thing. Ain't safe.'

I absent-mindedly correct my posture, though even beside him I barely reach his shoulders. He's a tall man, old but sturdy. 'Yeah,' I say, sweet, agreeable. 'I guess I learned my lesson.'

The door to the station creaks when it opens. Inside, it smells like the salty must of fish in here, and dust. I itch my nose. It's barely the size of a shed. I sit on a rickety chair in the corner. A radio is mounted on the far wall, beeping. Frank pulls open a mini-fridge – one tray is full of bottles of water, the other a six-pack of Bud Light. I think for a second he's getting me a beer but he doesn't, and I shiver when I wrap my fingers round the cool sweating skin of the plastic. 'Thank you.'

'Yeah, that's all right. And here, er, for your chin.' He deals me a napkin, dotted already at the side with the sweat from his hand. I take it politely, avoid his stain, hand still shivering with adrenaline, and press.

He's old enough to remember something and it's now or never. 'Your name's Frank, right?'

'Yes'm.' He uses another napkin to dab at the glistening expanse of his forehead.

'How long have you been running the ferry?'

He chuckles, and it's a throaty, ragged sound, full-bodied enough to hold in my hand. 'Well, wasn't always captain but I've been hauling people over this side of the Atlantic for close to forty years now.'

I blot my chin, pushing in too hard, the sting striking all the way up through my jaw. I grind my teeth as if to steady myself. I don't love what I'm about to do but I'm not sure how else to do it. 'Do you know a kid called Ellis?' I ask. 'I think he lives on the island full-time.'

I don't expect his discomfort to be quite so obvious, but Frank visibly shifts, his jaw tensing. He grunts in affirmation.

I worry I've already blown my shot with him. 'He's been talking a lot about his grandma. Roxy. Kind of a weird situation.'

He scoffs. 'Yeah, I heard he's been digging about it from Booker. Strange. Strange boy. Strange family.'

'It all seems kind of crazy, to be honest.'

'Well, sure. Though Roxy was kind of crazy herself.'

'What about her?'

There's a new energy emanating from him – bordering on giddiness, as if he *wants* to talk. I can't imagine I'd feel much differently. After thirty years of uncomfortable strained silence, maybe one would actually *love* to talk. And even with the little I have to piece together at this point, it's certainly a good story. 'Real spitfire of a girl. So damn angry all the time.'

'About what?'

'Oh, anything. Someone lookin' at her funny was enough to set her off.'

'She got in fights?'

'Oh, did Roxy get in fights. That girl was a walking skirmish. Would probably skewer people with her guitar if it weren't the thing she loved more than anyone.'

This is working. I do my best to keep the tone conversational – nothing too pointed, nothing too heavy. Actually, he seems to be enjoying talking about it. I laugh. 'Was there anyone in particular?'

'I remember she got into it with Lenore a couple of times, over jobs. Never got along.'

I don't know who Lenore is; I'll need to find out. 'But this wasn't real stuff, right? Like, I bet no one ever talked about really hurting her.'

He swigs his water. 'Oh, I think the whole of Sandown did, at one point or another. Things were different, though, after – that year no one saw a lick of her . . .'

'Before she disappeared, you mean? Why?'

'Well, she was carrying Sylvia,' he says, like it's obvious.

'Was she ashamed?'

'I don't know if she was. Constance was devastated, certainly.'

That must have been her mother's name.

'Assume they didn't get along,' I say.

'Oh, no. Constance smacked that girl around all day long.'

My stomach drops. 'What do you mean?'

'Nothing that kids ought not to be getting these days. Couple cracks round the head sometimes.' The steadiness with which he says this unnerves me and I suppose he can tell, based on his throaty chuckle. 'Not you, huh? Anyway, Lenore took up the regular slot at Indigo, so she wasn't missin' her too much. Tell you what, you reminded me of her a little, that first day you came. Same kinda fire. She was all into that, oh, I dunno . . . feminism and stuff.' He pauses, looks off elsewhere. 'I found it, you know.'

'Found what?'

He nods towards the sea. 'Her guitar. In the bay.'

I nearly twitch with excitement. 'Really?'

'That's right. Washed up right here, actually. Was a surprise at the time because the bay's pretty clean, and I didn't even know what it was at first, but the thing was so distinct, even though however long it'd been in the water it still looked like hers. I found it first thing while I was, uh, prepping the ferry. She'd painted these little . . . flowers all over it. Not to my taste, but, eh. Each to their own. That's how I knew it was hers, anyways.'

'Were you running the ferries around the time she went missing? Would you have noticed her onboard?'

'Might've, but I never . . .' In the wake of his speech's trail, Frank looks at me like I've insulted him – maybe realizing, after having been transported to what seemed like his own little world, that he's said far too much. 'What's this about, then?'

'Nothing,' I say. 'Just curious.'

'Well,' Frank drinks his water in quick jerks, swigs like it's whisky and smooths down his moustache. I notice now how small the shack is. A square of light filters through the window and spotlights him. 'I certainly don't know anything about that.'

'Thanks for helping me out,' I say. I go to leave. 'I'm feeling a lot better.'

'That Ellis is bad news, you know.' This makes me stop; I wonder if he knew that it would. 'You don't wanna get mixed up with any of this. That family is broken. Bad genes. Something. You can hear it every time he speaks that there's something . . .' He gestures, with an open hand, towards his own head. 'Wrong there.'

I turn, making sure I have one foot outside the hut in case I need to break. 'Really?'

'I think God doesn't make mistakes.'

'All right. Thanks for your help.'

I stride out of the hut, back to somewhere, anywhere else, I don't care where I'm going, I just care about getting away. If it's a murder suspect I'm looking for, then I think I might have just found the first.

CHAPTER 12

After what seems an impossibly long trek to the dorm, powered only by low-level impulse, I think of texting Ellis to tell him what's happened but decide he's almost definitely still asleep. In the meantime I write down every solitary detail about what just happened.

The sunrise cleanses everything. The sky has lightened to eggshell blue, shapes harder to pick out from my bleached memory – but Frank's still there, hazy on the borders, like the vestige of a dream. It did happen; my chin still smarts to prove it.

I'm not supposed to see Ellis until Saturday but this can't wait. Frank mentioned a woman named Lenore. We need to talk to her.

I don't sleep again. I leave for work at six without waking Peyton (for the second time this fractured morning – she sleeps like a damn rock), fifteen minutes earlier than before, and the sensation is that of walking through water, exhaustion the friction that makes every movement sticky and awkward. There's no wind down here but the clouds are practically skipping across the sky, still outlined with the pink vignette of early morning, like scabs.

The morning light, no longer sinister, clears my head and makes it possible to act instead of short-circuit. I text Ellis.

Me: Do you know anything about Frank?
The ferry captain?

I think about everything Frank said. Guitar made for skewering. A walking confrontation. Always fighting over something.

I feel pieces of Roxy form in my head and lock – pieces, maybe, that were already there, but now with names. I can almost see her in the room. Those bright green eyes, long blonde hair. I'm trying to decide what she means to me, what she is, what most accurately conveys the inimitable gush of her life – a knife of a woman who pushed until there was no body left to pierce. An alien. A feeling. A roll of thunder trapped inside a woman's body. I desperately wish to know her. I almost feel like I do. When I play any of her songs there's something intimate there, something almost too near – like she understands the badness. Like she was there to see it. I want to get back in bed and imagine her there with me. I can't explain why she feels so close to me.

At the diner, I say morning to Mary Anne and get started on the opening tasks, which she's now, on the second day, evidently decided I can already be left to do on my own (I can) – wiping down the tables and bar, refilling the receipt paper, turning on the radio. Mary Anne requests the sixties hits channel – presently playing 'Daydream Believer' by The Monkees. It's only my second day and, no, I haven't worked a busy tourist weekend yet but everything seems to be going fine so far. Generally Mary Anne is happy to leave me to my own devices, and I'm happy to leave her to hers – sometimes helping in the back of house with Charlie and Archie but otherwise mainly in her office, doing God knows what.

We open at seven, the sun warming the first thin strip of the island, and I flip over the paper OPEN sign that hangs in the window. Not long after this a familiar face sends the doors chiming: Booker.

My stomach churns. I think for certain that he must know, that he saw Ellis and me in the station on Saturday night, that he's come to confront me.

'Table for one, please,' he says, already a watery glisten on his brow.

'Sure. Nice to see you again.'

'Mm,' he says. 'Mary Anne already showing you the ropes, huh?' he asks with a grin. It takes me a second to realize he's looking at the bandage on my chin.

'Oh, no, I'm just a klutz.'

I lead him to an empty booth and deal him a menu and a white mug, top it up with coffee so hot there's steam licking the air before it hits the cup. I watch him scoop a cream and sugar from the container at the middle of the table. Is he looking at me differently? Have his eyes always been so pointed, so narrow?

'Thank you miss,' he says. There's a silence and I'm about to leave, having told him to enjoy, but he asks, 'How're you finding it, then? Sandown?'

'Yeah, I mean, good. My room-mate's nice,' I say honestly.

'And Mary? How's she?'

'Runs a tight ship.'

'That's her.'

I think about the blank space on the police report next to *Reporting Officer*, the empty folder in the filing cabinet, and can't help but wonder. 'Weird question, just wondering: how long have you been a cop?'

He leans back in his booth, a task, it appears, that requires quite a bit of exertion. 'Oh, Christ,' he says, his entire life up until this moment ostensibly flashing before his eyes. 'Thirty-two? No, thirty-four years, if you can believe it.'

Thirty-four years. 1986. 'And you've been in Sandown the whole time?'

'Had a couple of stints on the mainland,' he says, taking a bravely sizable swig given how hot the coffee is, 'but yeah, this is home otherwise.'

'Did you want something to eat?'

'Just the coffee's grand for now. Thanks, kid. Oh, and, uh, can you ask Archie to come out when he's got a free second?'

I do, and Mary Anne overhears and must register the confusion I'd attempted to hide. She tells me they're good friends.

He and Archie chat for about twenty minutes, Archie as animated as I've ever seen him, quietly enough for me to be unable to hear the words over 'Rock Around the Clock' (far too lively for eight in the morning on a Tuesday), then Booker asks for the bill for his coffee without issue and leaves. (His bill comes to a grand total of one dollar and seventeen cents, with tax; he gives me a fiver and tells me to keep the change.) I don't know if he suspects me of something, but I'm spooked enough to decide to lie low for the rest of the day, repeating our few exchanged words over and over, wondering if there's something I missed.

Ellis doesn't text me all morning. When lunch is in full swing – meaning, three occupied tables and two stragglers at the bar – I can't get to my phone again before the end of my shift without it being obvious I'm slacking. Meanwhile, on the radio station playing over the speakers, the DJ mentions something about a Hurricane Arthur building over the Atlantic.

Unusual for a storm to come so early in the year . . .

Visions of my dad storming off the next ferry in a mad dash to find me and right my wrongs soils my waking thoughts and I'm aware I'm running out of time – Ellis – *we*'re running out of time and I need to speak with him now. Saturday's practically another epoch, and Ellis still hasn't texted me when my shifts ends at three.

Dad will be here in two weeks, maybe less. This can't wait.

*

The face of the Willowwood is sporting a mid-afternoon glow of buttery sunshine playing in the crannies, casting deep purple shadows. The flower patches shudder, like they're waving me in. I open the front doors as if I live there.

It's an assault from the familiar scent of lemon. Ellis is sitting at the heavy front desk, reading something, and is startled when he clocks it's me. 'Mona! Wh-what are you doing here?'

'I finished up at the diner and I need to talk to you now. Did you see my text?'

'Yeah, sorry, I was gonna reply after work. But you can't come here now. What if my mom hears what we're talking about?'

'It'll take two seconds.'

Ellis pulls me aside and speaks sharply under his breath. 'OK, two seconds.' Then, for the first time since I've arrived, properly looks at my face. 'Hey, what'd you do to your chin?'

I lower my voice. 'I spoke to Frank today.'

'What?'

I tell him about the whole thing: the early morning run and the fall; Frank taking me into the ticket booth; him mentioning Lenore and Constance; getting really tense and strange. I leave Frank's implied vitriol towards Ellis. 'He said Roxy got in fights all the time; he mentioned Lenore specifically. I don't love the implications of a catty girl-fight narrative, but if it's true, then –'

'Couldn't he be lying, though?'

137

'Well, yeah. Definitely. But I get the sense there's more he's not telling me and he certainly seems off enough to have done something himself. Do you know anyone called Lenore who would have known Roxy? Hopefully still on the island?'

'It rings a bell; I'll have to –'

Sylvia appears round the corner, barely to our right. She stops in the arch of the doorway and scrutinizes us; I try to read her face in return but I can't tell what she's heard – if anything. She doesn't seem surprised enough to see me. 'Hi, sweetie,' she says coolly. 'How've your first couple of days been?'

'Really good, thanks.'

'Are you all right?' She's asking about my chin.

'Small tumble.'

'Listen,' she continues, arms crossed at her waist, 'I'm thrilled you and Ellis are getting along and that you're comfortable here, but please don't come by during work hours, OK? We're very busy.'

I glance at the registration desk to see what Ellis was reading; it's a women's health magazine. 'Right. I'm really sorry – I'll get going.' I turn on my heels.

'Do still let me know if you need anything, all right?'

'Bye, Mona,' Ellis tries behind me.

Outside, the red heat greets me, already an old friend.

CHAPTER 13

WEDNESDAY 2 JUNE

After the scene at the Willowwood, Ellis informs me via text that Sylvia is understandably suspicious; we agree to take it easy in the meantime. But I'm floundering, feeling useless. Roxy's alleged note didn't offer as much of a lead as I'd thought.

We need to speak to whoever Lenore is. I'm wondering if Lenore moving up to headline the Indigo in Roxy's absence would be enough of a motive to make somebody go missing to ensure she keeps the gig.

And I still need to figure out how to broach the subject with Mary Anne while evading the very real possibility of her wringing my neck.

During the day I realize the low hum of the diner, clattering of cutlery, whirring from the kitchen is actually kind of pleasant – it'll be nice to use as an ambient track for the podcast, I decide, and I record a bit of it on my phone, placing it into my pocket, microphone-side up.

Later I ring up an order but there's no more receipt paper left in the usual spot; Mary Anne's in her office and I go to ask her where she keeps the rolls.

I open the door to her office and she's there, huddled over one of her radios, some sort of beeping sound alongside – she leaps out of her seat when she sees me, moves to the door and ushers me out. '*Knock*,' she hisses, and she's right, I should have.

'Whoops. I'm sorry,' I say, a little startled by the intensity of the back and forth; that's the only odd thing that happens, but I curse myself for giving Mary Anne yet another reason to be put off by me.

In the dorm that night, I'm putting the pieces together but the pieces are more amorphous almost-pieces than anything concrete or worth acting on, and I'm not getting anywhere.

When Peyton gets back she immediately asks if I want to play cards. She, I already realize, is always wanting to *do something*: talk (most recently to discuss her reading of *Catcher in the Rye*), or go on a walk-turned-social engagement, or a trip to the store for things I'm not convinced we need. I can't decide if this is to compensate for something, the sort of thing people who don't want to be left alone with their thoughts do – or maybe a lack of private thoughts to want to be left alone with. And even though keeping pace with Peyton's whims is fast becoming my third job, the inclusion in the mundane highlights a quality in both Peyton and Ellis I quite like: how they treat me as though they've known me for much longer than they have.

I finally agree to play because the world is hot and boring and makes no sense and there's nothing better to do. But I'm not paying attention. I'm playing horribly. I think of Celeste. Dad. I lose three rounds in a row.

'Your game's off,' Peyton says. 'No fun if you don't wanna kill me. What's up?'

'Nothing.'

'Liar.'

'Do you ever just realize . . .' I say. 'Never mind.'

'What?'

'That you have nowhere in the world to go back to?'

Peyton blinks. 'Don't you?'

I shake my head vigorously. The leaving has felt too good. The leaving has made me realize that, no, I can never go back.

'I'm sorry, Mona,' Peyton says. 'You seem . . . Don't take this the wrong way. And I've known you for, like, five days so this might be totally out of line and off the money, but, you're really heavy, sometimes? Most of the time. And serious. Very brooding.'

I blink, suddenly shy.

'Like, sometimes I look over there at you at your desk and your face is –' Peyton performs a not-especially flattering expression, lips tight, eyebrows furrowed, eyes angry.

Pink blooms across my cheeks. I want to apologize for my face, for her having to look at it.

'And it's nothing bad, and it's just you, but it does make me sad. Because I think probably something happened to make you that way. And I don't know what it is. I mean, what, you can't go home? Is that what it has to do with?' she asks. 'Your family?'

I don't know why I say this, but after a moment I say, 'Maybe I'll tell you someday.'

'How very cagey. Well, you're nice deep down, anyway.'

Her certainty makes me angry. 'And what makes you say that?'

'You offered me the bed,' she says. 'The first day.'

I'd forgotten about that. 'I was trying to get you to leave me alone.'

'No, you weren't,' she says. 'You weren't.'

'Oh, sorry, didn't realize you know every one of my motivations for everything I do.'

'Not all of them. Just that one. And Ellis likes you. I can tell. Not that there're people Ellis doesn't like, really, but . . . he really likes you. Anyway. Any other weird questions you want to get off your chest?' she asks.

'Yeah, actually. What did you mean when you said that you don't even know me?'

'Did I say that?'

'I said I was sorry for lying after I talked to my dad,' I remember, 'and you said it's OK because you don't even know me.'

'I think sometimes people expect too much from others. As far as I'm concerned, an easy way not to get hurt is not to expect anything from anyone.'

No one would say that unless they've been hurt. Maybe I was wrong about her.

After a moment Peyton rummages in the gap between her bed and the wall and emerges with a bottle of rum.

I raise my eyebrows at her. 'Didn't see you put *that* away when you were unpacking.'

'I didn't know what kind of person you were yet. Have you seen yourself? Absolute snitch. Now that I know you're another heathen masquerading as a quiet little freak, we're golden.'

'But *rum*?' I say, and take a swig.

'We're out at sea, aren't we?' She takes a swig in return, then says, her eyes screwed tight and voice gravelly and half-missing, 'Yo-ho-ho.'

And the welcome throat-burn distracts us, at least for a while, distracts *me* well enough to concentrate, and I win the next two rounds.

'I was, uh, wondering,' Peyton says after, face rosy now, lips wet. 'Do you, uh, have a boyfriend? Back home?'

I scoff without meaning to – Peyton looks hurt by it so I proceed gently into whatever new frontier of conversation this is. 'Definitely not.'

She shifts, timid, casting for something. 'Girlfriend?'

I've never been asked this directly. 'Used to.'

Dawn broke up with me last summer. I liked Dawn. She had the worst laugh I'd ever heard and could fix just about anything with her hands – was good with cars, computers, wiry things, which I found attractive. I wasn't sure I loved her as I had nothing to compare my feelings to, but I knew

I liked her well enough. I'd catch myself thinking of her while I was bored in class, kissing her, her in various positions, sometimes sexual and mostly not, sometimes quiet, comfortable intimacy – moving my hair from my face or picking lint from my shirt. Towards the conclusion of 'us' I realized that I liked to think of these things more than I liked for them to actually happen, but hated the thought of officially breaking it off. It might have been cowardice, or fear of retaliation, or the anticipated tedium of a serious, overly sentimental conversation – even still, my general enjoyment of her company was enough to make her words sting when she eventually ended whatever wilted thing there was between us with a seemingly premeditated speech in which she listed every single one of my flaws as I sat there, silent, listening.

I'm sorry, she'd said to open the tirade, *I know you're messed up from your sister . . . but . . .*

I'm too distant, she says. I let no one in. I don't trust her. I'm mean. I want to hurt others before they have a chance to hurt me. I'm too single-minded, too willing to manipulate to get what I want. Even when I'm being genuine, or what she thinks is me being genuine, she says, it seems like I'm playing a part, I'm reading lines, and I'm waiting for her to say hers back to me.

She might have been right. Maybe I could have loved her if I'd tried. Trusted her if I tried. Same thing.

I like Peyton. I don't really feel like inviting anything more into the equation. Not here, not now, where the very nature of my being here is a lie, a secret in itself. How could anything meaningful be built on top? And I don't like people looking at me like that, generally, anyway. But I think that might be how she's looking at me and despite all of this and my reservations I can't bring myself to put an end to it.

Peyton's eyes flicker downward. She picks at a bobble on her sock. 'Was wondering. Don't want to make things too awkward and we're, you know, stuck in the same broom closet together for three months, so. And Liam and I are just *seeing* each other,' she says, and tosses the foam ball up to the miniature basketball hoop affixed to her wall. It misses and bounces back in her lap. 'And I bore easily.'

'Oh, my God,' I realize. 'You're nervous.' It's flattering, obviously.

'I'm not fucking nervous.'

'You're a little nervous.'

She hurls the basketball at my head. It hits. 'You are a cantankerous bitch and I do not care if you live or die.'

'Same.'

'Don't cut yourself on that edge.' Peyton considers something for a moment, then slaps both hands down on her lap and says, 'Walk? Little air? Little ice cream? I think Liam's at the boardwalk.'

'All right.'

I pull on my windbreaker and open the door for her when we leave. Peyton looks me up and down when she passes, standing on her toes to reach my face. 'You have a scar.'

'A two-day-old scratch is not a scar.'

'No,' she says. 'A light one. On your cheek.'

'No way?' I'm kidding. I know about the scar on my cheek. What I don't know is why she's looking so closely at my face.

Then she's closer than she's ever been and without missing a beat pecks her lips against mine. 'Whoops,' she says, and scurries ahead of me down the corridor. I'm too surprised to speak.

You're nice deep down.

I'm not, I'd wanted to say. The sooner you come to terms with it the better for us all.

The boardwalk really has no right to be open on a Wednesday. Aside from a couple of quiet stragglers, the only ones there are the Seasonals, mainly hanging out with their friends required to work there, and we're evidently no exception. All lit up, and for who? Above us there's the purple summer twilight, the heat licking at the edges of the air but not stifling; fluffy mauve clouds cling to the edges of the horizon. It's a really nice night.

I'm, admittedly, quite buzzed. Peyton and I both devour a burger and portion of seasoned fries while talking giddy and delirious nonsense about nothing, and, after, Liam lets us ride the merry-go-round for free. For some reason it's the funniest thing in the world and we can't stop laughing; I don't know about Peyton's joy, but mine comes so unexpectedly easily that I almost stop, and I'm not sure whether it's from the shock of having it or fear of losing it. I'm ghostly, but not in a bad way; I just feel as though I need to keep clinging to the moment so as not to be thrown off.

Four rounds is our limit before we get too dizzy to go on again and have to stagger off.

Peyton's giggling behind me. I get the sense it's about me.

'What is it?'

The multicoloured lights play on her face, pink to purple to aquamarine, and she's such an unintended vision that I almost think about dropping this whole thing, about having an average, unfettered Sandown Bay experience, waiting tables and sitting by the rocks with a girl who I'll say goodbye to at the end of the summer without too much heartbreak, but with enough fondness to wish it had lasted a little bit longer. Meanwhile Roxy is in my blind spot, just out of view.

But I already know what this is – one of those things, a situation born from convenience and boredom and nothing more. Something for now.

I smile despite myself.

Peyton clocks something behind me; I turn to look.

'Uh, hello?' It's Ellis, from further up the dock.

'What are you doing here?' I ask him.

'I was gonna look for sea glass,' he says. 'Want to see?'

'Hell *yeah*,' Liam says, leading the pack.

Peyton grabs him by the arm. 'Um, excuse you, where do you think you're going?'

We regard the near-empty boardwalk all at once. Above us, a rollercoaster whizzes past with nobody on it. Liam snorts. 'Oh, you're right. Someone might *steal* the *carousel*. Come on, Ellis, show me some of your fancy glass.'

And we all follow him down the length of the boardwalk and down the steps I'd taken the first day I was here, down on to the beach.

'It's so cool how it's m-m-made,' Ellis explains. 'Like reverse n-nature, I guess. When we find gems and stuff in the w-w-wild, we have to refine them, but with these, the glass is m-m-man-m-made but nature refines it.'

'Nature *refines* it, huh?' Liam says in a way that's not mean-spirited but still mocking, and Peyton walks up ahead and punches him on the shoulder.

Once Liam and Peyton have moved out of earshot I wrap an arm around Ellis. 'Ellis,' I say, 'do not ever let anyone make fun of you for knowing more than they do.'

'It's not a b-b-big deal,' he says, but looks at me with a tight smile anyway, and I know he's heard me, understood what I meant. 'Oh, actually –' Ellis slithers from my grip, bends down and emerges with a piece of it, smooth and sapphire. 'That's a good one,' he says, and pockets it.

Meanwhile, ahead, Peyton and Liam have seemingly forgotten the task at hand and are stripping down to their underwear. 'Come and swim!' Peyton shouts.

I look at Ellis, who shakes his head. 'I'll stay with Ellis!'

'*Pussies*,' Liam shouts back, and lifts Peyton into the black waves. Watching this strikes me with a sharp pang I can't name at first; jealousy, I quickly realize.

Ellis and I sit on the rocks.

The night is as illusory as a memory, light reflecting oddly and dreamlike off the water, moving edges blurred, the humming glow of the mainland hazy in the far distance. Above and behind us, the mechanical whirr of the scrambler and waltzer. Wildflowers jitter in the occasional breeze, and the salt in the air is so thick I could lick it. My breath whistles loudly in my ears. I am alive. I don't have to be – perhaps shouldn't be – but I am. All at once, watching Liam and Peyton try to trip each other up on the tide, hearing Ellis's feet shuffle on the rocks, I become aware of the story of my life folding out in front of me. There's so much good, I understand, as easily as breathing. Why can't it always be like this?

'So, I think I figured out who Lenore is,' Ellis says, breaking the spell.

'You did?'

'Well, I thought maybe I remembered the name but I wasn't sure. Her full name's Lenore Worthy. She's a musician too – or at least used to be, I guess.'

'That's a motive. Jealousy, money. She lives here?'

'I think so.'

'Think? I thought everyone knew everyone around here.'

And I remember by the pain in his eyes. 'Everyone except us, I guess. People keep their distance.'

'Right. I'm sorry.'

'Anyway. I was looking at the census information and I think I have an address.'

I punch him lightly on the arm. 'All right, sir. Look at you, investigating.' Ellis smiles shyly. I am aware of a few others scattered along the shore – not that they're paying any attention to us, but to be safe, I say, 'Let's talk about this later.'

'OK, sure. That works actually b-because I have something to show you.'

'What?'

'It'll be better if you see it. But my mom can't know. We can meet at the N-No-Names? At n-nine at night tomorrow?'

I nod. 'You're on.'

Peyton tires herself out after only thirty minutes or so, and she and Liam go to leave. As we're saying our goodbyes she regards Ellis and me and says, 'You guys look so *cute*. Couple of little cuttlefish,' and takes a picture.

'I do sort of want to swim,' Ellis says after they've gone. 'It's just that Liam always tries to dunk me.'

I snort. 'I'm not totally sure if I can swim.'

'Want me to show you? All you have to learn is how to float.'

We wade out, past the point of the breaking waves, until the water is just bobbing and lulling and my toes are barely scraping the bottom, catching occasional sharp bits of shell.

'B-basically, we're two-thirds water anyways, so we're, like, designed to float, and it helps if you're taking deep breaths too, b-because it's easier the more oxygen you have in you.'

I do as Ellis says. Relax.

I wonder, briefly, if Roxy's bones could be here. If we could be just above them.

Deep breath.

And there we are, floating in the black.

'Sometimes I come out here,' Ellis says, 'like, probably further than what's safe, and float for ages. Especially at night, depending on which direction you're facing, it's hard to tell where the sky stops and the sea starts.'

'Kinda nice,' I say about the phenomenon. He's right; there're moments I can even see the stars reflected in the waves.

'Out here I feel like no one is their own person, maybe.'

'Hm?'

'I guess, trying to relate to people, you think about how different everyone is from you. At least, I do.'

'I do too.'

'And I wonder silly stuff now. Like who I'd be if my family had b-been normal. And who I'd b-b-be if I'd grown up somewhere normal.'

I don't speak. Saltwater laps my ears.

'I didn't know my grandma well. Constance, I mean. Kinda cold and angry. Even she seemed like she didn't want anything to do with me sometimes. And I love Mom. Obviously. I get why she wants to keep me safe. It's just us. But, I don't know. I wonder how things might be if it had been different. But I don't know if knowing that would make me happy. Because then I might start wishing for it. Or, even, I don't know . . . maybe that version of Ellis is worse.'

My throat contorts in on itself and I can't speak. I want to speak to him but I can't let myself.

'But then I think,' he says, 'after all that, out here, in the d-d-dark, I don't really feel like anything. But in a good way. I feel like a thing in the water.'

'A thing in the water.'

'Bodies in the water . . .'

We're quiet.

'I think about this a lot too,' is all I can muster.

'I know. That's why I'm telling you. Like, I talk to Peyton about things sometimes but I don't know what she'd say to this kind of stuff.' Maybe I prickle at the mention of her name, because he asks, 'Is there something going on with you guys?'

The question is so grounded that I'm nearly shaken from my float. I angle my head towards him. 'You noticed?'

'A little. Do you like her?'

'Well enough.'

'That's funny,' he says. 'She said you guys fight like you hate each other.'

'We do.'

Ellis and I stay for only a little longer, until the night is too dark and the water too chilly to bear. Swimming back to shore inspires a fit of nerves, my muscles too sharp and locked to bring any grace or confidence to the task, but I'm safe under Ellis's watchful eye. Nothing we talk about on the way back approaches the heaviness we had breached. He recites childhood swimming anecdotes. We both point out the constellations we know well enough to name (Big and Little Dippers, Orion's Belt; Ellis impresses with a sighting of Scorpio). Where our paths diverge at the nape of the neck, our clothes still damp, I feel like something has changed, as though some new and delicate intimacy has grown between us that wasn't there before. I want to touch him, somehow, a hug, or a hand on his shoulder, but every way I can think to initiate feels odd and contrived. 'Get some rest,' I say finally, and that feels like enough.

'See you tomorrow!' Ellis says, already starting up the lamplit drive, a boyish tug of a smile across one side of his face.

There's a spring in my step as I walk back to the dorm.

A dimmish streetlight flickers above me as the pitchy buzz of a mosquito brushes against my ear and I realize that I've only been in Sandown for five days. Can that be right? Not only has this felt like a lifetime in and of itself, but I feel my other life, whatever the thing I'd arrived with was, fading from reality as easily as a dream.

Maybe it's because I'm now so untethered that I'm seeking things to tether myself to. Peyton already feels like a safety line. So does Ellis. I'm surprised by how soft I feel towards them, these people I've only just begun to know, who would have never appeared in the story of my life if I hadn't come here to find them. There's a power in how I've catalysed my own profound experiences. Would this have happened anywhere, no matter where I'd gone, no matter whose bones I went looking for? Is the world full of Peytons and Ellises? Or is there something about Sandown, something about the two-dimensional main street, the clean boardwalk, the omni-embracing sea, reflective from all sides, that forces one to confront the truth of oneself no matter which way one looks? Something about Peyton and Ellis themselves? I can't say. I'm hypnotized.

I think of Roxy. I wonder if she felt this same thing too, and who she felt it for, and why.

Maybe it's a combination of all of it, I think, as I remember Peyton moving, all of her bouncing and sheened in the moonlight, her and her mouth, still sharp with cinnamon; as I think of Ellis, head bobbing in the water, face melted with overwhelming and uncharacteristic calm.

I'm so nowhere and so everywhere. It's already tomorrow, I realize, looking up at the expanse of indigo sky. *It's already tomorrow.* I keep saying it to myself tonight. I'm aware of my hands moving alongside me, my feet on the pavement, my hair blowing in my face, my sunburnt lips sore from smiling, my warm skin tinged with coconut. I'm very light right now. I don't know if I feel a sense of peace towards what's to come or if I'm not thinking about it at all. Or a sense of peace towards what's happened. That too.

None of them know. None of them have to. None of them will know to ask.

It's already tomorrow.

Celeste isn't with me tonight. In a way, neither is Roxy.

And I don't know if this Mona that's left is me, but I like her.

CHAPTER 14

THURSDAY 3 JUNE

In the morning before I leave, I fold back the curtains a fraction so as not to wake Peyton. The calm of her sleeping face and the relaxed and repetitious motion of her body make me think of last night. On the way back to the dorms I was mentally preparing for *something* to happen, but Peyton was already passed out on top of her bed – spirit-sleepy, maybe – and I, overcome with a desire to do anything gentle to her, had covered her in a blanket. Then it'd taken ages to get to sleep because I'd wanted to redream the whole night. Peyton, in technicolour, bounding in the sea.

My stomach seizes suddenly.

The dreamy unreality of the night before shifts so violently out of focus that I'm furious with myself for having felt any of those things at all. What did I think I was doing? I'm wasting my time. How could I have let myself think this is a vacation? How dare I make this time out to be an inconsequential detour when it's the main story? It is an insult to Celeste, to Roxy, to myself, to even be thinking about this trivial bullshit.

Two weeks. Probably less. That's what my dad said.

I leave for the diner in a huff, Peyton still asleep, resolving not to waste another second.

I'm only working for a couple of hours before I realize I'm growing impatient. The situation with Frank still has me on edge. I didn't like the way he spoke about any of it – about Roxy. About Ellis.

And Mary Anne was the only other name listed on the police report. No, I didn't want to interrogate her so early on, without any leverage. But I'm still riled up about my earlier revelation of wasted time, and though perhaps it'd be wise to observe a bit longer, I'm not feeling particularly wise.

It's quiet towards the end of the lunch rush at two, when my shift's almost over. I'm scribbling doodles on the back of receipt paper when I hear her come out of her office and then exit through the door at the back of the kitchen. I follow, my eyes needing to adjust to the whiteness of the outside, and I find Mary Anne sitting on the lounge chair behind the building. She hears my approach.

'If you're allowed to take a smoke break every hour then I think I should be able to as well,' I say.

Mary Anne takes a long drag through her teeth and looks at me, gentle exasperation in her eyes. 'Everyone in there taken care of?'

'Yep.'

She gestures with her cigarette to the log stool opposite. 'Then siddown.'

We're quiet. Gulls scream from somewhere and a hot breeze sizzles past. I scrape at the blistering asphalt with my feet and can't tell if Mary Anne is the type to appreciate the silence – probably. I'd like to break it. I look at her – she seems tired, jaded. I imagine myself at her age and wonder if I'll have the same fatigue oozing out of every part of me.

I wonder too, brief as lightning, what Celeste might look like now, had there been no wood to be tempted into.

'Have you lived here your whole life?' I ask.

'Born and raised.'

'It seems like it'd be difficult to go to a school with so few people. Like you're forced to hang out with them.'

'You know, you'd think,' she says, taking a drag. 'But the circumstances are so odd, us being here, that I suppose we sorta . . .' She gesticulates, looking for the words. 'Bonded over that.'

'Are a lot of the people you grew up with still living here?'

'Oh, a few – well, come to think of it, probably most of them.'

'Did you know someone named Roxy?'

The glance she casts up at me is so unforgiving that I shudder. She speaks slowly, dripping venom. 'I'd heard word that some kid was going round asking questions about Roxy – didn't realize she'd be the one under my own roof.' She points at me with her cigarette, so near the smoke licks my nose. '*You stay out of this business.*'

The reaction is so unexpected that I don't know what to do next – steely is my neutral state and I hope that's how I look now. 'Who told you?' I ask. Based on the sort of casual misogyny which seemed to come easily to Frank, I decide he probably wouldn't have confided in her. So who else – Booker? Sylvia? Ellis?

'It doesn't matter,' she snaps. 'What matters is you are a guest here, on this island, and guests keep their noses out of business that doesn't concern them.'

'Maybe it should concern me.'

'Tell you what, I didn't buy the whole *Seasonal programme* in the first place and we don't really *need* you here. Understand? I complain long and loud enough and they'll boot your ass to the mainland quicker than you can beg. Not just *fired*. I can do that. I can make that happen.'

I narrow my eyes. She's trying to scare me. 'I could stay with Ellis.'

Mary Anne scoffs. 'You think Sylvia is happy about any of this, either? You think she wants this anywhere near her Ellis?' She crushes her cigarette into the asphalt under her booted foot. 'You leave him out of this. He's a good kid and good kids don't belong anywhere near dangerous business.'

'It's *his* business. As much as anyone's. *More* than anyone's. And why is it dangerous?'

Mary Anne stares.

'Because of someone?' I ask. 'You?'

And she's really angry now, moving towards me when I haven't dared move a muscle this whole time; if I stand still enough I can grow roots in the ground and won't be knocked. *I dare you*, I want to say. But I lose my nerve when I see how her eyes are flaring; I know nothing about her but in this moment I learn everything I need to know to make a start. 'Because of everyone, honey. Because we've been trying to forget this hurt and it's taken decades but we've done it, and people here are gonna choke on the dust you're riling up. Selfish only to think about danger to yourself; it's danger to *us*. Folk'll get hurt.'

I smear a bead of sweat from my ear. 'It sounds like someone's gonna hurt me.'

'I will myself, if you don't leave these good people alone.'

'What if they're not all good?'

'You think you can come here, not knowing no one or nothing, and decide after a day or two that some of us that have been sticking together for thirty-odd years are not all good?' Mary Anne says, stumbling a little over her words. 'You don't know *anything* about what's gone on here. What matters to us. Insulting, really.' Then says again, as if reaffirming to herself, 'It's insulting, that's what it is.'

'I want to understand.'

'You've got no right to.'

'I want to help, then,' I say.

'That's rich.'

I apologize even though I don't want to, even though it's a lie. 'I'll stay out of things. I was just curious.'

'You're not here to be curious. You're here to work. And it's a privilege.'

I bite my tongue. 'You're right.'

And she gets in close again, so close to my face that I can smell the mildew on her apron. 'Now, go on. Back inside.' Just like that it's business as usual. 'I wasn't gonna say nothin' but I thought I saw Betty short of coffee. And go say something sweet to Carol, woman in the dress. Her dog died, sweet old Labrador, and she's not taking it well.'

I text Ellis on the walk back to the dorms.

> **Me:** Did you tell Mary Anne that we read Roxy's police report?

> **Ellis:** No. I swear.

> **Me:** Someone did.

> **Ellis:** I promise it wasn't me. Who do you think it was?

> **Me:** I don't know. It could have been either Booker or Frank, because we've spoken to both of them personally.

> **Ellis:** Weird.

> **Me:** Would your mom have said something?

> **Ellis:** Idk. Maybe.

> **Me:** Mary Anne basically threatened me. She said she didn't want us speaking any more + would fire me if we did. Do you know why she'd be so upset over this?

Ellis:	No, I'm sorry, my mom might know more but I don't think it's a good idea to ask.
Me:	Well, I'm not listening to her, obviously.
Ellis:	Idk. Aren't you worried about if she does actually fire you? You'd have to go home.

It occurs to me that Ellis thinks I came to have my summer vacation on Sandown Bay and would be disappointed, primarily, by alleged good times cut short. The reality is more that there is no reason to be here at all, *unless* I can speak with Ellis.

Me:	It's OK. I don't start what I can't finish.
Ellis:	I didn't know we started anything.
Me:	We definitely have, based on Mary Anne's reaction.
Me:	Are we still on for tonight?

My heart quickens at the thought. What had Ellis said? He had something to show me?

I'm excited.

Ellis:	Yes. No-Names parking lot. 9.

Mary Anne's reaction has shocked me and so I desperately want to know more. I want to speak to Archie but this, of course, is complicated. He might not know – more accurately, remember – anything, and if I ask I'm risking him telling Mary Anne, which seems a predicament ending well for nobody.

Is the town *hurt* by Roxy having gone missing instead of relieved by it? Is that what Mary Anne implied? She could have been lying.

I can't wait to see what Ellis has to show me.

CHAPTER 15

Peyton's nosy when I leave; I tell her I'm going for a run.

The sky's weird tonight, almost green, thick clouds rolling in from the mainland, angry and seemingly ready to burst. I catch intermittent flashes of lightning.

I use one of the dorm bikes to ride there. It takes maybe fifteen minutes – for Ellis, I think, it's just a walk down the street. This isn't the wood behind their house – further down the road they live on, there's a cul-de-sac circled by temporary-stay cabins. Past an unthreatening wooden barrier, there's an empty parking lot, presumably there for when the woods were open. Now it's encircled by that same barbed-wire fence and the same signs as the stretch of wood behind Ellis's house. The greenery, though, isn't as dense here as it is in the Willowwood's backyard; with no defined treeline, the barbed fence seems not to have known quite where to go and meanders unconvincingly between wide gaps in the trunks.

Ellis is already there when I arrive, sitting cross-legged on a long stretch of grass next to the fence. I make my presence known at once so as not to spook him, let the soft rubber of the tyres scratch against the asphalt as I brake. 'Hey, bud,' I say. Above him, there's a flickering lamp post that casts shadows straight down. Even baby-faced Ellis looks creepy in the harsh half-light.

'Hey.'

'Sylvia give you any trouble?'

'No, surprisingly.'

'What do you have for me, then?'

He exhales, quick and hard. 'OK. So.' He unzips his backpack and rummages inside until he emerges with a container the size and shape of a shoebox, but made of sturdy dark wood, with a metal clasp. 'As far as I'm aware,' Ellis says, in such a low and serious register that it gives me chills, 'this all belonged to Roxy.'

I suppress the urge to grab the box straight from his hands, instead asking quietly, 'Can I see?'

'Well, yeah.' He undoes the clasp and the lid pops open with a wonderful creak, revealing nothing at all at first, until I shine the flashlight from my phone on it. 'This is almost everything, all I could take for now.'

There's a photo on top. I recognize the spot – by the pier, facing the park opposite the main strip. It's Roxy. And she's young, maybe my age – she's wearing forest-green flares and a grey sweater, her long blonde hair blanketing her shoulders, arms crossed over her chest. She's leaning against a boxy red car.

'Wow. Is that hers?'

'Yeah. It's a seventy-five Camaro.'

'You know stuff about cars?'

'I mean, whatever I can google. I've fixed M-Mom's a couple of times. But it's kinda nice, right? I wasn't for sure it was hers but . . .' He digs a little further inside the box, moving aside all manner of alluring treasures. Keys. He jangles them in front of his eyes. 'Still have these.'

'What happened to the car?'

Ellis shrugs. 'I guess they would have impounded it or something. Which sucks, b-b-because it was really nice.'

Further inside is a trinket, a guitar pick, a Morse code key, a couple of books – philosophy – and a birth certificate. *Mother: Constance O'Hare*; there's no father listed.

Then a journal.

I flip it open, hungry, and shine my flashlight on this too. I recognize some of them as finished lyrics. 'Glass Daughter', 'Orion', 'Anywhere, Anywhere'.

'This is amazing,' I breathe, feeling like I've caught a glimpse of something very intimate but not compelled enough by ethical deliberation to want to stop.

There's tons of unfinished lyrics too, throwaway phrases and words and thoughts, penmanship tidy. It's fascinating to watch in real time the ticking of her brain. None of it makes much sense; in a margin she'd written *a whole day in heaven and teeth-cracked pistachios*, and *give her the peach-blush and risen sky in a syringe, give her peace and quiet,* then, in massive letters, on the same page, *bright ascetic dissonance!!!!* Lists of words elsewhere: *moss / maggots / fly trap / tendril*. Then, *The demand to be loved is the greatest of all arrogant presumptions, Friedrich Nietzsche.*

'*What is a poet?*' I read aloud from a page to Ellis. '*An unhappy man who hides deep anguish in his heart, but whose lips are so formed that when the sigh and cry pass through them, it sounds like lovely music.*'

Ellis watches me.

'*And people flock around the poet and say, "Sing again soon," that is, "May new sufferings torment your soul but your lips be fashioned as before, for the cry would only frighten us, but the music, that is blissful."*'

I feel my mouth go dry. 'That's, uh, Kierkegaard, apparently. Danish philosopher.'

'Yeah,' Ellis says. 'There're some quotes. It's mostly unfinished lyrics. But in the back there's something – "Baby Blue".'

'That's a song of hers.'

'No, that's what I thought too, but – they're not the lyrics to the song. They're letters. *Addressed* to someone called Baby Blue.'

I look at him, breathless. 'Baby Blue was a person? Do you have any idea who it could be?'

'Not a clue.'

I flick hungrily to the back of the journal.

The letters are heavy. Talk of new lives, using words like *forever* and *immortal* and *intertwined* and *heat*.

There's no greater earthly phenomenon than you,
in the dark, reading my mind.

All beginning with *Dear Baby Blue*.

'No one has mentioned anything about this,' I can't help but whisper. 'Who are these letters to? And she obviously never sent them.'

'Are there any p-pages torn out?' Ellis asks astutely.

I check along the binding but it doesn't look like there are. The mystery within the mystery. 'We need to find out.' And then it occurs to me, hits me like a beam of light. 'Ellis. The handwriting.'

'What about it?'

'Have you compared the handwriting in her journal to the note in the car?'

'N-no. Oh, man, n-no.'

'I read some stuff about handwriting analysis in high school.' I had – around the same time I got good at picking locks, followed by a brief obsession with the FBI. Never thought I'd actually get to use any of this stuff for anything.

Ellis pulls up his photo of the car note on his phone and we set it beside a journal page. My absolute first instinct says that the handwriting is similar – both quite difficult to read, all sharp lines and small letters. My brain is already firing. How could this be Roxy? But I look closer and realize that, actually, Roxy's y's and g's on the lyric sheets are looped and stylized, mixed intermittently between cursive and regular, mainly her r's – some the print shape and some plateaued. And more obviously – Roxy's spelling and capitalization are correct and consistent; the note is neither of those things. I point this out to Ellis and I can't quite read what he thinks about it.

'That's crazy. Well, that means –'

'Something's amiss on Sandown Bay.'

We're quiet for a moment but Ellis's eyes have already lit up in a sort of hungry way, and now I know he's addicted to the chase too, and the sight of it excites me like a shark drawn to copper mist. 'This is insane. I can't believe I didn't think to –'

'It doesn't matter. Now you do.'

'I can't believe it.'

'All mysteries are made up of a bunch of smaller ones, and that's mystery number one solved, anyways.' I close the journal gently. 'Did Roxy write the note? No. We know that for sure.'

'Right. So what are the other m-mysteries?'

'Why wasn't her file in the folder at the police station? What do Frank and Lenore and Mary Anne have to do with this? Who's Baby Blue? And if Roxy didn't write the note . . .'

'Who did?'

Thunder. All at once, seemingly from everywhere, seemingly in my brain. To our left, from inside the forest, bark shatters like glass and shoots towards us like an assailant. The shards clatter to the ground.

'Holy shit,' Ellis breathes, nervously running his hands through his hair.

I smirk out of fear, maybe, or the timing. 'Someone is telling us we're on the right track.'

'What about an exploding tree says *right track* to you?'

'Intrigue; very ominous. Good things.'

'Then what do we start with?' Ellis asks. 'If those are all the mysteries. Where do we start?'

'I want to talk to Frank again,' I say. 'Or talk to someone who knows something about him.'

'Do you really think he could have done something?'

I chew on the thought. 'That's what's weird. I asked him, when I was fake-interrogating, if around the time of Roxy's disappearance he'd seen anyone on the ferry who could have been her, and he was about to say no. *If* you were guilty and needed a reason for people to think you're not, wouldn't you say you think you might have seen her on the ferry?'

'Yeah. You're right.'

'He still creeps me out, either way,' I say. 'And, Lenore.'

'What did Frank say about her? That they fought?'

'Apparently. If they're both musicians, it could have been jealousy? Competition over jobs? He mentioned Lenore taking over Roxy's slot at the Indigo while Roxy was pregnant; that's a motive. Either way, it would be helpful to speak to someone who can set the scene, at the time. We should pay Lenore a visit.'

'We? I don't know. I think it's working out fine now, where you're the upfront abrasive one and I n-n-never talk to anyone ever.'

I still feel there's something Ellis isn't saying and I need his confidence that we act as a team. This separation of duty wouldn't be anywhere near conducive to that – he needs to feel like he's on the frontlines as well. 'You should be there. What if something goes wrong and I need backup?'

He smiles. 'I don't know what kind of backup I'd be.'

'More importantly, I'm sure there're things about all this that you know and I don't.' Gently, upfront – *I know you're keeping things from me*. I had pegged him as transparent as a window but I am coming to terms now with the fact that I was wrong, and I feel bad continuously badgering; not just bad, but unwise to badger continuously. I can't lose his trust. *Trust me*, says the snake with the apple. *Trust me*, says the girl with a tape recorder in her pocket. Pang of guilt. It's for the best.

Ellis casts his gaze downward.

'And maybe you can catch her in a lie. Or maybe you have some genetic connection. Or even something your mom said, something Mary Anne said – anything might jog your memory. Right?'

'Yeah.'

There's something about the night that tells me I can say more, I can push him a little further, so I do. 'You can tell me stuff, you know.'

He feels called-out by this, I can tell, and shuffles a bit, breaks my gaze. 'Mom says I trust p-p-people too much, funnily enough.'

'Well, she might be right. But trusting me isn't the same thing as trusting *people*. I don't think you ever said – where are you guys moving to?'

'Uh, M-Michigan.'

'Any reason?'

'She met a guy there. Online. So. I think we're gonna stay with him for a little b-bit while she finds her feet. I don't know. If she's happy, I'm happy.'

'Oh.'

'We probably can't get our own pl-place because it's gonna be hard to sell the Willowwood, I guess. Sandown isn't as b-b-busy as it used to be; it sort of looks like no one even wants it.'

'So what, then? What if she can't sell it?'

He shakes his head. 'I don't know. Probably just leave it there.'

'That's sad,' I say, quite upset actually at the thought of the Willowwood abandoned, the door boarded, the tastefully overgrown flowerbeds and bushes whirling up the sides of the black shutters. 'I mean, not that she's done something wrong. But that it's got to that point.'

'Yeah. But it's not – I'm not even sure she wants to leave because of my nana. I think she cares too much about what everyone else thinks of us.'

'You don't?'

He shrugs. 'I guess not. I mean, what *really* b-b-bothers me is when people think I can't talk because I don't have the words. I always know exactly what I want to say. I'm not unsure. It's so frustrating, to know what you're like in your h-head but not be able to be that in front of people. I guess I just want people to like me.'

'I like you.'

'Hey, you just said you're not p-people,' he says, snickering. 'Well, I like you too.'

And my insides scream. Guilt. Absolute unadulterated guilt. He can't like me, because he knows nothing. He doesn't know enough about my foundations as a person to be able to make an informed decision about whether or not he likes me.

'Thank you for all this,' Ellis says. 'For helping me look for her. I feel like it's what my nana would have wanted, in a way. Everyone's felt so much pain. And I just don't think Roxy would have killed herself. I don't – I don't think she would have left Mom like that. I don't like people thinking that's what she did.'

'I mean, I think that stuff is more complicated than that, Ellis. Not just a matter of leaving or not leaving. I don't know tons about it myself, though.'

He gnaws on a sunflower seed and spits the shell on to the grass. 'Sure. Family's weird, b-b-because you never get to have any more, you know? What you've got is all you've g-g-got. And ours, it's – I mean, now it's literally just me and my mom.'

What you've got is all you've got. I scrunch my face as a reflex.

Ellis suddenly remembers. 'Oh, your – I'm sorry, I –'

'It's OK.' He doesn't know that, yes, what he said has hurt me, but it's hurt me in the exact opposite way he thinks. I'm not upset that I've lost something irreplaceable, but that what I had in the first place was always what I was due. I understand what Ellis was saying even if I disagree completely.

What you've got is all you've got.

'C-can I ask you about your sister?' he says finally.

I shift. I'd sort of forgotten that I told him about her. 'Sure.'

'What was she like?'

'Well, she was six years older than me, first of all. Bit of a strange gap when you're little, I guess.'

'Oh. Wow.'

'My dad wanted two kids but my parents had trouble conceiving.' I don't mention what became of my mom as a result of my existence. 'But it all worked out because she was amazing.'

Ellis's expression opens up.

'She was smart. Smarter than just about everyone. This is such a small thing, but I remember – I had this crappy flip phone when I was nine, for emergencies, and something had happened at school. That's the funny thing, I guess – I don't even remember what it was, but I was so upset that I called her from the bathroom and she cut class to come and pick me up. She'd said it was a family emergency. And it was, in a way. She called me out of school and took me to the mall where we got looks all day because, you know, they were, like, why aren't they in school?' I let the artificial memory ooze in between my teeth, treacly and thick, lost in the mythology of who she might have been.

Ellis is quiet. 'What happened? You said she disappeared, b-b-but . . .'

'We were hiking. I lost track of her in the woods and she never came out.'

Even the trees lean in to listen. 'I'm so sorry.' And he's crying again, like he did that night outside the police station. One fat tear that rolls quickly down his face and splats on to his exposed shin.

'I do miss her,' I admit.

He pulls me into a hug. I'm surprised when I don't flinch, and even more surprised at my disappointment when he pulls away.

'I-I'm sure you do,' he says. 'I would've loved a brother. Or a sister. Doesn't matter.'

'It's not true that your family's all you have, though, is it? You have me,' I offer. 'You have Peyton.'

I don't know why I find myself wanting to convince him of this, of the comfort of belonging to someone. Of wanting you both to belong to each other.

'I wanna find Roxy for b-both of us,' he says.

'For *everyone*,' I say. 'Everyone.'

Ellis nods, steadfast, but looks around, something spooking him. 'Can we get out of here? This is giving me the creeps.'

I perform a melodramatic huff. 'You want to get in trouble until you're in trouble, and then you wanna get out.' I don't say it but this is also giving me the creeps. It seems like these sorts of places – empty parking lots – only appear during the quiet hours. It's the weird quiet, the silence, the dark, the muffled hiss of waves on rocks.

My terrible lies.

Though there's a comfort, admittedly, about the perpetual crash of waves against shore – the inevitability of the next and next and next, like days. 'But, yeah. We should get you home.'

'You don't need to b-be my chaperone. I can get home myself. And I'm f-from here.'

'Was just offering.' I smile. 'Clearly something's after us tonight. I might need to protect you from rogue lightning.'

We leave in different directions, the echoes of what I'd told Ellis pounding in my ears, the night-time air dry on my eyes.

All I can think is that I didn't mean to lie again.

I really didn't.

CHAPTER 16

Celeste lied.

She lied so often and easily it was as though she had a parasite that spoke the words for her, an evil little mouth only capable of spouting cruel, strange things.

She was six years older than me and it was a reasonable expectation that, even from the time I was very small, she'd be able to look after me. I was left alone with her most days. On a Saturday when I was seven years old Celeste sauntered into the room looking too much like me – my blonde hair, my jaw, my dark eyes – but arranged on her in a better way, somehow, in a way that was more proportional, more interesting, made more sense. She insisted that we should go out for a walk in the woods on our property. We lived in a suburb of Indianapolis, and our house was on a plot of land acres wide – the woman who gave birth to me had apparently loved the outdoors.

When Celeste asked me to do something, I did it.

Unseasonably cold even for November and I hadn't brought a jacket. After a five-minute walk, which isn't negligible when one is a child who can no longer see the house poking from between the trees, Celeste said we were to play hide-and-seek, and I needed to spin and count at the same time, all the way up to thirty. I closed my eyes, counted, shuffled my feet. It took eleven seconds of counting but I realized what had happened, what I had fallen for, but by this point I'd already spun, and opening my eyes gave me no more insight than I would have had while they were shut.

The woods weren't big. An acre at most. I could have walked in any direction, emerged into open suburbia and I would have found my way back to the house – but I was a child and I couldn't move. That was the first time in my life I remember feeling raw, jagged panic, the bone-hollowing sort that teaches how easily one can slip into suffering over things you once used to enjoy; the smell of the forest, the rustle of leaves in wind. Of course I didn't know this at the time. Or couldn't articulate it, at least.

Trees became looming, malevolent beasts. I gripped on to one of them while the world spun. Only recognized the true icy-coldness of my baby skin once the warmth trickled down my leg and pooled.

I don't know how long I stayed there for. I just know that by the time Dad came looking for me it was night-time and my hands were dripping with blood from gripping so hard on to the bark.

'What were you doing out here, my girl?' Dad asked.

What was I doing out here, Celeste? What was I?

Celeste came with him and after Dad held me up to his chest to carry me back to the house, all precious and doting, she lingered behind to create an unbreakable line of sight between us. *Tell and you die*, she mouthed.

Even on the walk back I felt I was different.

I still have scars on my hands. They're not the only ones.

Just after my ninth birthday. 'I hate that mole on your face,' she said, unprompted. 'Ugly. Like a witch.'

From then on, she wouldn't stop talking about the *mole*. That was the year I scratched at the raised brown skin with my soft little fingernails until all that remained was a yawning red crater which gushed blood like I'd never seen before in my life. I was hoping to cover it up before Celeste noticed, but she found me rummaging through the medicine cabinet, took one look at the red puddle creeping across the white tiled floor, and laughed in my face. She grabbed me by my cheeks, hard, and jerked the offending hollow up and into the light. 'Oh, that's even worse,' she said, flicking it, then sucking off the blood that transferred to her finger. 'It'll scar, you know.' I impulsively wore a plaster over it for the rest of the school year, even after it'd healed.

More scars. More hurt. More, more, more.

I've rolled it over in my head, of course: her cruelty, the reasons for it, the boundlessness of it. It seems as though being lovely was so adverse to her nature, but she wanted so badly to be – so she'd keep the act up at school, exhaust herself, then dedicate her domestic life to making mine hell. She told me aged five that Dad was not a real person and he was actually a robot incapable of loving me. I could not process this. I was too young to recognize the lie, to recognize the pain pouring from her like a tap. I watched her, once, press her thumb down on the back of a frog until it burst. This sent her to therapy. The collection of bloody pads strewn across my bed sent her back. And she liked to watch me cry; whenever I'd run off from her and hide away in my room, there was always a click of the door, an eye through the crack.

There's one moment still as fresh as when it happened. I was six. I had a colouring book, a beach-themed one, and I was scraping indigo into the ocean when Celeste sat down next to me and said nonchalantly, 'Myrtle, I've been thinking about something. Do you know what parasitism is?'

'No,' I said. 'Paris-tism?'

'*Parasitism*. It's a relationship in science where one organism benefits at the expense of the other.'

'Do you mean animals?'

'Sure. Any animals. We're organisms. Or,' she said, 'a leech.' She pulled my crayon from my hand. I looked up to meet her eyes. 'Do you know what a leech is?'

'An organism?'

'Yes. They're big and fat black slugs, but with tons of sharp teeth that can latch on to people and suck out all their blood.'

The words made me want to vomit. 'Celeste –'

'Do you know what happened to Mom? Has Daddy ever said? I think you're old enough to know now.'

I couldn't speak. The familiarity with which she said *Mom* to refer to a person she once knew, where in my mind's eye there was only a feminine shadow, an idea of a person, unsettled me so deeply I didn't know how to respond.

'You were her leech.'

'What do you mean?'

'While you were in her. Sucked out all her blood. Made her weaker and weaker and weaker so that when she finally pushed you out, all fat with her guts, there wasn't enough left for her and it killed her, and you moved all her organs around inside her and those came out too. You're a parasite, like a leech.'

I cried then, quietly, because this was so disturbing, and of course she wouldn't lie about Mom, about her dying, about the guts bursting forth from her like red glistening worms.

'I'm just letting you know. I'd want to know too, if it were me.'

'No, Celeste –'

'Oh, pull it together.'

Or maybe she could. Lie, that is. Of course she could, I realized. Yes, it all made sense now: 'You're *lying*.'

I didn't have time to flinch before she reeled back her hand and sent it flying down across my face.

One of the worst things that happened as a result of this was how these things lingered. Scars – physical ones – I can attribute to her, as a result of things she'd done. But parts of me have been shaped – are being shaped – in an unnatural way, a trajectory initiated and seen through by Celeste, even in her absence, because of her absence. Were these traits natural or branded? I don't know if I dress in the uncaring way I do because I like how it looks, or because I don't want to be seen. I'm not sure if in second grade I'd bitten Dave Frederik until he bled when he pulled my hair because I didn't like being touched, or because Celeste made me fear other people's hands. I wasn't sure if I barely spoke because I didn't want to or because she'd taken my voice.

I can't answer and that, in and of itself, has changed me too.

And all of this is why I struggle to assign a quality to that memory, a feeling to that day – the day Celeste slipped into the dense wood and never came back out.

I push everyone away and I know this. I will not let them close in case they get the chance to slip a knife between my shoulder blades. This is not because I'm afraid of betrayal. Celeste never *betrayed* me, unless, by being my sister there was an inherent obligation not to hurt me, which I don't think is true. I guess I'm as worried about having a knife stuck into my own back as I am about feeling the need to stick one into someone else's. My own bloodlust. I am so scared that I am like her. I am so scared to be her. Not her – the worst parts of her. Hell is other people and also yourself, if you look hard enough.

I smack a tear off my face.

Where did Celeste go that day? Why couldn't she find her way out? What inside the dank dark deep was so compelling to her she had no choice but to seek it out?

I have no interest in immersing myself in the chaos of the human race. I've learned that I can't interact with it or add to it in any valuable capacity, and when I try, I remember I only know how to manipulate. I need to admit I find it difficult to think of people as full people – to think of them as anything but extensions of myself. I'm not sure if that's my fault. I hope it's not – oh, oh, I hope it's not.

I am bad. I deserve this. I deserve to experience the arresting and unlikely joy of living only to discover I'm an irredeemable soul.

I ride on past the isthmus, the infinite eyes of sea watching me go from every direction.

I'll learn to love the fire.

Fine, I'm not here to save Celeste's skin. Just my own.

I plan to start writing quietly once I'm back inside. I'm still composing myself but I don't want to forget what Ellis and I spoke about.

I'm opening the drawer to my desk when it's Peyton's voice. 'Mona,' she mumbles behind me.

I wince, though even now there's something pleasant about her sleepily uttering my name. She sounds sluggish enough to be lulled back to sleep so I tell her a friendly lie. 'Sorry,' I say gently, 'I was looking for something.'

But she's more alert than I thought. 'What on earth are you doing meeting up with Ellis in the middle of the night?'

A spike of fear. 'How did you know?'

Peyton clicks on the lamp beside her bed. Her eyes are tired, smudged with day-old liner. 'He told me he was seeing you.'

Damn it, Ellis. 'It's between us.'

'*Between you?* What sort of *between* is happening there?'

Her tone invites a new possibility of untoward intention, and I know I need to shut it down immediately lest this conversation becomes something else. 'What? Peyton, do you think I'm –'

'You better fucking not be.'

'I'm not. I sort of can't believe you'd even say that.'

'Then what are you doing?' Nothing. I don't want to say. 'Mona. *Mo. Na.* What are you doing?'

I've been caught, I realize, and I'd try to weasel my way out of any similar situation but Peyton is the sort of stubborn person to sit here interrogating me all night until I've given her a satisfactory answer. 'Fine. Roxy.'

'You're *doing* Roxy?'

'We're investigating. Her disappearance.'

Peyton lets her head fall into her hands. 'Oh no, oh no . . .'

'We don't think she killed herself.'

'Please don't encourage him, Mona. Please.'

'*He* approached *me* about looking into it, and of course I'm curious. I want to help him.'

'Oh, so you're gonna casually mess up a kid's life to satiate your curiosity?'

'What do you *mean,* mess up his life? And he was gonna do it anyway.'

'That's a *shitty* reason!' There's a knocking from the other side of the wall that makes me jump. Peyton speaks in a hiss. 'That's a really *shitty* reason. By that logic, you know, fuck laws, right? Who needs 'em! They're gonna do it anyway. People are gonna murder people anyway!'

'OK, fine. Here's a reason – I think he might be right.'

'How? You don't know anything about these people. You literally just got here. This place is fun for the summer, and it's fun to sort of dip in and out, but you can tell they're heavy, Mona. Heavy with . . . something. All quiet and weighed down. You should know that better than anyone.'

'Because of *Roxy*. And that's what we're unpicking. We're righting things.'

'They all hate Ellis enough without him snooping around for no reason.'

'Him and Sylvia are moving away at the end of the summer, anyway. Ellis wants to know. You said to take care of him. That's what I'm doing.' Using him. *Using him.* Shut up. 'I'm keeping an eye on him so he won't get hurt. Isn't that better than letting him stumble blindly into this himself?'

'You're letting him buy into false hope.'

I bite my tongue. Not false hope. Not a fantasy. His life. Everyone's lives. 'But I think he's right.'

'Then you're much dumber than I thought you were and maybe that's why Harvard said no.'

'And here's something – even if it is a fantasy, who cares?' I keep speaking so as not to let her know she's got to me, with such a *childish* remark too, and something has maybe actually ruptured. 'He's miserable. He's miserable

184

enough for the both of them. And I'm giving him, I don't know, something to do, if nothing else, something that feels important.'

'You've been here for a *week*. You don't know anything about him.'

'Maybe more than you. I'm not a bad person. I want to help him.'

'*Do you?*'

Another knock. 'Shut up!' someone says.

'*Two fucking seconds!*' Peyton hisses to the wall, then lets a beat pass, eating the two of us up and then sighs. She looks ghostly in the dark. No, I don't want to argue with her necessarily, but I can't say I'm not at least partially enjoying the attention, the intensity. She's down to barely a murmur. 'I believe that. But I don't believe you know what you're doing.'

'I guess we'll have to agree to disagree.'

'Yeah,' she says, rolling over to face the wall, 'I guess we'll have to do that. Great. Perfect.'

'I don't want to hurt him,' I say, and I swear it's not a lie. It's the sort of half-truth that forgoes words like *won't* or *refuse*. But it's true on the surface. 'I want to help.' I picture Ellis bobbing in the dark water. Bodies in the water. No. I don't want to hurt him. 'You have to believe me.' There's a beat while I wrestle with something I still don't quite understand. 'Why are you so protective over him?' I ask, finally.

'Does it matter?'

'I guess not.'

Peyton huffs and rolls back to look at me. 'Dustin. My younger brother. He's Ellis's age. You're going to say it's stupid because it's not the same thing.'

'I'm not going to say it's stupid.'

'There was an accident in our house, when I was little. A fire. Super scary. Nobody died but my brother got burnt and he ended up with a scar on his face, a little down his neck. He got bullied for it mercilessly. And it's not the same thing as Ellis, I'm not saying it is, but my brother turned out the exact *opposite* of him. Super angry, always starting some new fight, thinks everyone's out to get him. And God, it's not like I blame him – I can't even begin to imagine what it's like for *every new goddamn person's* first impression to be the worst thing that ever happened to you – I'm just worried one day Ellis is going to have enough and he's going to snap.'

I'm sympathetic, and I understand, but I can't tell her how this makes me uncomfortable – some sort of fetishizing of youth, of innocence, that makes me wonder, given these hang-ups, what she could possibly like about me. 'That's really why you're worried, then? That we might find something and it'll change Ellis for the worse?'

'Do you have siblings?'

I almost smile, everything she doesn't know too delicious even to bear. I shake my head.

'So you don't understand, Mona. I'm sorry. You can't.'

'Goodnight, Peyton.'

She says nothing.

What she doesn't realize is I'm probably exactly what Ellis needs right now – someone who wants the same thing as him, clever and bullheaded enough to get things done, to show him that his desires and ideas aren't inane. How ironic she wants him to stand up for himself, and all I've seen her do since I've arrived is patronize him.

I'm the only one who will gladly fight for Ellis and won't ask for anything in return.

And when I go to sleep, there's an expanse of nothing and I'm glad for it. There's no Celeste, no lies, just churning black and in my ears, the dull thud of my heart, the only beast I know who keeps to a sure rhythm and doesn't pull tricks.

CHAPTER 17

SATURDAY 5 JUNE

Saturday morning, a mighty fog has draped itself over the island, the non-view from my dorm window all but swallowed up by the haze, the railing of the balcony giving way to a descent into grey nothingness. Everyone's kind of giddy about it, the halls already bounding with activity.

Friday was odd – Peyton made no effort, really, to clear the air from the night before, but today she's back to her normal self, acting as though nothing had happened.

I wake up thinking of Lenore, of Mary Anne and her anger, of Archie, of Baby Blue.

Ellis wants to meet up at ten in the morning to try and talk to Lenore – Sylvia will be on the mainland so he can leave without questions from her. I delight in the fact that I've clearly riled something in him, that he's excited to proceed, to be thrust out of what was once his comfort zone into the full unyielding current of the investigation.

Lenore's house is apparently near Ellis's side of town, so I walk over the neck and towards the Willowwood and linger outside for about five minutes.

'Everything go OK?' I ask when Ellis emerges.

'Yeah, all good. Peyton's working the front desk and she asked where I was going – I said I had to get flowers. Which isn't a lie because Mom *did* actually ask, so I should still do that.'

'We can go afterwards.'

'How is this supposed to work?' Ellis asks once we approach Lenore's street, Rockglenn. 'Is this like a good cop, bad cop kind of thing?'

'Why, change of heart? You wanna be bad cop?' I say, laughing a little at the thought of soft-spoken Ellis slapping his hands down on an interrogation table.

'D-definitely not.'

'Don't worry. I'll do the talking. I need you to listen for important information that I might miss as someone who's not from here.'

'OK.' Ellis nods vigorously. 'That makes sense. B-b-but what if she doesn't want to talk about it at all? Then what do we do next?'

'We'll get there when we get there,' I say, trancelike. I turn to meet his gaze; there's a mayfly on his shoulder. I peel it off by its wings. 'Those fuckers only have a lifespan of five minutes, did you know that? And each one dedicates its impossibly short life to being as irritating as possible.' *Just like you,* I imagine Peyton saying. I strip away the thought.

'Mona, what if she's not even home?'

'You're right. Let's leave.'

Ellis turns to me with a wry smile. I plough into him with my shoulder.

'Is that what you want me to say?' I ask.

'No.'

'Then what do these anxiety-ridden questions even accomplish, huh?'

'Force of habit.'

'Break it. We'll get there – when we get there. If she doesn't want to talk, we'll figure something out. If she's not here, we'll come back.'

'Oh. I think this is it,' Ellis says.

It's a small house that evokes the aesthetic of a barn – bright red with a sloped roof and an ill-fitting conservatory addition, framed with thin white netting. It looks like it might crumple under a strong breeze. We stomp up the depressed wooden steps and swing open the first screen door, which is unlocked and about as heavy as a breath. It groans when it opens. A copper sun hangs on one side of it, a moon on the other. A windchime sings. I'm not nervous. I largely feel nothing when I ring the doorbell, and only a slight leap of surprise when the door swings open to reveal a woman.

She's in her late fifties, maybe, and she's wearing this corduroy two-piece suit despite the heat, curly black hair on the top of her head, black make-up that has smudged slightly round her eyes. Her skin is a warm brown, barely shiny. The artificial pink of her lips cracks when she purses them. 'Oh. Hello. Can I help you?'

'Are you Lenore?'

She blinks. 'Yes, I am.'

I figure an upfront approach will work best. 'We wanted to talk to you about Roxy Raines. Did you know her?'

Lenore looks around, like she might have fallen for a trick, and her first instinct seems to be to close the door slightly. 'And why would you want to do that?' She has a voice that sounds like a xylophone being tapped, staccato and high and tinkling.

'We just have a couple of questions for you. It's for a . . . school summer project. A heritage thing.'

She looks for confirmation from Ellis, who frantically nods after a beat. Maybe it's a hint of sympathy that crosses her face but either way she sighs and says, 'Well, all right. Come in.'

We follow her inside, the path behind her scented like expensive woody perfume.

Her house is borderline unnavigable. A hoarder's narrow walkways, glass display cabinets piled with thrift-store trinkets – the furniture, too, is mismatched and well-loved. I'm not even sure what colour the walls are – they're choked by an abundance of picture frames, maps and art and dreamcatchers and clocks. A cross dangles precariously above a cluttered mantelpiece. The living room smells like lavender.

'This is interesting,' Lenore says. 'Interesting. Have a seat.'

Ellis and I sit on a floral-print tapestry couch, scratchy to the touch.

'Either of you want coffee, tea?' she asks.

Ellis declines for the both of us.

Lenore regards Ellis in a friendly way, but with a look that's still shrouded in thinly veiled pity. 'How's your mom doing, honey?'

'Yeah, she's good.'

'And the hotel? All business as usual?'

'Yeah,' he lies.

'Well, that's good,' she says, and presses down her skirt with the palms of her hands.

Is she stalling? Nervous? But why would she even let us in, in that case?

Lenore turns her attention to me, unwavering. 'And who might you be?'

'My name's Mona Perry. I'm a Seasonal. But Ellis was a little nervous to come alone so I'm accompanying him.'

Lenore leans forward towards the oval coffee table where there's a glass dish full of cashews. She digs out a handful and throws them into her mouth, crunching with her molars. 'That's nice of you.'

'This is a nice house,' I say, not necessarily truthfully, but better than saying, *This is certainly a house*.

'Thank you, sweetheart. It was my parents' until they passed and their parents before that – a few generations' worth of treasures in here. Anyways. How can I help you, then?'

I look to Ellis, trying to get him to speak. He realizes.

'Uh,' he says, 'well, it's not b-b-business as usual, actually. Mom and I are moving at the end of summer and before I go, and with, you know, everything that's happened, I wanted to learn more about Roxy – my grandma, I mean – and her life, I guess, because I won't get to do it again.'

Learn more. Little genius.

Lenore retreats in on herself slightly. Settles into the couch, like she'll be here a while. This is good. 'Well,' she says, 'sure, I knew her. Everyone did. I knew her since she was Catherine.'

'Did you know her well?' I ask.

'We certainly weren't good friends, but we'd both lived here our whole lives and, well, every child knew each other because there were so few of us.' She speaks almost like she's narrating a play, a considered, theatrical inflection to her words.

'Was there anyone she was especially close to?'

Lenore shakes her head, brow furrowed. 'The most solitary girl I've ever met. Everyone knew about her temper and stayed away. Except, well . . .'

'Who?'

'Mary Anne was the only one who was never afraid to really dig into her. They fought *constantly*.'

'What did they fight about?'

'Oh, nobody could ever keep it straight. They were always at each other's throats. Everything. Might as well have been arguing about the colour of the sky. They *were* friends, I suppose, but the sort of friends who have another falling-out every other week. When they got along, they got along swimmingly. Roxy always had a way with words and Mary Anne had quite severe dyslexia; Roxy couldn't keep her mouth shut to save her life and Mary Anne was more of a people-pleaser. They did different things for each other. But as we grew up the fights got worse. Messier. Knew more ways to hurt each other, it seemed.'

Hurt each other.

'Kids,' she says flatly, 'I'd love to keep answering your questions, but before we get too immersed in this, I'd like to ask you one thing. Do you really think I don't know what you're doing here?'

We're quiet.

I can practically feel Ellis vibrating with anxiety beside me. Even I'm taken aback.

'Hm?' she says. 'I understand the implications of what you're asking me.' She cracks another handful of cashews between her teeth. 'You're trying to find out what happened.'

I feel Ellis look at me, undoubtedly panicked, no poker face.

I might as well try it. 'Yes,' I say. 'Yes. That is what we're doing.'

'And how exactly were you led in the direction of *my* home?'

'Frank mentioned you,' I said.

'Oh *really*? And what did *Frank* have to say about me?'

I look into her eyes. 'That you had it in for her.'

Lenore scoffs, a high-pitched bark of a sound. 'Ah, so I'm a *suspect*, am I?'

Ellis is trying his best. 'Just o-of interest.'

'That senile old coot has no idea what he's talking about. Did Frank mention giving Roxy money under *unusual*

194

circumstances? Bet he hasn't shared that damning titbit of information with you.'

'Money? For what?'

Lenore shrugs. 'Who knows? I just remember him complaining, letting it slip at the time.'

'Were they friends? Why would he give her money?'

'If you ask me – I reckon she had some dirt on him.'

'Dirt? Like –'

'Oh, she knew all kinds of stuff about everybody. I don't know what his specific poison was, and I don't know what she'd need the money for, but I certainly wouldn't have put blackmail past her.'

'OK. Wow. That's a lot. We – are you OK with answering more questions?'

'It depends. If you're here to interrogate me further as a suspect, then –'

'No, we're –'

'I was always the musician. Before she was. Dorothy in the community *Wizard of Oz*, if you can believe. Meanwhile Roxy didn't pick up a guitar until she was sixteen, maybe, and of course she was the best right away with the voice of an angel. I was making good money in the summers, playing for tourists, but after, Roxy split my profits in half. Then by a third. I never hated the girl, though. How could I? Damn if I wouldn't use my pipes and eyelashes to get one up on her, had I been blessed with her set of pipes and eyelashes. And that's my truth.'

I don't want to lose her. 'I bet you weren't too upset while she was hidden away, then?'

'*Ha.*'

'Do you remember anything about the night Roxy went missing?' I ask.

'Before she'd fallen pregnant with Sylvia, she'd been offered a contract or some beginning stage of a record deal – I don't remember any more. Obviously things changed – but in any case, she still wanted to move to Nashville and she was playing her last show that night, some kinda big send-off hurrah. I didn't stay for her whole set because I wasn't feeling well that day, but I still made an appearance as I wanted to make amends. I congratulated her and she seemed fine. Happy, even, which wasn't like her. Oh, actually . . .'

Lenore wanders into another room without saying where she's going or what she's doing, and returns with a photo album. She drops it on the coffee table with a deafening boom and flips through, humming to herself – I think it's 'I Wanna Dance With Somebody' – before landing on the page she wants us to see. She jabs the picture with her finger. 'There.'

And there they are, clear as day – a young Lenore and Roxy in The Indigo Lounge. Both smiling, Lenore moreso than Roxy. Roxy's wearing an emerald green jacket, her guitar slung round her. Ellis exhales in delight.

'That's amazing,' I say. 'Do you mind if I take a picture?'

Lenore shakes her head. 'Again, I didn't stay for long, so *I* hadn't noticed anything odd. Word after that night, though, was that Roxy and Mary Anne had argued about something, as always.'

'Do you know anyone who was there that night, who might have seen what happened after?' I ask.

Lenore considers for a moment, softly pensive. 'You'd be good talking to Henry. He owns The Indigo Lounge now but was there that night, bartending. Oh, and –' she leans in close – 'Have you met the police chief?'

'Booker?'

'He might have been paying her close attention, if you know what I mean.' Mine and Ellis's collective confusion is enough to get her to elaborate. 'Had a bit of a crush from what I recall.'

This is fascinating. I'm typing everything into my phone. Booker? 'Do you remember the day everyone realized she was gone?'

'God, yes.'

'Can you talk a bit about what you recall?'

'Well, that it all started wrong. I'd wanted to get the earliest ferry to the mainland – which, my mistake, it was Labor Sunday anyways so the first ferry wouldn't have been out till noon – but by then everyone had got word that Frank had found her guitar and that nobody knew where Roxy was. Which, of course, wasn't unusual in itself. The guitar, though – that was hideously unusual. Loved that thing more than life. That's how everyone knew something was different this time.'

'It wasn't unusual that nobody knew where Roxy was?'

'Oh no. Roxy would disappear for – God, days at a time, really.'

'Where would she go?'

'Who knows?' Lenore sips her drink. 'She'd get the ferry to the mainland and hitch-hike. I remember someone had even mentioned they found her lumbering out of the woods one time, all straggly with leaves in her hair and her guitar slung on her back. But that was only a rumour. Be gone for days in a row, worry her poor mother sick. It's an absolute miracle she lived that long after the way her daughter treated her.'

I'm suddenly very conscious of Ellis next to me.

'Constance never came to her gigs. I'm not even sure she'd ever heard her sing.'

'Do you think it would have changed anything? If she had?'

Lenore shrugs. 'Well, how would I know?'

'Did they have a bad relationship?'

She seems less conscious of Ellis. 'Oh, dreadful. Terrible. Roxy was always free-spirited, and her mother wasn't especially spirited in any sense of the word, more spiri*tual*, and her daughter worried her sick. Here's what you need to know about Roxy. Has anyone told you about her? Ellis, did your great-granny ever tell you what she was like?'

Ellis shakes his head.

'Beautiful, truly, but mean. So strange – she hated everyone. You'd warm to her right away but you'd never, never truly know where you stood with her. As far as I know – I'm sorry, but though she spun all these tales of moving on and new lives, deep down I don't think she knew how to live anywhere but here, how to go anywhere her mother wasn't, and the thought of that tore her up – she had a death wish and I'm pretty sure she got what she wanted.'

Ellis shifts beside me. I feel an urge to protect him in maybe a maternal way but I can't. But he signed up for the knowing – he'll get the knowing.

We're quiet for a moment. 'What do you think happened to Roxy?' I try, hoping to simplify things.

Lenore leans back in her chair slowly, as if to prove a point, with a wry smile on her face. 'Your guess is as good as mine.'

'But it isn't,' I say. 'You lived this. You knew her.'

'I didn't,' she says. 'Nobody did.'

'If you had to guess?'

Lenore chews her cheek. 'I can't answer you, sweetheart.'

'All right. This has been really helpful. Thank you. Just – one more question. Do you know anything about someone called Baby Blue?'

'Baby Blue?' she asks, incredulous. 'Did she know somebody called that? No, no. Maybe one of her weekend boys. That's a bit sentimental for her, though, to call someone that.'

'Are you friends with Mary Anne?'

'We don't speak much, no.'

'Good. Please don't tell her we came.'

'You don't think Mary Anne might have . . .'

'We don't know. But she told us not to look into any more of this. Really angry about it. We're not sure why, but, yeah. It doesn't read as an innocent thing to do, does it?'

'I wouldn't read too much into it,' she says. 'Mary's always been especially secretive. Never took kindly to outsiders.'

'Yeah. Well, we'll keep that in mind.'

'Listen,' Lenore says. 'You'll both learn this as you go, but there are things in this life that we never find the answers to. Our guts speak volumes, though, and, fine, if you want to know what my gut has told me about this whole event? Because, believe me, I've flipped it over. My gut says that Roxy took her own life that night.'

We're quiet. The words settle.

'But everyone has something to hide. And you both ought to be careful, if you're really doing this. You might find you're uncovering things in the process that don't concern you or Roxy, that people don't want you to discover.'

'Sure.'

'Be careful.'

Ellis and I head out, back into the day.

'OK. So. That was interesting,' I finally say. 'Anything in particular stick out to you?'

'I don't know yet.'

'Frank giving Roxy money is . . . something to note. Potentially blackmailing him.'

'I guess she was closer to Mary Anne than we thought too. That explains why she's always been so nice to us . . . oh, hey.' Ellis looks at me nervously. 'Sorry I didn't tell you about this right away. I honestly forgot. But something Lenore said m-m-made m-me think of it.'

'What is it?'

'You have to come back to mine to see.' He kneads his brow. 'We d-d-do actually need to get flowers first, though.'

CHAPTER 18

Ellis and I buy the cheapest bouquet we can find from the florist on Porter – a bunch of yellow chrysanthemums padded out with baby's breath – and march them back to the Willowwood.

Once we arrive at the head of the street, Ellis, ever-cautious, instructs me to wait for the all-clear signal to assess Peyton's whereabouts and make sure Sylvia hasn't returned early, and scurries off alone with the flowers in hand.

Ten minutes of unexpectedly relaxing under-tree sitting later, I get the text.

> **Go inside and straight up the stairs**
> **through the kitchen. Go quick.**

I do as he says, passing the front desk, now adorned with our bargain bouquet; first up a cramped staircase, walled in on either side with barely enough room to raise both my arms. The top floor is clearly where Ellis and Sylvia reside, much more lived-in than its lower counterpart; a basket of laundry sits in the hallway, a pair of shoes, an overfilled

201

bookcase. More compact than downstairs, it's got that musk-tinged, slightly balmy smell of human occupation. There's a ladder swung out from a hole in the ceiling that I assume leads into the attic – and I nearly jump out of my skin when Ellis pokes his head through from above.

'Hey,' he says. 'Come on up.'

The attic's not much bigger than my dorm, which is already small, but is rendered claustrophic due to the clutter: instruments, stuffed toys, a rail of moth-nibbled clothes, a crib, a castle of boxes – *Halloween, Christmas, Ellis – School*. An interminable dust-current is spotlighted by a ray of light streaming in through slatted windows on the far side. Every breath in is another powdery torrent of mothballs and must.

'So, there's . . . there's one m-more thing,' Ellis says, cross-legged on the floor. 'That I haven't shown you. I really d-didn't think it had anything to do with this.'

I lower myself to meet him.

He hands me a piece of white paper that had obviously once been crumpled into a ball, slightly coffee-yellowed at the edges, dry to touch. 'This turned up in our mailbox right after Nana died this April, without a stamp on it. My mom doesn't know that I know about it.'

'Why wouldn't you know about it?'

'She threw it away. I found it in the trash and hid it up here.'

be Happy she's gone, Honey. your better off. always
Here for you. always been

I read it again; note the strange capitalization, the misspellings. 'You said it wasn't stamped?'

'Right. It was in an envelope but I don't even think it had our address on it.'

Not mailed, then. 'Why would your mom throw this away?'

'I don't know. I think she thought it's someone messing with us. But I . . . I wasn't sure.'

'Who do you think sent this?'

'Well, I remembered what you said. About the handwriting. I didn't even think of it until you mentioned it. So I compared, and . . .'

We're looking at the same time and I'm waiting for one of us to deduce, to figure it out, and I'm looking at Roxy's handwriting from the journal and the note and, no, those don't match, but the note and the letter –

'Holy shit, Ellis.' I tie knots with my line of sight, and he's right. They're the same. 'OK,' I say, as if to ground myself, because I know this means something but can't decide what. I look at him, making sure my eyes are properly expressing the seriousness despite the heavy yellow light in the attic. I say it for the first time, alarmed by my own certainty that I break out in goosebumps. 'So whoever left the note in Roxy's car is the same person who sent this letter.'

And then, thumping downstairs. Door opens. Shuts. My gut flips. 'Oh no.'

As if on cue, Sylvia's voice from downstairs. 'Ellis? The flowers are nice, sweetheart, thank you. Are you upstairs?'

Ellis's eyes are enormous, his voice no more than a hiss. 'You have to go. *Now.*'

'OK. How?'

'Window.'

'Window?'

'Yes. Out. Window. Now.' He eyes the sliver of window above us, on the slanted portion of roof. I swing open the window and all my limbs are seized by rigor mortis. It looks so far down. Ellis, between glancing wildly at me and the attic's door, clocks my hesitation and says, 'There're slabs of roof all the way down! I've done it a million times. You'll be fine. *G-g-go. Now.*'

My eyes well up with tears – why are they doing that? – my palms filmed in sweat, my brain a mass of barbed wire. I can't move.

The footsteps are getting closer.

'M-Mona, please! She'll tell M-Mary Anne and we'll be done.'

It's so high. It's so high. Why am I afraid of heights? What is happening? 'I can't. Ellis, I can't –'

'Ellis? Why are you in the attic?'

Ellis whisper-screams. '*You have to go. She'll never let m-m-me talk to you ever again.*'

This is the right thing. I'm sure. But I can't tell if I think that because it's actually the right thing or because I'm too scared to go through the window.

Ellis hisses again. 'Shit – fine. Take this.' He squashes the letter into my hand and I jam it in my pocket. 'Yeah, Mom.'

The door flips upwards and there's Sylvia's head, like a mole, and less like a mole when her eyes open wide and she sees me. 'What are you doing up here?' She pieces it together quickly. Sylvia is resolute. 'Right. Get out of my house.'

In my peripheral vision, Ellis moves towards me, his voice small and wavering. 'M-Mona . . .'

I stay firmly rooted to Sylvia. 'Please. I'm sorry we're here and sneaking around but it's really important that –'

She sets her jaw. 'Get out. Get out, or I'll rescind your accommodation in a heartbeat.' Not even a sliver of the agreeable, soft-eyed woman from before.

'Just go, Mona,' Ellis says miserably.

I stomp down the cavelike staircase without looking back, and realize that Peyton's at the bottom, close enough to have heard the whole thing. Behind me, Peyton says my name weakly. 'What's going on? Mona?' I don't stop for her.

What happened to the process? The careful chess moves, the beat-by-beat, the considered method I'd come here intending to uphold? What happened to 'nothing like the police station'? Why can't I do any of this right?

That's what Celeste would be saying, if she were here.

I grind my teeth all the way home, the white sun assaulting my face, sweat tumbling down my back the way the world is collapsing around me.

I'm in the dorm writing everything down, trying to rid my mind of the embarrassing confrontation.

Lenore said Frank had given Roxy money, that Roxy might have been blackmailing him.

And whoever wrote the note in Roxy's car all that time ago wrote the one delivered to the Willowwood, only a few months before now. Tormenting, for some reason. Had a reason to hate Constance, for – what?

How long have I been on Sandown? I arrived last Friday. A week and a day. Time moves so unusually here, rushing and dragging at once.

Lenore said we should speak to Henry, the guy at The Indigo Lounge. We – or, I – will talk to him next.

Peyton gets back later in the day, smelling of sunscreen and sweat, the bridge of her nose a little rosy. 'What'cha doin'?'

At this point I've been staring mindlessly at my journal for the past half-hour, practically drooling on to it, so I say, 'Fuck all, apparently.'

'What were you talking to Ellis about today? You guys were upstairs. Which is. Weird. Suspicious. Secretive. Sort of like you're still . . . hm. Oh, right, doing exactly what I said you shouldn't.'

She heard. She knows. 'Peyton –'

'Mona, I know this is important to you for some reason. But, please. Sylvia's really upset. I've never seen her like that. She was in a bad mood for the rest of the day – pissed off with Ellis. He doesn't know how to feel.'

I am physically incapable of saying no to her at this precise moment, so I lie. 'I understand.' It's easier to lie and cover it up later.

'Come for a walk with me,' she says.

I'm making no progress anyway so I do as she says, follow her down to the boardwalk, sun beginning to set in the cloudless sky after the fog from this morning.

We have an unusual encounter on the way to the boardwalk.

'Oh, hey, it's the *detective*.' It's a group of Seasonals, guys who I remember vaguely from the bonfire. They're laughing. I can't tell if it's derisive or not. I don't really like the attention, either way – and I don't know how they know to call me that.

I feel Peyton's eyes on me. 'What do you mean?' I ask.

'Haven't ever seen the locals so riled up about anything. They're all talking about it,' one says.

They move off, laughing to themselves. 'Hope you unmask the killer,' another mumbles as they pass. '*Scooby dooby doo.*'

Peyton and I keep walking in silence. 'Well. That's embarrassing.'

Peyton says nothing but I can tell she's maybe secretly pleased that they might have dissuaded me.

The boardwalk is way busier than it was three nights ago; this is maybe the first real tourist night. We have to weave in and out of the crowd until I follow Peyton down to a ledge above where we'd swum. Tenacious sea grass bursts through some of the cracks on the rocks, brushing against my ankles as I swing my legs. We sit there for a moment. I'm waiting for something to happen; her arm jerks and for a terrible moment I worry she's going to reach out and grab my hand.

'Am I in trouble?' I ask her finally, then, to her silence. 'It feels like I'm in trouble.'

'Tell me you care about me.'

I don't know what to say. 'What do you mean?'

'Just tell me.'

'I don't even know you.'

Peyton recoils, face etched with, seemingly, genuine hurt, as if this is anything different from what she'd said to me before. 'That doesn't mean you can't care about me.'

'I care about you.'

'And tell me you care about Ellis.'

'I care about Ellis.'

'Tell me you care about his well-being.'

'Of course I do. More than anyone else around here, it seems like.'

'Not more than anyone.'

'I know you've known him for a long time, and I know I just got here, but we're not playing around, it's real-world stuff, and it puts you under an obligation to someone, Peyton. I . . .'

Suddenly I want to lay it all out for her, everything Ellis and I already know, how far we've come already. If she tasted what I do right now, if her insides felt like mine, all rioting and magnetic, moving towards something instead of away, finally – maybe she'd understand then.

'Some things aren't worth knowing,' she says.

'You're misunderstanding all of this.'

'You know, sometimes, when people get shot – OK, firstly, I watch a lot of those ER shows. Right?'

'Yep.'

'And sometimes, when people get shot, the bullet will still be lodged in them in a sort of sensitive place. Like, I saw an episode about this guy who got shot *in the back. Of his neck*. And if it had gone a millimetre left or right, he would have *died*, right?'

'Sure,' I say, already arriving at the point of all this, but not minding the intense gush of the diatribe.

'And once they treated the wound, they decided it'd be way more traumatic to his body to take the bullet out rather than leave it in.'

'Yeah, I get what you're –'

'They left the bullet in.'

'Peyton . . .'

She swivels round and grips my biceps. The way she's staring shuts me up, with these bright and pleading philosopher's eyes. 'They just left it.'

I hope for an earthquake, a sinkhole, any natural intervention to force the moment to end, but nothing comes, so I finally nod to get her off me.

'I like you,' Peyton says.

'Yeah, I like you too.'

'I want to have a summer with you.'

I look up at her. 'What?'

'I like you and I want to have a normal, non-mystery-plagued time with you. It's Saturday. I'm meeting Liam and some of the guys at Indigo. Come with me. I'm a second away from begging you.'

'I –'

'Please, Mona.'

This, I realize, is a moment of choice. She's saying drop it, now. Let's have a normal time. Let's be teenagers in a lazy almost-paradise where there's nothing to do besides populate your coming life with memories. *But you have to decide.*

She's too close. *No one's ever been closer,* I keep repeating, and I don't know why. I want to kiss her and I want to throttle her and I want to do neither; I don't want to touch her at all, I don't even want to look at her; I wish I'd never met her, I wish I'd never come here, and I tell her to fuck off.

'What?'

'Fuck off, Peyton.'

I turn on my heels and stomp off in the direction of the dorms, seething, new barbs slashing my insides. What Peyton doesn't understand is that the comparison doesn't work. Trauma is never benign, never simply *sitting* there. If Roxy's Sandown's bullet, then she's leaking fatal quantities of lead. Even if she weren't, is that really any better? To leave the bullet? Spend the rest of your life walking around tacked by that unnatural metal mass, its origins in violence, and know it's there forever and there's nothing you can do about it? A symptomless infection changing you from the inside. *Changing you.* There'd be nothing more satisfying than to see that alien object finally emerge, red and wet and glistening. Even if its removal were a terrible risk. Even if you might rupture.

I'm dizzy with horror at the thought of Celeste having left an actual, physical thing inside me – how I'd revel in tearing it out with my fingernails, with my teeth.

Take the bullet out. That's what I'd want. Gouge the flesh, if necessary. Even if, maybe, there's nothing left of me by the end.

Take the bullet out.

CHAPTER 19

SUNDAY 6 JUNE

Work's busy today, packed with the hangover crowd, which I'm sort of grateful for – I don't feel like thinking. My mind keeps flicking back to Peyton despite this. She was friendly enough in the morning but I could tell she'd been especially hurt by last night, slinking through the dorm with a sort of quiet and pathetic resignation, changing in the bathroom instead of her usual move of making a point of doing it in front of me.

Peyton had said it herself: she doesn't even know me. But if she doesn't know me, she *certainly* doesn't know Ellis either, or what's best for him, or for this place. Faux-ethical, holier-than-thou posturing, and for what? So she can feel like she knew best all along? So she can pretend that this whole place isn't fracturing underneath something more sinister than she could ever even conceive of?

I refuse to waste time on her.

What does matter is that whoever left that note all those years ago could still be here on Sandown Bay.

I have my guard up the whole day, wondering if Sylvia mentioned to Mary Anne what had happened, but she doesn't seem any the wiser, her usual grumpy detachment plastered on her face; on good form, the only interaction we have is when she shouts at me after I get distracted and burn a round of toast.

Towards the end of my shift I text Ellis to confirm plans for meeting up to talk to Henry, the bartender-now-owner of The Indigo Lounge. I'd spoken to him only one other time today to apologize for not being able to get out of the attic. *And I thought I was the scaredy-cat*, he'd said.

I expected, but am still displeased with, his hesitation.

> **Ellis:** Idk, Mona. Peyton said we shouldn't be doing this.
>
> **Me:** Peyton doesn't know as much as you think she does.
>
> **Ellis:** I guess.
>
> **Me:** Ellis, think about it. If she knew everything that we do, she'd understand.
>
> **Ellis:** Then can't we just tell her? What we found already?

We could. Selfishly of me, I don't want to; she's earned none of it.

Me:	I don't think that's a good idea.
Ellis:	Don't you trust her?
Me:	It's not that.
Ellis:	Mona, I'm sorry I just don't think so. Everything is weird and on edge.
Ellis:	You dont need me anyways! I don't do much besides sit there and I get too nervous to talk!
Me:	Ellis, that's not true, you're vital.
Ellis:	I'm sorry I can't. Just not right now.
Ellis:	Sorry : (

I need to get him over his reservations at some point – but for now, I'll do this one alone.

Once my shift lets out, I cycle five minutes down the road, past the butterfly house and a brewery, to Indigo. It's dark when I enter, barely any natural light, and the light that does come in is through porthole windows. There's all manner of sea paraphernalia hugging the wooden panelled walls – anchors, skulls and cross bones, black and white photos of ostensibly sea-faring men gathered around ships. There's an assaulting stink of stale beer, grease, sugar gone bad. My tennis shoes keep sticking to the floor. Given it's the first real weekend of the tourist season, it's modestly full – the crowd is patchy but loud. There's the dull thudding of dart against board, sizzle of taps, clatter of glass. I worry I've timed this poorly.

There's a kid working the front, tall with downturned eyes and reddish, pockmarked skin, who I recognize as one of the Seasonals.

I say hello. 'Do you know if Henry's here?'

'Yeah, he should be in the back – oh, aren't you Mona?'

'Sure.'

He grins wildly, shaking his head. 'Holy shit. Is this part of the – *investigation*?'

I blink at him. 'Might be.'

'Aw, man,' he says with a big cheesy grin. 'Yeah, yeah, Henry? Yeah, I'll get him for you.'

'Thanks a lot.'

'Take a seat. Oh – not at the bar, obviously.'

I find a spare circular two-seater table – it's shaped like a barrel – and position myself into the rickety wooden chair poised at the side. I go to rest my head in my hands but my elbows stick to the table and I decide against it.

Henry, I learned, still owns the place; his son's the boss. I think that, too, is what draws me to all this – children assuming the lives of their parents. I understand why Roxy didn't want that. I understand it *intimately*. I feel such a particularly misplaced revulsion at the idea, that simply being in this place feels like exposure therapy. Sylvia inheriting the Willowwood. Lenore still living in the house she grew up in. What do you do, if that's not what you want?

I suppose you become Roxy Raines.

Henry, a stout man with a head full of dark curly hair, emerges from the back, wearing an expression like he's being inconvenienced. He lowers himself on to the chair opposite me. 'What's this about, then?'

'Hi, my name's Mona. I – I wanted to ask you about Roxy Raines.'

He leans into me, taps his temple with a forefinger. 'Well, I'll have you know, I don't blab for *free*.'

I blink. Oh. This is actually happening. I've never bribed anyone before. I search through my pocket for a crumpled-up tenner and pass it to him, and wonder, briefly, if it's tax-deductible.

'Do I remember that spitfire,' he says, folding the bill and slipping it into his shirt pocket. '*Yeesh.*'

He tells me the standard fare – talented but difficult, beautiful and mouthy.

'What about the night she went missing?' I ask. 'I've talked to someone who said this was the last place she was seen. I'd love to ask you some questions about the night.'

'Was so damned long ago – and, Christ, I barely remember what I had for breakfast.'

'Whatever you can think of will probably be more helpful than you realize.'

'All right. Well, firstly, none of us had seen much of her in a while because – well, it was understood she was being *kept in*. We all knew what happened there, of course. Mood had changed. If she was dark before, well, after she had Sylvia – that girl was a black hole.' Henry palms his face. 'Anyway, it's Roxy's last set, everyone's drinking. And even if you didn't like Roxy, you sure liked her music, so people were listening. Towards the end of the night Roxy's in the middle of her set and something spooks her. Walks clean off the stage in the middle of the song, and Mary Anne follows her out. We all shared a kind of glance, you know, *oh, they're at it again*, but the night was flying by and they did this all the goddamn time. They were out there for a while, bit of a commotion. Archie and Booker are inside nursing a couple drinks, shooting the shit, and eventually Mary Anne comes back in all distraught, like she's been crying or something.'

'Then what?'

A man approaches Henry from behind and claps him hard on the back, laughing about something. 'Hey hey hey, hold on a goddamn second, I'm being *interviewed*!' Henry says in veritable hysterics, then turns back to me and asks, 'What the hell was I talking about?'

'Mary Anne comes back in distraught.'

'Right, right. Mary Anne's pissed, then her and Archie have some sort of back and forth, then all of a sudden *Archie's* packing up and blowing out of here, like it's the end of the world or something. I think Booker and Mary Anne went along with him. Night was pretty much fizzled out by that point. This poor guy who went on afterwards, don't remember what the fuck his name was but it was his first time playing here, came all the way from the mainland, and it was just about the worst crowd you could imagine. Was playing shitty Police covers and no one gave a single –'

'Did they say anything about where they were going? The three of them?'

'Not a word.'

'Would any of them have wanted to hurt Roxy?'

'Mary Anne, well, I didn't know her well. Booker neither, but Archie wouldn't hurt a fly as far as we all knew; and Archie, yeah, good luck asking *him* about any of this, because, well, you know, nobody's home – but he's always been protective over Mary Anne, so, I don't know, maybe he *would've* hurt a fly for her.'

'Someone mentioned that Booker might have had feelings for Roxy.'

'Well, geez. Nah. I don't know much about that.'

'Are you aware if Roxy knew anyone on the mainland? Like, here's what I'm saying – is there a universe where she *did* what she said she'd do, left and never came back?'

'She could've. Everyone knew about her secrets. Not what they were. Just that she had 'em.'

'Do you know anything about Frank? The ferry master? I heard something about Roxy blackmailing him.'

'Sounds like her.'

I don't know what else to ask. At this point I feel like I'm going in circles. I thank Henry for his time and go to leave, but remember one more thing. 'Do you know about anyone called Baby Blue?' I ask.

He furrows his brow. 'Not the Badfinger song?'

I almost laugh. 'No, that's all right. Thanks again.'

Henry sings behind me – '*Guess I got what I deserve, kept you waiting there, too long, my love*' – as I walk back out into the blaze.

*

218

I leave but don't feel like going back to the dorm yet. I ride all the way up past the isthmus, the sun setting now, the horizon pink-edged and smouldering. Warm air on my face. I'm feeling alive.

I'm thinking about everything Henry said. Mary Anne and Roxy fought; Booker, Archie and Mary Anne all left together.

A sense of calm falls over me, the world rolling underneath. I think we're close to something now.

I circle the Willowwood just to greet it, almost hope Sylvia catches me passing from the window. Everything is going to be OK. Great, even. We're going to crack it. This whole thing is going to split open.

I ride past the edge of the No-Names, branches beckoning with their long skeletal fingers from the perimeter, and I don't like them, as always, but I get to thinking about forests.

Maybe we're all full of an empty plain but then with every memorable moment, good and bad, there's another tree planted. Then another then another then another. And maybe we convince ourselves that, as we become increasingly tangled in the mass of trees and divots that are us, life is about looking for the clearing, the bit where all of it breaks. But maybe that's the secret. Maybe the secret is that it never breaks. Not really. It never breaks, and the only thing that's really gratifying is pressing the bark against your face and delighting in the thought that this is me, and this is real, and this is true. Just lying down in the undergrowth, in a wood made of all of you, of every joy and every terror, and saying this is me, and this, and this. The difference between feeling lost and feeling fine isn't a change in circumstances, it's a change in behaviour.

Truth of circumstance isn't the same as truth of the self, I decide. This search for Roxy is powered only by events, actions, things that people actually did. But maybe truth of the self is whatever I'd damn well like it to be.

When I arrive back at the dorm Peyton pretends like I haven't, a menacing quiet between us reserved only for unsaid things, not even glancing up from the idle taps of her phone.

I spend the night transcribing Henry's interview and change into my sleep clothes in the bathroom.

Before I go to bed, I tell Peyton my theory about people and forests, not even as a peace offering, but something more sinister, maybe, forcing her to listen to my voice, forcing her to experience me.

The silence settles like grave dirt when I'm done. Cicadas trill sharply from outside. The nape of my neck prickles with sweat. I can't help but look at her, the gentle rise and fall of her stomach, the pale soles of her feet, dusty with sand. But I don't expect her to have any thoughts, so I turn over and face the wall, experimentally shut my eyes, but after a moment she says, 'That's really sad,' then nothing else.

I turn, my pillow softly ruffling, and ask her what she means.

'So hopeless.'

'Man. At least I was polite about the unsolicited wisdom *you* subjected me to yesterday,' I say, and shut my eyes again.

I wonder if she hasn't quite understood what I mean about the forest, because it's actually maybe the most hopeful thought I've ever had. Then we're quiet again and I swear she's moved on to something else, but another moment passes and she says, almost a whisper, 'Maybe you're a forest. I'm not.'

I roll back round to look at her staring at the ceiling, her silhouette in profile: the soft scoop of her nose, the petals of her lips. 'What are you, then?'

Peyton spreads her hands high above her and moves them from each other, like she's parting the sea. 'A big open sky.'

CHAPTER 20

MONDAY 7 JUNE, 4 a.m.

I'm becoming acquainted with the stars.

The moon is through the window, three-quarters wide, clear enough that I can make out the craters collapsing into each other, making up what I can't help but see as a sort of anguished face.

I finally shake myself out of an interminable torture of half-wake, half-sleep, slip on my tennis shoes and go. I pass the ferry, docked in the harbour, massive and bobbing in the sluggish waves, rising and falling like someone asleep. I'm still thinking about Celeste. Not even the motion outmanoeuvres her this time; she's clinging hard.

Like a leech.

There are no sisters. I even learned to hate the word, the hissing and the hard consonants prodding around, restrained in the very front pocket of your mouth. It's an ugly word.

I could never discern what I was to Celeste. I wasn't sure if she even saw me as human, as animal, as bug. Which made little sense because we were always told – by everyone – how alike we looked. In the mirror I saw her black-brown eyes under glasses, her blonde shock of hair. I hated it. I wanted to pluck out each hair that reminded me of her. I wanted to scrape away at my skin to the bone, till it could grow back new.

But even now, feeling my body hum beneath me, I know, deep down, that no amount of dyeing or peeling or scraping will ever separate me from her. It's just DNA. She's family.

What do you do when these people you've been designated to have in your life are the worst thing that's ever happened to you? I suppose you hope they go missing.

I pinch myself for the thought but it happened, so there's no point in backtracking now.

I kept a secret part of me that not even she could touch. It was small, and quiet, and I only brought it out in places I knew were safe – three in the morning under the covers, when she was out with her friends, when the house was quiet and still. But it isn't enough to have the option, to know it's there, to have the assurance that that part of you will always be there when you want to return to it – because it won't. Nothing will always be there. Parts unused will grow weak and shrivel and die. They will be unrecognizable and you'll try to fish them out and you'll realize you can't even feel them any more when you dive into the murky waters and reach for them. Those muscles of selfdom, of personhood wither away if neglected.

And I'm angry now, mostly. Most things make me angry. Most people. I find it hard to make friends. Maybe I'm cruel sometimes. I don't intend to be.

But we all try to hurt people on purpose at some point or another. Sometimes it's revenge. Sometimes it's petty cruelty, dangling tadpoles between our fingers because we haven't learned the value of life, and everything that breathes exists for us.

Some never learn the value of life, except their own.

I don't want to be this way but I will if I have to.

But it occurs to me – all the Seasonals know about the investigation. Word's got around now. Someone could find out about the podcast. All it would take is one person saying the wrong thing and this would all fall apart. I should have been more careful. But how did people even find out about it in the first place?

Then, more seriously, it dawns on me. If Ellis and I are right, which we are, about it being the same person leaving the note in Roxy's car all those years ago and the letter in their mailbox just months before, it means there's a possibility they're still here. Maybe we've already talked to them and don't know it.

I'm thinking about all this when I remember it's Monday at four thirty in the morning and it is completely, utterly silent.

No noise. No stirring. Nothing is open yet. No one is preparing for the day yet.

Not even Frank.

Call received approx. 4 a.m. Sunday morning from resident who discovered property known to belong to Catherine O'Hare [alias Roxy Raines].

Then where was he today – on a Monday morning? Surely he should be prepping even *earlier* on a Monday. And maybe it was decades ago, but these people don't seem the sort to change the way things are done.

And Lenore had said she wanted to get the ferry early the day Roxy's guitar was found, but it was Labor Sunday and ferries weren't running until later. Frank wouldn't have been prepping the ferry then. So what was he really doing out by the docks so early – and whatever it was, why did he lie about it?

CHAPTER 21

The sun is setting on the way, red to pink to purple, stretching all the way across a clear expanse of sky, the ocean reflecting it back at itself. The edge of the heat has burst and my perpetual trail of sweat in between my shoulder blades during the day has mercifully dried. And there's the No-Names parking lot, spooky and empty as ever.

Ellis and I had arranged to meet after work; this time I'm here before him and my aloneness unsettles me. The woods are just as sinister as I thought them the day I arrived, glaring in through the backyard of the Willowwood. I get up close to the border of the No-Names and read the same signs I passed that first day. NO TRESPASSING.

The toothy scratch of tyres on asphalt behind me makes me jump. Ellis pulls up. 'Hey. What are you doing?'

'Have the woods always been blocked off? And is it all of the woods?' I ask, realizing immediately that I sound a little dazed.

'As long as I've b-b-been around, I'm pretty sure. And yeah, the fence runs from side to side.'

'The signs look beaten up. Like they've been there a while.'

'P-probably.'

'It seems weird that they'd have this whole bit of the island – like, way more than half of the total land mass – blocked off. Wouldn't developing it be at least a sort of tourism pull?'

'Yeah, I guess you're right. I don't know, I guess it p-probably is unsafe back there. Apparently – I m-m-mean, you can see, it's so dense that it's hard to even m-move through some of it. And it's all a mess now; it'd take ages to m-maintain it. And I guess m-most people don't come here to go hiking.'

'Mm. You're probably right,' I say. I catch Ellis up on the week's findings – namely, recounting the conversation I'd had with Henry. 'And then – Frank. I had an epiphany.'

'What do you m-mean?'

'He said he found Roxy's guitar, and the police report said the guitar was found Sunday morning. Right?'

'Sure.'

'Really early. The report said four in the morning. But what did Lenore say? What day would that have been?'

'The Sunday before Labor Day.'

'Yeah.' And I'm eyeing Ellis because something about him changes, and then I see, he's figured it out before I've told him but he wants me to ask him the question. 'Ellis, what time do ferries normally leave on Labor Sunday?'

'On holidays it's usually noon.'

'So what was our friend Frank doing out at the shore so early? Shit, Ellis, think about it. Maybe he needs to get rid of the guitar but he knows it's light enough to get washed back up to shore . . . or, maybe, not even that. I don't peg him as an especially clever guy. Maybe he wants to insert himself in the investigation to make him look like an innocent bystander. Right?'

'Yeah, OK. Right.'

'So, either way, he calls in this guitar, and it's four in the morning –'

'Why would it be in the m-morning two days after, though?'

'Any number of things, I guess. Shock. Fear. Maybe he'd been trying to get rid of it in other ways. I mean, Ellis, we caught him out on his alibi. And he has a motive. Lenore literally said she thinks Roxy could have been blackmailing him.'

'What do we do?' Ellis asks.

I chew my thumb; confronting Frank again with this information seems unproductive at best and dangerous at worst.

This is when the siren blares and we both practically jump out of our skin – but I hide it better than Ellis, who's trembling. It's Booker who emerges from the police car.

'Of course it's you two,' he says. 'Jen at the post office calls me all distraught, says she thought she saw vandals out here. What the hell are you –'

'Booker,' I say, glancing at Ellis, 'we need to tell you something.'

He shuts the car door behind him. 'If it's about what I think it is then I'm not interested.'

'Or, what if it is the same genre as you think it is, but it's more than you ever could have imagined?'

He grips my head playfully like he's palming a basketball. '*No*.'

'Frank's alibi d-doesn't hold up.' This comes from Ellis, who speaks so loud and so clearly that it gives us both pause. He seemed to have been harbouring all his nerve for this one declaration, however, because he says nothing else.

I fill the dead air. 'Frank says he found Roxy's guitar early. Report said it was Sunday morning.'

'Sure, if I remember correctly.'

'It was Labor Sunday. Frank says he was out that early prepping the ferry – which would make sense if the first ferry was leaving at the usual six thirty, maybe, but it wasn't. The first ferry wouldn't leave until noon on holidays. Why was he out there so early?'

'Oh, Christ, Mona. That's all you've got?' He leans back on to the cruiser, arms folded across his chest.

Something in me deflates. 'What do you mean?'

'Miss Perry, I appreciate your stick-to-it-iveness. And I normally wouldn't tell you this, but if it'll get you to calm down – it was a poorly kept secret at the time that your friend Frank –'

'Not my friend.'

'– would often sneak away into the night to meet up with ladies in a manner that his then-wife would have found reprehensible – notably Denise, God rest her soul. I think he was on his way home. You'll find this was of course not documented in the official record.'

I let the words settle. I think back to what Lenore said: *blackmail*.

'Then why wouldn't he have just said that?'

'Because he – understandably, might I add – probably didn't want to tell law enforcement at the time, and certainly doesn't want to tell a couple of teenagers decades later, about his private affairs.'

'Lenore said Frank was giving Roxy money.'

'Jesus Christ, you've been talking to Lenore?'

'Yeah. She's nice.'

Booker throws his hands up, exasperated. 'Understand something, kid. We cared about Roxy,' he says, and I can tell I've hurt him. It's odd hearing someone say it. That no, maybe they hadn't all conspired to keep quiet about her supposed death. 'Of course people cared. But she hadn't had an easy life. She was troubled. And simple logic said she was going to do something drastic eventually.'

'Did you know Roxy well?'

'Everyone knew her in passing. And she was a very disturbed young woman who hurt a lot of people, including herself.'

'Those are strong words.'

'And you're making serious accusations about innocent people.'

'We heard a little bit about you, actually.'

He scoffs at this. Not the freeze and side-eye I was hoping for. 'Oh, I'm sure.'

Ellis pipes up. 'Lenore said you liked Roxy.'

'Christ, what have you done to this damn place? I swear, ever since you rolled in, everyone's talking, *gossiping* like we're – like we're *teenagers* again.'

'Did you see her? The night she disappeared?'

'No, I didn't.'

'Why not? It was her last show. Wouldn't you have wanted to go see her?'

'It was a Friday night, still tourism season, and I was just starting at the force. Of course I was patrolling.' Both Lenore and Frank said he'd been there, so why is he lying?

'What about Mary Anne? Was she there?'

'You've got some gall asking about her now.'

'Were you the one who told her that we were looking?' I ask. 'Is that why she knew? Are you covering something up?'

'I don't know if Mary Anne was there, because I wasn't, and I recommend you don't ask anyone else about it.'

'Who's Baby Blue?'

'You're trying to look through a brick wall, Miss Mona. And there's nothing on the other side of it. I know you think you're digging and digging and eventually you'll strike something, but –'

'We don't need any more metaphors. It's fine.'

'No, it's not fine, actually. Listen very carefully.' He's deadly serious now, his register so low it makes me shiver. 'I saw you on the cameras. Both of you.'

I try to speak but my usual veneer has cracked and I'm certain everyone can see right through it.

'There's a silent alarm that trips if anyone's around the station out of hours. I came by to have a look but there wasn't anyone there by that time – or, at least, I didn't think so. I checked the cameras the next morning. You're smart, obviously, kid – but not smart enough to realize there were *cameras*?'

'I – no, I just assumed there wouldn't be a reason for anyone to check them. And – then you should be able to explain why Roxy's case file was empty.'

His words are heavy and staccato. 'You have committed a federal offence. You broke into a police station to look for confidential documents, a crime for which I've just got a confession. Do you understand?'

The blood drains from my face.

'You think you're on some grand adventure, and you think you're cleverer than you are. I understand. I understand that maybe you think you're a bit brighter than everyone else and that what you're doing here is important.' I'm embarrassed; he's not talking to me and Ellis, just me. 'I'd even say I felt like you too, when I was a kid. I think Roxy would've liked you and she didn't like anyone.' Despite everything, all this, I swell with pride. *She didn't like anyone.* Me neither. 'But you need to watch yourself.'

'People keep telling me that,' I say.

'Maybe because it's true.'

'Thank you. I'm sorry. I know you're doing us a favour.'

'More than a favour. If anyone found out about this? And I'm not sure if you're actually sorry, but it doesn't really matter. Take that energy and make sure it stops you from doing any of this again while you're here. I won't say anything if you drop this now. I don't want to hear a *word*. About *either of you*. Understand?'

Booker goes to leave, then, like an afterthought, turns.

'You think I haven't thought about everything you're thinking about, thought about her, every day since she left?'

Ellis and I both nod.

'I swear,' he says, 'I swear, I still see her sometimes . . .'

We're all quiet. A sea gull screams above us.

'And . . .' He kneads his brow, like he's in pain. 'I certainly don't need to tell you this, but the folder was empty because I sent it off for you.'

I blink. 'What do you mean?'

'All file requests are sent along to the county office on the mainland. I was gonna try and see if I could get the information to you. What a sucker, right?'

My chest, already strained from his chastising, finally crumples. 'Thank you,' I say.

'Well, doesn't matter much now anyways, now you've got Ellis on your team.' He eyes the two of us. I worry we look pathetic. 'Truly, what are the chances?'

'We're sorry, B-B-Booker,' Ellis says.

'Look, I don't know you especially well . . .' He's looking at me. 'So I can't speak for you – but I know you, Ellis, and I wouldn't have expected you to get mixed up in all this.'

Ellis's expression is downcast.

'It's his family,' I say, a spike of anger underneath my words.

'And that's exactly why he ought not to be. Sometimes nothing good comes from digging.'

'You won't see any more of us,' I say.

Booker gazes back, but past us, at the barbed wire fence. 'And stay out of there,' he says, finally. 'All kinds of dips, ravines and that. One of you could get hurt.'

Booker drives away, the shock of the siren still floating around near the back of my skull. Ellis and I are silent until the sound of tyres on gravel has faded into the far distance.

Without looking at Ellis, I say, 'He was lying about not being there.'

'I know.'

'But *why would he lie*? More importantly, why would he lie about where he was, and defend Frank at the same time, and then also send the files off for me?'

'What do you mean?'

'If I was a police officer who had killed someone and some dastardly kids are sticking their noses in, I'd be the first to hope that they pin it on somebody else. Why wouldn't he just let us think Frank had done it to get us off his case?'

It's all a bit hopeless now. Mary Anne and Archie. Booker. Baby Blue. Sylvia. How does it all fit together?

'So what do we do next?'

But neither of us have an answer, and we're both a bit shaken, so Ellis and I cut our losses and go, the No-Names breathing behind us.

After I say goodbye to Ellis, on the way home, because everything is very confusing, I'm thinking of Booker and where he fits in, but I also can't stop thinking about the deep, dark woods, and I'm searching for information on my phone. No dice; I'm looking maybe for something in the local paper about the woods being blocked off, but the archives only go back so far and it doesn't look like they've digitized any of their papers pre-2005.

But I'm stuck on this now and I can't shake the curiosity.

Finally I come across a digitized collection of news from a small publication that is primarily focused on locations from the mainland but also includes news from Sandown. I try the search. *Woods closure Sandown. Forest. Shut.* I close a warning about Hurricane Arthur.

Finally I find it – an article headline. SANDOWN SURPRISES WITH IMMEDIATE FORESTRY CLOSURE.

Sandown County has announced the official closure of its forest today after a series of accidents city officials attributed to the untamed nature of the wood. Police chief Clark says it's for the best. 'We're lucky it's so beautifully preserved, but until we can ensure our visitors can safely experience the beauty Sandown has to offer, we can't in good conscience leave it open to the public.' A ten-year beautification project has been proposed but is yet to be approved by the town council.

It's dated 4 November 1986, a little more than two months after Roxy's disappearance.

My heart quickens.

This strikes me as unusual timing.

I don't have too long to linger on this, though, as I open the door to my dorm and I realize –

Somebody has been here.

CHAPTER 22

The mess is hard to identify.

It doesn't look like anything, really. Debris. Detritus. Black bits of string and plastic, like the viscera of a roll of film. I actually worry at first that something has happened to Peyton – although she leaves behind the occasional cold cup of coffee or shirt on the floor, she wouldn't leave the room in this state.

And then I realize what it actually is on the floor, based on the one drawer of my desk that is flung open wide, the explosion radiating from that central point.

It's all the equipment for *How to Disappear*.

My microphone is shattered. Closer inspection reveals the wires have been cut into little segments, in some places meticulously but in others they're completely ripped. A tape recorder has been smashed to bits. My headphones dashed. Even my pop filter is torn up.

My body seizes, knowing before I do that maybe this place is still unsafe, that someone might still be here. The thought shakes me and I immediately check under the beds, beneath the covers. I check the hanging light, beneath the shade; someone in a movie I saw once found a bug there.

Once I'm satisfied there's no active danger I shut the door, press my back against it and let myself fall to the floor.

I'm not safe now. This proves it.

And if I wasn't sure whether there was a killer on the island before – if I thought maybe it was someone who'd gone, or died, and that I was reopening a case that had croaked long before I had laid eyes on it – then I certainly don't think that now. There's still a killer on Sandown Bay, and they've been in my room. *Our* room. They know about what I'm really doing here and aren't happy about it.

In a panic I try Peyton's phone but it goes to voicemail.

But it's not that the killer was trying to *prevent* me from telling – they can't be that dumb. I can get new equipment, obviously, and even if I couldn't there're ways of information-sharing unencumbered by whether I own a microphone. This wasn't strictly prevention – this is a message meant to frighten me.

I realize I'm muttering to myself, a steady chorus of *shit*s that I make an effort to stop to focus my thoughts. I feel like I've been playing pretend this whole time and only now am I being tested, and I'm alarmingly underprepared. Not just unprepared. I didn't even know there'd be a test.

Idiot. Did you think you could waltz on to an island and piss everyone off and solve the mystery with flying colours?

You have no idea what you're doing. You're a historian. Not even that. You're a record-keeper. You're a leech.

Sylvia was right; Peyton was right. I shouldn't have done any of this.

I take a picture of the mess with my phone before moving anything, just in case.

There's nothing out of place on the front door – handle on, lock works, door clicks when it shuts. I check the window and the balcony door – both shut, and there aren't any footprints along the side of the building, on our balcony. I doubt whether anyone would even be able to scale the wall in the first place.

If the windows are fine and the door isn't marked then they must have had a key. Or Peyton left the door open, but I don't think she'd do that, and they would have had no way of knowing definitively that she would have.

We can go with the key for now.

Ellis and I must be getting close, I realize, if whoever it is has now gone to the trouble of threatening me directly.

I curse Peyton, willing her to pick up her phone. I need to know if she saw anything, or ran into anyone on the way – but a wave of clarity crashes over me. I can't tell Peyton. Peyton, who's already worried about Ellis's well-being, who will certifiably rage if she thinks our endeavour, previously only *maybe* emotionally manipulative, has somehow actually turned dangerous. And neither can I tell Ellis, who, too, would be dissuaded by the threat of reprisals, who at this point could possibly be scared enough to confide in Sylvia.

No forced entry, no breaking and entering. So who has keys? Sylvia, I realize.

This is getting complicated quickly. Maybe I have to tell Ellis. And I realize we haven't yet spoken about Ellis's great-grandma, even after Frank's intimation that she'd abused Roxy.

I try to picture the scene: Sylvia comes into the dorm, smashes everything, because – because of some terrible family secret. Because what if *Constance* had killed Roxy that night? I suddenly realize I know hardly anything about her. This is an enormous oversight, even after everything Lenore had said. Maybe an argument got too heated one night; I picture the B and B, a body slumped over a couch, in a bed, a thrown glass striking a temple.

Maybe Ellis's mom knows more than she is letting on.

But Ellis has just given a speech about family. About family being the only thing you really have, about family being irreplaceable, and – oh God, I can already see the glossy film of his eyes if I even so much as hint that maybe instead of all-loving his was self-destructing.

I can't ask about this yet.

The same person who sent them that letter put the note in Roxy's car all those years ago. Or, at the very least, would have written both of them.

And based on the absolute state of my dorm room – they're getting closer. They're *already* closer.

Could it have been Ellis's great-grandmother? Is that the theory I was banking on? For the note, maybe, but the letter – obviously the letter came after she died. She couldn't have sent both. Even if she arranged it in a retrospective 'put this in my mailbox after I die' way, why would she have done that? And about herself?

Nothing makes sense. A headache coils around my forehead. This is all wrong.

What do I tell Ellis? He can't know about the podcast and he can't think I suspect his mom had anything to do with anything.

Peyton gets back around nine at night. She's unusually cheery – not that it's unusual generally, but it certainly is lately, given the new sombre tone of our relationship and our string of disagreements.

'Where've you been?' I ask.

'Could ask you the same question, sunshine.'

'For real, Peyton.'

'A few of us went swimming. I was gonna ask you to come, but you weren't –'

'No, it's fine. Did you notice anything weird when you got back from work?'

She blinks. 'Like weird how?'

'Here? In the dorm? Anything taken or moved?'

'Can you be more specific? You think I'd touch your shit?'

'No. No, not at all, not you, I was just – wondering. And, uh, at work, was Sylvia there all day?'

'What are you *talking* about?'

'Was she, Peyton?' I ask, exasperated.

She softens. 'I don't know, I mean, no – I think she left around lunch today. Was gone for a couple of hours.' Peyton knits her brow. 'What's going on?'

'Yeah, it's fine. Sorry. I'm just being weird.'

'What else is new,' she breathes, then lowers herself on to my lap, facing me, and throws my hair over my shoulder – something curiously tender, even for her on a good day, and I feel myself tense. She must sense it, because she doubles back and asks, 'Really. What's the matter?'

I want to tell her. She's so pretty there in the light of the desk lamp that I'm compelled to tell her everything. I do feel bad about our fight, and the loneliness. About Roxy, Ellis, the podcast, why I'm really here. Even about Celeste. Maybe then she'd understand. Maybe then she'd be able to spar with the heaviness in me that she can't name. There's its name. It's Celeste Perry.

But instead I tell her nothing's the matter and quietly get ready for bed, at moments unsettled by the sense of a third ghostly presence in the room.

CHAPTER 23

TUESDAY 8 JUNE

I wrestle with the new information in my mind, trying to unpick the knot of it.

I'm paranoid out of my mind at work. I can't let go of the thought that Sylvia is the only one with keys – her or, theoretically, Booker. I imagine it wouldn't be too hard for him to finagle some.

I call Ellis during my lunch break, outside and a good few paces away from the back of the diner so Mary Anne can't hear.

'Hey, Ellis,' I say. 'Do you remember where your mom was yesterday? Around the afternoon?'

'Um, I think at the B and B for most of the day? Until night-time at least. She might have left for a bit around then.'

'Did she say what she was going to do?'

'Seasonal stuff. Accommodation checks.'

My legs prick with goosebumps. If it *was* Sylvia, and she knew about the podcast, then she would have told Ellis by now, surely, to keep him away from me. And Ellis doesn't seem to have a clue in the world. I decide not to test it.

'Why are you asking about my mom?'

'It's nothing. Really.'

'You can tell me whatever. We're a team.'

'I know, Ellis. Really. Don't worry.'

Nothing good will come out of me telling him my suspicions. It could go two ways: he'd either be upset at me even for suggesting that Sylvia could have done something like that, or – well, he could never trust his own mother again. I can't do that to him.

Unless I had definitive proof.

'So what's our next move, then?' Ellis asks.

For the first time I don't know and I tell him this. 'Just – let me think today. I'll let you know.'

I surprise myself with how afraid I am. Maybe I'm imagining it, but Mary Anne seems to be keeping a closer eye on me than usual.

I have the inexplicable sense that everything is on the verge of falling apart. We've reached the precipice and we're seconds away from the descent.

I'm feeling like I have less and less to lose. I don't care about Mary Anne's temper. I need to speak to Archie. Archie, who I've barely seen say two words to anyone my entire time here.

My mouth runs dry. What's the scenario? Something happens in the woods, no one wants anyone to find it, or see what it is, someone who probably has a high standing in town, who's capable of making a change like this so quickly. I re-read the article I found last night in a fever.

When there's a slow moment I catch him in the kitchen.

'Archie, I desperately need to talk to you.'

'OK.'

'Do you remember the night Roxy went missing?'

'Roxy?'

'Roxy Raines. Or Catherine O'Hare. Do you remember her?'

'Listen.'

'What, Archie?'

'Listen. That's her.'

'What?' There's nothing; the only sound I can hear is the light chatter from the diner and the beeping in Mary Anne's office.

'That's her.'

'What are you –' I look behind me, in case Mary Anne is coming. I'm floundering. 'Do you know anything about the woods? Have you ever been in the woods?'

He doesn't say anything.

'Archie? Do you know about the woods?'

'I'm sorry,' he says, 'but I can't help you. I just can't help you. I just can't.'

'Archie?'

'I just can't help you.'

'It's fine –'

'I just can't.'

*

It's one in the morning and I'm thinking of the woods.

I need to go out now. Night isn't the best time but I don't want Peyton asking questions, so I sneak off into the darkness again, vaguely aware that Booker might catch me. But everything is falling apart anyway so nothing matters. Someone is after me. Someone's been in my room. Someone knows everything I've taken measures to hide and it could all come out at any moment, so everything needs to happen *now*.

I don't want to tell Ellis about this, for some reason. I don't like that I'm keeping secrets from him. Though this isn't a secret, really. But something about this feels personal and I want to do it alone.

The woods.

There's a mile of fence. Some of it runs through the back of the Willowwood.

The whole thing is streaked in long, dirty shadows.

I illuminate the chain link with the flashlight on my phone, not totally sure what I'm looking for, then I see it. There's a section of the chain link breathing and flexing of its own accord with the wind, not in tandem with the rest. I approach and wrap it in my fingers and pull – it gives in nearly a straight line, all the way down. The edges are as evenly silver as the rest of the fence – not rusted. It's almost as if it's been intentionally cut away. Quietly, without drawing attention to itself. My blood runs cold.

I take a breath that feels cold and sharp even in the warmth. The beam of my flashlight flicks over the treeline, searching for any sort of guidance, clue – reassurance?

But the woods owe me nothing. They never have. Certainly not today, with me here, planning to gut them.

Go in.

I don't know what part of me says it. The yawning darkness in front of me. It's the way forward. I can feel it. For a moment I think I actually might. I actually might cross the barrier. I peel back the fence to see. Right size for a person, exactly.

I swallow, but my throat is swollen and it's painful.

Not now. I can't do it now.

And then – movement. Movement from beyond the trees. A lumbering figure. A flash of hair.

Celeste. Celeste Celeste Celeste –

I turn away, goosebumps prickling the back of my neck. Why am I welling up? What am I doing?

I set off for the dorm and whatever ghost there is haunting the No-Names tonight watches me go.

Memories always come at night.

There's something about the dark that evokes monsters that don't relent once roused. Maybe it's because in the monochrome of darkness one's mind can project easily on top of it.

After the terrifying intensity of what had happened that night, it's no wonder how my mind has got to this place. Booker left with Archie right after Roxy that night from The Indigo Lounge.

Someone looking back at me from the No-Names. I'm thinking of the woods, and unmarked graves.

Celeste.

The first thing I thought when Celeste went missing was that she was trying to scare me.

Black plays in front of my eyes and spreads through me like ink.

I loved her missing. When she was missing it was easy to pretend that she'd never even existed at all.

I didn't react when Dad told me she'd died and he interpreted this as me not understanding death, which I did, but he didn't realize. So he explained it to me and I pretended this had illuminated some deep truth and I forced myself to cry, but the reality was I was ecstatic. Maybe unable to *truly* comprehend the finality of it – a feeling I still have, even now – but aware enough to know *here is what it means: that she's not coming back*.

This is why Dad has always hated the podcast. He interprets its existence as some obscene vestige of grief, a coping mechanism, when, of course, that's never been what it is.

Roxy Raines. I remember the first time I heard her name: in my sister's mouth.

Celeste liked the nihilism, the sort of searching of the lyrics – she was weird because her tastes changed as suddenly as her mood. She liked to play parts. Roxy was the catalyst for one of them, a welcome folky reprieve from the occasional screamo. It was when Roxy's album was rereleased that Celeste found her on Spotify, I think, and wouldn't stop listening.

Now I remember. *Now I remember . . .*

It's true that I'm even here because of Celeste. The one autonomous decision I've made in my whole life is still because of Celeste.

And I see her. I don't know if I'm asleep and I don't know if I'm awake but I see her again, staring at me.

It's normal at first, as I knew her. Forever seventeen. I'll soon be older than she was when she disappeared. But maybe she's been ageing. Maybe she's still out there and she's older now, and while I'm thinking this and she's staring at me through the fog, her hair grows in front of me, all the way down to the ground – but it's not just her hair, it's her hair and her nails and her face, bits of rotted flesh sloshing off her and slapping against the ground.

I can't even scream.

Weeds grow from her hollow eye sockets. Slowly at first, but then they're growing towards me, and there're vines and thorns and they're digging into my eyes too, and it burns. It burns – *I'm sorry, stop, stop!* – and I try to bat them off but they won't go, and it feels like I'm striking something solid and I –

Open! My! Eyes!

Hit, hit, hit.

'I'm sorry, I'm sorry! Mona! Mona, stop! Stop! Stop!'

Peyton. Not Celeste.

I settle my arms and lower them to my sides. I'm straddling her. Her stomach rises and falls rapidly.

She stares up at me, face ghoulish and shadowed, eyes cutting through the dark. 'Mona?'

I'm here. I'm in the room.

'Peyton – what was I . . . ?'

'Were you asleep?'

'Yes. Oh my God, I was dreaming.' I hold my head in my hands, squeeze my skull together to try and stop the throbbing, try to coax myself out of the murky fog of unconsciousness. I move myself off her bed and hover there, next to her, unsure what to do now. 'I'm sorry. Are you hurt?'

Even in the dark I can see the inflamed rims of her eyes. 'No.' Peyton rolls over and faces the wall. 'No, I'm not hurt.'

I can't stop clenching and unclenching my fists. 'Peyton, I'm so sorry, I –'

'Just go to sleep, Mona.'

Clench, unclench. 'I get nightmares sometimes; it's not me, it's –'

'Go to fucking sleep.'

I'm losing it. I can't stop seeing the woods. I want to vomit. Her face my face her face my face.

I get back into bed and close my eyes. I count to ten. I count down from ten. I think of drowning. I think of falling from a height. I lie in the dark like a corpse until the day's first small light, an awful dead forgotten thing.

CHAPTER 24

WEDNESDAY 9 JUNE

I'm in bed all morning, motionless, I think, because I can't stand the thought of opening my eyes. Especially not while Peyton's still there – her stirring wakes me up but I don't let her know. I can't bear to face her. I almost want to sit up, to mutter an apology bleached and exposed by the daylight instead of my hurried and strange night-time one, but I have no idea what the words even are. Humiliated is an understatement.

I've got a closing shift at the diner. It's a Wednesday so it's slow – only two tables are full by about seven that evening (a thirty-something man I don't recognize, and a woman from the florist's) and I'm drawing webs on the back of receipts. I'm out of my mind with anxiety. My cuticles are shredded to bits, and I keep forgetting to put sunscreen on, so every movement makes my skin pinch. I catch myself in the reflection of the toaster; the skin beneath my eyes is heavy and purple.

Then Frank comes barrelling through the front door. His eyes meet mine with a rage. 'You,' he says. 'Where's Mary?'

Mary Anne hears the commotion and comes out, wringing a rag through her hands.

Frank's forefinger jabs in my direction. He licks his lips, shakes his head. 'Mary, I gotta tell you something. Your girl here – she's nothing but trouble.'

A maybe imagined hush falls over the whole of the diner. Clanking stops. Everyone turns to look.

Mary Anne glances between us both. 'Is this about –'

'Oh yes. Oh yes.'

Mary Anne turns to me, dripping venom. 'Out,' she says. 'Out, now.'

'Please, can I explain –'

'No explanations.'

'I want to help you! I'm trying to help you, and the only reason you wouldn't accept help is –'

'You're out. I should have done this in the first place. I should have done this as soon as I knew what you were up to.'

For a moment I don't move, as if inaction will force the situation to dissolve, but there is no choice, I have to – and I smash open the front door and storm out. I should have finished the sentence. The only reason you wouldn't accept help is if you had something to hide.

There're two things on my mind on the way back to the dorm.

First, *into the woods*. Then, *Booker must have told*.

Peyton's in the room when I get back.

'I thought you were closing,' she says. Not even daring to address what happened the night before. Good. I like it that way. Let's dance around the point, dance around the strangeness and horror of what I did until both of us go blue.

'I think I just got fired,' I say, still in a sort of daze.

'You think?'

'I did get fired.'

'Why? What the hell did you do?' And her face changes as she realizes. She doesn't know exactly what's happened, sure, but she's pieced it together. 'Mona . . .'

I want to do it by myself. This is the last shot. There's nothing else to do at this point. No more interrogating. No more interviews.

I grab what few belongings I have, wrap my windbreaker round my waist in case I need it, and bolt for the door.

'Where are you going?' Peyton asks.

'For a walk.'

'Want me to come?'

I pause. Peyton must sense the mania now. She's looking at me, eyes pleading for something I can't place.

'No,' I snap accidentally.

Peyton recoils.

'I'm sorry. I'm really stressed out. There's a lot happening. I really don't want to go home.' I can tell that something about this has hurt her. I'm not sure there's enough will left in me to mind. 'See you later.'

I hate what's happened. I hate myself for letting it happen. I want her. Of course I do. Honestly, maybe I want anyone.

Why have I been wired this way? God, I want to join the human race. Even when I like people, I feel different. I want to explain everything to her. I almost want to tell her about Celeste, so she'll understand, so she won't be hurt. As far as she knows, I'm an entirely normal person who's making awful decisions for – I don't know, my own strange pleasure. And maybe that's true anyway.

I hate how I've made her feel. I get the sense of a time and place wasted – something that doesn't even come round that often. Not even wasted it – obliterated it. What have I done? What have I done with yet another chance to be loved?

Even though I desperately want her to, Peyton doesn't watch as I slip out of the room.

Into the woods.

I have no choice. The situation has brought itself to me and now I'm being forced to participate.

I don't tell Ellis. I don't even know where he is now. I feel sick with paranoia, retreating further and further into my own head.

The woods were shut to the public officially two months after Roxy's disappearance.

I roll up to the No-Names parking lot with the flashlight on my phone and that's all. I'll have to look again in the morning. I couldn't sit in that dorm knowing there might be something here waiting for me.

I walk along the fence, weaving the chain link in and out of my fingers.

My palms are filmed in sweat. Maybe I should've brought Ellis after all. Or Peyton, not that she would have agreed to come, or agreed with any of this. But the aloneness is overwhelming, the aloneness that results from a force of nature duelling with a much, much smaller force of nature that is barely a force at all. My teeth crack against each other. The trees tremble and the sound of leaf scraping leaf shoots goosebumps across my body. There's birdsong from somewhere.

I want to do this by myself. I want to keep Ellis from what I might find.

But I'm worried it's more selfish than that.

I return to the cut section of fence. I have to go in.

And *now*, quickly, before anybody sees me here.

I grip the cool spindly metal of the chain link with my fingers and peel it back, which is easier than expected. Like someone has been here doing exactly this many times before. My hair catches on the sharp edge as I pass through.

And then I'm on the other side.

Sick. I already want to be sick. I grab the fence again to make sure it hasn't grown over, hasn't raised ten feet. I can get out if I want. I can get out whenever I need. My phone is heavy in a welcome sort of way in my pocket – there's a compass on it. Civilization will always be almost exactly due south. I'm fine. I can't get lost. I have my compass. I'm fine.

I get the sense that something is watching me. My heart quickens in my chest. I'm moving quickly now and I can't make myself slow down. The forest floor is so textured and uneven that the noise of it makes it seem like I'm being pursued by footsteps other than my own, and I fall over myself and bash against a tree.

I rest my head against the bark and look up.

There's something tied to the tree. I stand, shine my phone's flashlight on to it – it's a black ribbon, vaguely shiny and reflective in the light.

If someone was identifying a path, why would they mark it with *black* ribbon?

And I realize – if it's reflective, then . . .

I move slowly in a circle, shining my flashlight deliberately on to each section of trees, and my breath hitches again, my heart hammers.

Something's caught in the beacon. There it is. A path. Ten or so ribbons, in what's nearly an orderly line.

I know I'm breathing too quickly but I don't know how to make it stop. My mouth is bone-dry.

There's nowhere to go but forward.

The way the branch diverges from the trail looks deliberate. Like somebody had pushed it out of the way – and recently. Further along and my flashlight is searching for a moment, but then I see it.

There's a makeshift cross, shoddy, two planks of wood tied together. A circle of stones, too precise to be natural.

This is a grave.

My heart pounds in my chest.

I dig. Dig without thinking. I shouldn't be digging but I am. I should leave it and call someone and I'm thinking all of this as I unearth that good silk-spun stuff, that soft forest soil. Dig with my hands and fingernails and that's all. *Idiot*, I should have brought a shovel, I should have brought something, but it's shallow, and something's taking form – fabric, silky against my fingers compared to the grit of the dark, and I hold on to it for dear life.

This is all that's there. What is it? I lay the fabric down and direct the flashlight on to it. Green. It's a shirt. Or thicker – a sort of jacket. And it's stained. Different from the stains caused by the dirt – these are darker, more sporadic. Bloodstained.

And I've seen it before. I'm certain I have. I pull up the picture of her on my phone, the one Lenore showed Ellis and me of Roxy on her last night alive. And there it is.

Wrapped round her shoulders like the end of the damn world, there it is. Corduroy collar. Tortoiseshell buttons.

This belonged to Roxy.

I want to collapse, jump out of my skin, scream. I kneel, kneel, kneel. The forest is looking at me. I can feel it. But where is the rest? I dig further down but there's nothing, no body, no bones – I'm screaming internally. I'm so close. What is this? Where is she?

I don't know why, but I sit there and cry for a few moments.

I'm lost. Calm down. *Calm down*. The woods are closing in on me and I need to get out.

I feel myself panicking, losing control of my body, but I find the path marked by the ribbons again and do my best to remember the route. It occurs to me that I could end up stuck out here and then nobody would know what I'd found, which, right now, almost feels more important than my life. Fumbling around in the dark, it's as though I have no past, no memories – just whatever physical thing I am, panicking in the fragmented moonlight, and slipping against the forest floor, which feels weirdly natural, like I wasn't meant to do anything before or after this. I'm surrounded by ends. I was born to an end.

My breath comes in shallow spurts, dry and unsatisfying, dizzying.

Eventually I clock the hazy glow of the streetlights from the parking lot and I breathe the bluest breath of my life.

I'd cockily assumed I wasn't only going to find something, but I was going to find *everything*, but even this significant something has me trembling.

I am in a world of chaos and unknowns and the only thing I can do is go to the person who can do something about it.

Booker.

I don't know what else to do so I walk forty-five minutes to the police station, lie on a wooden bench by the entrance, and shut my eyes.

After a horrible non-sleep beginning at midnight even though I knew no one would be there until seven, my back aches horribly, my neck stiff with exhaustion, and I have no dreams – I'm not even sure that I've slept. Until someone's shaking me awake.

'Kid.'

It's Booker.

'Kid. What in the hell are you doing?'

It takes me barely a second to come back to reality. 'I found something,' I say, weak, strained and croaking, as if I've survived something awful, and I feel like I have. 'I found something.'

CHAPTER 25

THURSDAY 10 JUNE

Booker and I travel to the No-Names in his squad car. The mood is unexpectedly sombre. Not that I'd thought this would be an especially joyous occasion, but I'd imagined more verve, more excitement. To fill the silence I ask him about the concern I originally had yesterday, which is now largely overshadowed by this more pressing one.

'Did you tell Frank?' I ask. 'What Ellis and I said to you?'

He doesn't look away from the road.

'I've been fired. He came into work yesterday and told Mary Anne and she fired me.'

Booker is silent. 'Well, no, I don't know anything about that.'

When we arrive at the forest, I walk Booker to the gap in the fence, show him the part that I suspect has been purposely cut away. 'How hasn't anyone noticed this?' I ask as I slink my way under, and he follows.

He kneads the back of his neck. 'These woods – the city won't do anything with them. Nobody comes out this way. Except, I guess, for you.'

I explain to him what happened – that I'd got spooked and run, and had accidentally come across a ribbon on one of the trees, which led me to my discovery.

The woods are huge.

The woods are as big as the ones Celeste disappeared into.

I'm leading the Sandown Bay police force to the unmarked grave I dug up with my hands and I cannot believe I got here. I can, but still can't. What would I have said a week ago, if I'd known this was going to happen? Everything came about so quickly. I feel like I haven't even had enough time to think about any of it.

I worry for a moment that I won't be able to find the precise location again – the only reason I was able to find it in the first place was because the ribbons reflected the flashlight, but now, in the day, they're not registering. But I remember landmarks, the dips in the earth – it's all inexplicably branded on to my brain, and we're back.

'I dug it up,' I say, watching Booker regard the ravaged plot, as if something new might still crawl from inside. 'I'm sorry. I shouldn't have. I'm worried I've ruined everything by touching it. But it's probably been buried so long, I don't know how much evidence there would even have been on it in the first place.'

Booker's face is unreadable.

He takes his phone from his back pocket and calls someone on speed dial. 'Hey, Chuck,' he says, 'we're gonna need – shit, I don't know. Mainland force needs to get here, at least.'

'What going on?' I hear faintly from the other end of the line.

Booker looks me up and down. For a moment, I almost think he's about to break into a smile. His eyes hold mine. 'Kid found something.'

When he gets off the phone, Booker tells me to go home. I protest – I feel like I should be overseeing this, somehow – but he insists. He offers to drive me but I want to walk.

I can't remember if I've texted Ellis yet so I check, and I did, last night, saying what I'd found – the jacket, bloodstained. He hasn't replied.

I can't stop looking at Lenore's photo of Roxy, the emerald jacket hugging her arms, the same one that's in the woods, covered in thirty-five years of decay and dust and maybe one moment's worth of very important blood. Proof. Something that's not words or hearsay or speculation. Proof of something real, finally. Something physical.

Something violent.

Peyton's there when I finally return to the dorm – I don't know why I wasn't expecting her and her presence makes me jump.

'You never came back last night,' she says automatically. 'The whole night. I was awake waiting for you, worried sick. Where the fuck were you? Where did you even sleep? Don't lie this time. Please don't lie to me, Mona.' Her hair's a mess. I'm secretly pleased she, for some reason, has matched my level of distress.

I remember, suddenly, that I'm starving. 'Do you have any food?'

'Mona.'

'I absolutely wasn't with Ellis, if that's what you're asking,' I say.

'Then *where*?'

'I was in the woods.'

'Oh yes, of course you were. Of course you were inexplicably *in the woods*. And what did you find there? Bigfoot?'

Sick of this. I pull up the pictures on my phone and show them to her. 'This.'

Peyton quietens as I scroll. 'And what is that?'

'The jacket Roxy was wearing the night she was last seen. With bloodstains. Buried in the woods, with a cross.'

I show her the picture of Roxy on that night and watch her flick between them. Her seemingly stone-faced indifference makes me want to grab her by the shoulders and rattle her until she shouts, until she wails, *You maniacal genius, you marvellous fool, I'm so sorry I doubted you . . .*

'Police are there now,' I say. 'Whole area's blocked off. I'll go back if you want. I'll show you.' *I'll rub your face in it.*

Peyton rolls her lip between her fingers. 'Are you sure?'

'Positive.'

'Does Ellis know?'

'I texted him last night but haven't heard back.'

A wave of nausea curls around my stomach; I don't remember the last time I've eaten, brushed my teeth, partaken in small and simple human pleasures. I feel as though I'm the physical form of something much bigger than myself now. Maybe those things don't matter any more. That quiet night we had on the beach, the night Peyton kissed me, feels like it happened in another lifetime, to another girl.

I believe things are going to move very quickly from here.

Peyton sighs. 'Well, shit, Mona, what are you gonna do? What's gonna happen?'

'I don't know yet.' *I'm scared*, I want to say, but I don't. *I'm scared. Hold me.* I don't like whatever this feeling is, how at odds my desire to grab her by the neck is with my other equal desire for her to be tender and familiar towards me. I don't know what I need. I've never known what I need. I don't even know her. 'I want to talk to Ellis first.'

Peyton exhales, finally realizing that she is in over her head, and I get the sense there is something she wants to say that she isn't saying, but I have neither the time nor the mental faculties to sit here wondering what it might be. 'Here,' she says, walks behind me and gently places a granola bar and an energy drink on my desk. 'You look awful.'

'Thanks.'

So what do we do? Just wait? What evidence are they going to find on a coat that's been buried for thirty-five years? Even if they test the blood, even if we know it's definitely Roxy's – I mean, we already know that. It's in the picture. Clear as day.

Somebody buried a bloodstained jacket that had belonged to Roxy Raines – with a cross.

But *why* would they do that? Where is the body? You leave a cross for someone who you know has definitely died. But a bloodstained jacket doesn't mean they knew that. Maybe whoever killed her had dumped her in the sea, but felt sympathetic enough to leave something behind – but what kind of so-called sympathetic killer violently murders someone and throws them in the ocean? And then leaves notes behind mocking Roxy's mom – who, in fairness, she hated – after her death? It doesn't make any sense. A murder? An accident?

Where's the body?

I feel my mind slipping. There must be something I've missed. Something that *we* missed.

Now more than ever I mourn my destroyed notes. I scroll through my phone, looking for something, anything. Snippets from conversations. The interview with Lenore, my interview with Henry. How can there be nothing? How have I been working all this time, this *whole* time, feeling like my fingers are gripping a crumbling cliffside, barely holding on, and have nothing to show for it?

I reach the end of my activity, the ambient track I took in the diner on Sunday, and that's all. The chatter of the diner blares in my headphones. This is it. There's nothing here. What do we know? Where do we go? Who do we talk to? I could go revisit Roxy's notes, but I'm not prepared for another false path – I mean, what else could we do at this point? Dissect lyrics? Hidden meanings? *Code?*

I flick through the recordings. Anything.

Then I realize that when I was recording the ambient sounds in the diner that day, I was still recording when I went into Mary Anne's office.

'*Knock*,' I can hear her say.

'Whoops. I'm sorry,' I reply.

I remember now. What I'd only before caught glimpses of: all that equipment in her office. What looked like radios. And the clicking: it's there, faintly, in the recording.

What had Archie said? *She's there?*

It's not just clicking, is it?

I play the recording again. I think back to Roxy's notebook – the Morse code key. All the radios in Mary Anne's office.

It's Morse code.

'Oh my God,' I breathe.

Peyton thinks something's the matter, and it is, but I don't have time to explain and I don't care because, for the second time in the past twenty-four hours, I've finally stumbled on something I can sink my teeth into.

Ellis picks up on the second ring.

'Ellis,' I say, 'I need you to get over here *now*.'

'I know, you said. Are you sure it's Roxy's jacket? Mona, I don't know if –'

I can't believe how quickly I've moved on from that being my most pressing concern. Everything is happening so quickly. The moment threatens to tumble away from me. 'That, yes, but not that. Something else. Come over now. Like – run. Take a golf cart. I don't care.'

'Is everything OK?'

'More than OK. Get over here.' I hang up.

Peyton's eyes bore into the back of my head. 'You scared him, Mona.'

I'm not sure what compels me to snap at her, the adrenaline from the potential of this discovery or my utter exhaustion. 'You think so little of him – you *do*,' I say, when she tries to speak over me. 'You think he's weak and needs to be protected and can't make his own decisions. One of the first things you said to me was that you didn't like that Sylvia treated him like a child, but this whole time you've been acting the exact same way.'

I don't turn to her but by the rasping of her breath I imagine she's seething. 'Sure. Whatever you say. I'm late to see Liam, anyway. Bye.' She leaves quickly, her bag nearly falling from her shoulder in the process, and shuts the door too hard.

I'm lost in my thoughts until Ellis arrives. Of course I want to look up the answer to this new question myself but I think it's important that he's here, and I can hardly make myself wait, but thank God the inhabited portion of this island is practically a square metre because he's at my dorm in ten minutes.

I tell him what I've realized and he pulls up a Morse translator on his phone.

'Ready?' I ask.

We play it back, click by click.

'Long, short, short, short,' I say.

'Uh, long, short, short, short . . . B.'

My heart, too, is beating with the irregularity of the code.

'Short, long?'

Short, long . . . A.

Long, short, short, short . . . B.

'Ellis, if the next one is what I think it is, then –'

Long, short, long, long . . . Y.

Ellis and I share a look.

'No fucking way.'

'Keep going.'

And it finishes as we expect.

B. L. U. E.

Baby Blue.

CHAPTER 26

The look Ellis shoots me is delicious. All at once, his wonder and fear and well-meaning confusion plastered across his face. He rakes his hands through his hair. 'I m-mean, of course that's crazy, b-b-but I don't know what that means.'

I'm angry more than anything – that I've had this information, hidden though it was, the whole time; that I hadn't thought to check. But why was Mary Anne sending this, and to who? Why this phrase?

'We need to get into her office,' I say, without thinking of the implications of the statement, the potential consequences that could follow. Maybe it was naive of me to want to stick to the process when I first arrived here, to play nicely. Maybe that isn't how the world works. Maybe playing by the rules doesn't ever get you what you want.

Maybe I should always have known that.

'We need to go now,' I say.

Ellis's eyes widen. 'Now?'

'Yeah.'

'Mona, it's like, nine in the morning. The diner is literally open right now.'

He's completely right, of course. My sense of time has been obliterated. 'Fine. Meet me here at midnight.'

'I don't know – I don't know if I can.'

'I mean, you don't have to. But it'd be nice to have you there.'

Ellis nods resolutely. Good soldier. 'I'll think about it.'

He's about to leave and this is when Peyton opens the door. She glances between the two of us. Ellis doesn't say anything, just slinks past her and out of the door. He's fully on side now. It's a wonderful sight. If only Peyton could understand.

She watches him go and for a moment I think she's actually hurt, but the hurt just turns to her volatile brand of passive-aggressive anger that I can't even bring myself to entertain the idea of assuaging, and she turns away from me. She's made herself an enemy, not the other way around. I'm sympathetic to her; how she, too, is only trying to fix the perceived wrongs of the world, to make things right. But no one will be protected from this life. I decide to tell her this, someday. That there's no escape from suffering. That perhaps, instead of this horrible desperate dance to avoid it, we should seek it out and learn its name.

CHAPTER 27

FRIDAY 11 JUNE, 3 a.m.

Ellis and I step into a night impossibly dark and littered with stars.

Crickets are trilling lazily from somewhere when I meet him outside my dorm. His hair is dishevelled, the skin beneath his eyes heavy and pale purple.

'Did you sleep at all?' I ask him.

'N-no.' Our walk to the diner is quiet and seemingly formal; Ellis says not much of anything until we finally catch sight of the diner in the distance and he says, 'OK, I'm actually really scared about this now.'

'This is the most exciting part. Ellis –' I grab him by the shoulders – 'we're gonna figure out what happened to Roxy. We're gonna crack this mystery that's been weighing your family and this place down for literally generations. It's exciting. It's a good thing. And we have no other choice.'

'You're right, like, I know, logically or whatever, that you're right. That this is exciting. I don't know – I guess I just feel like something b-b-bad is going to happen.'

'Nothing bad is going to happen. I promise. I won't let anything bad happen to you. OK?'

Ellis resolves something within himself and puffs out a shallow breath. 'OK.'

We slink around to the rear of the diner. I've come prepared with my array of lock picks.

I get started with the first pick when Ellis starts to rock on the balls of his feet. He's looking around but it's the early hours of Friday morning – there's no one out this late, not in this part of town. Even if there were, they wouldn't be able to see us: the island isn't well lit and we're concealed beneath the veil of night.

'How long does this take, normally?'

I chew my tongue, thinking I've nearly flipped the tumbler, but no dice. On to the next. 'It depends. On the type of lock.'

'Well, like, at the police station, how long did it take?'

'Maybe five minutes? But that was an easier sort of lock. This one is proving a little trickier.' On to the third.

'What if you can't open it?'

'I don't know, Ellis. We'll figure it out.'

'Well, should we m-m-maybe have thought about that before w-we –'

'*Please!*' I whip my head round to look at him and he deflates. 'Ellis. I'm sorry for snapping, OK? But you're making me nervous. Please trust me. What happened to the version of you who followed me into the police station? Totally unprompted, before any of this?'

'That was different. There wasn't a m-murderer on the loose then.'

'If anything, the fact there's a murderer on the loose should dial you in.'

Except I try the fourth and fifth and by then it's been ten minutes and I'm out of picks.

I curse. 'I don't know what's wrong.' We can't just leave. If everything we've learned is a funnel that's coiled around us, this place is our only exit. The only way out is through.

'You could try the front door,' Ellis says.

But I'm looking somewhere else: the window. It leads straight into the office.

Ellis knows what I'm thinking.

'M-Mona, no. No. Have you lost it?'

I don't know whether or not I have, but I know my blood is boiling and it's erupting and it needs out. I know whatever I have is less of a haunting and more of a possession – it's not something outside me that wants to come in, but the other way round. I created this feeling and it needs somewhere to go. I didn't always use to be the kind of girl who could do this but I know more than anything, more than a bullet to the brain, that I am now.

I palm a heavy rock from the building's perimeter and experimentally toss it between my hands.

Then I chuck it at the window with everything I have.

Ellis yelps, but the window doesn't even shatter – it bounces straight off and nearly hits me in the leg.

'M-M-M-Mona,' Ellis says. 'I can't do this. P-Please. I really, really can't do this.'

I pick up the rock again, ready for a second go. My shoulder's throbbing in the socket. 'Then go,' I say. 'Go home. You don't need to be here.'

He looks at me, hurt, and my chest crumples. 'M-Mona . . .'

'*Go, Ellis*. Go. Or shut up and let me do this.'

I regret the words as soon as I've said them but they'll mean nothing if I don't stand by them.

He doesn't say anything and doesn't move so I assume that's the green light for throw number two. Reel back and lunge forward – the glass cracks, but doesn't shatter.

'Shit me,' I say. 'Someone's gonna hear.' Then I get an idea. I peel my shirt off my body, damp with sweat (I've got a sports bra on underneath) and wrap it tightly round my fist, holding the rock.

'Mona! Mona Mona Mona, no –'

Too late. Punch. My whole arm screams and my brain lights up red, but the glass shatters. I wail, at first worried the sound is an alarm.

I look down and see blood.

'Ah . . .' I drop to the ground in an attempt to escape myself, to try and crawl away from my own arm. I can't even look at it. I think I might be sick.

In my peripheral vision I sense Ellis coming down to help me but everything is going black. 'Is it the pain?'

'The . . . blood,' I manage.

I cringe, unwrapping the shirt from what I assume will be a mangled knot of flesh.

'It's not bad,' he says.

'I'm sorry I shouted at you,' I say, and my eyes are prickling with tears. 'I'm sorry.' That's not me, I want to say. *It's her. It's her. It's her.* 'I'm sorry.'

'Relax,' he says.

I listen for an alarm and nothing comes. Maybe it was a big deal when Booker caught us on the station cameras but now we have nothing left to lose. We need to get into this office and it was the only way.

Ellis helps me to my feet. There's no time to linger. I use the shirt to clear out all of the shards still clinging on to the sill, and mange to pull myself up and over the wall, through the window, into the office.

I gesture to Ellis to come inside but he shakes his head firmly and takes one step back. I shrug.

Now I see the radio in its full glory but I still don't completely understand what I'm looking at. I fiddle with a couple of the knobs and nothing happens.

My attention turns to her desk.

'Mona, please hurry,' Ellis hisses through the broken window. I don't listen.

I open one of the drawers – a photo. Mary Anne, Archie. And Roxy.

She's in the middle, beaming wide, sunglasses covering her eyes, but it's her. They've all got their arms round each other.

Further digging and – and there's a car key. A ring of keys with one unattached. And it looks *old*. Mary Anne didn't have a noticeably old car, I didn't think – so what is this the key to? I gesture Ellis over to the broken window and show him the photo first. 'Have you ever seen this?'

His eyes grow wide. 'N-no. No, definitely not.'

'Ellis,' I say, 'why would Mary Anne have an old car key tucked in the back of her desk drawer?'

'Oh my God. This looks like –'

'Say it.'

'The key to Roxy's Camaro.'

'*Her motherfucking Camaro*,' I repeat. 'It could be a spare. But –' I remember something else. 'The letters. The note in the car and the one sent to your mom. Didn't Lenore say Mary Anne was severely dyslexic?'

'Oh God. Oh my God.'

My brain is collapsing. I'm functioning on autopilot. I'm not choosing to think – my thoughts have left Mona somewhere else, too fast, somewhere along the shore. 'So Mary Anne left the note in the car,' I say. 'But why? Why would she have done that? Roxy *said something* to Mary Anne that made even Archie angry. But what was the row about? Maybe Archie gets all riled up, shoots Roxy. It's an accident. Obviously Archie would want to keep that quiet – but why would Booker?'

'I – don't know. I don't know. He must have done something bad himself.'

'And then why would Mary Anne write the note? She wanted to get rid of Roxy? Or cover up for the two of them?'

But Roxy was supposed to leave for Nashville the following week. She was already going. It doesn't make any sense.

'We need to talk to Mary Anne.' I slump against the wall. 'I don't know what to do. I don't understand. I'm missing something. And Baby Blue . . .'

'We should go home, Mona,' Ellis says, finally.

I don't know why, but at first I think when he says *home* he's telling me to go back to Indiana.

He's not wrong. We should get some sleep.

Before we say goodbye at our classic breakoff point at the isthmus, Ellis stops. 'Did you mean what you said?' he asks. 'About me not needing to be there?' The words are so vulnerable they're practically flayed.

'No, Ellis, of course not. I'm sorry. I snap when I'm nervous. You're so incredibly important. I mean it. Please believe me.'

His half-smile is the saddest thing I've ever seen.

I hug him for eleven heartbeats. He's the one to break it. 'Night,' he says finally.

On the dark walk back to the dorm I remember I'd told Ellis I wouldn't let anything bad happen to him, even though I keep happening to him, over and over and over.

'There's a bunch of cops outside The Island Spot.'

I think I'm dreaming at first. My eyes adjust to morning. I don't remember falling asleep, nor do I remember taking any of the contents of the spilled bottle of pain medicine on my nightstand. I'm groggy enough to suggest I've slept for longer than I ought to have. Peyton is standing, arms crossed, at the far end of the room, as far away from me as she could possibly be. She's not even looking at me. She might not have said it.

'There's a bunch of cops outside the diner, Mona. Mainland police too.'

I prop myself up, a prickling line of sweat dripping down the middle of my chest, hair glued to the nape of my neck. Peyton's bathed in velvety orange, her skin rich and glowing. *I love you*, I think sleepily. *How angry you are, how much you love Ellis and despise me.*

'That's where you went last night.' She's still not looking at me, eyes flitting between the floor, the wall and through me, out of the window. Maybe she's a mirage. One of her heels bobs up and down at a dizzying pace. 'Whatever you and Ellis were doing had to do with that.'

'Yeah. It was. How do you kn–'

'How do I know it was *you*? Man, I don't know, an educated guess.'

'No – how do you know there're cops?'

'Your weird small-hour escapades must be rubbing off on me. I guess I wanted to see the damage.'

I'm fully awake now, my mind ticking along steadily. 'Did you see anyone else there?'

Now Peyton finally looks at me and scoffs. 'Are you interrogating me?'

'No, I'm asking as a friend. Was anyone else there? Did you see Mary Anne?'

'And I'm more likely to answer to an interrogation,' she says. 'You're out of your mind.'

I get up and dress, unconcerned by Peyton's eyes on me. I have to leave. Peyton notices my arm. 'Oh my God. What did you *do*?'

I'd almost forgotten about it but, yeah, it smarts as I tug a fresh shirt over my head. I fell asleep with my old shirt wrapped round it and bursts of red are peeking through the fabric. 'Doesn't matter.' I pull on some shorts and tie my hair in a ponytail, which takes a moment longer than usual on account of the wound, and I'm ready in maybe thirty seconds flat. Peyton watches me leave. She's eerily silent as I open the door.

'Mona,' Peyton says, and I turn back to face her. 'I'm going to kill you if anything happens to Ellis because of this.' Without a hint of irony, hyperbole, teasing. I've never heard her voice so dark. She means it. *How much you despise me. How much like home it feels.*

'I know.' I step outside the room, and right before I've disappeared from view I drum my fingers against the width of the door and say without looking at her, 'We're almost there, though,' and I go.

Classic move of a breaker-and-enterer – to return to the place they have just broken into and entered.

I don't know what else to do. I walk there in a daze.

The morning is radiant and bleached, blue in an almost surreal way; the moon, I see, is pressed against the sky like a semi-translucent stamp, hovering a finger's length above the mainland.

I feel inexplicably like I've found all the pieces but not the order in which to arrange them, seemingly unrelated information like the limbs of an exquisite corpse impossible to neatly bind.

There's a mass of cops situated around the diner. I don't see Booker anywhere. Mary Anne stands at their perimeter. A woman wearing thick gloves prods at the jagged glass of the broken window. A blackened wave of numbness rushes through me; how easy it was last night to shirk the consequences of a necessary act – how easy it'd be now to prove that I'd done it. Though at this point, I'm unsure if that matters.

Mary Anne and I are locked in a gaze from maybe thirty paces away. She moves from the cops to meet me. 'Suppose,' she says, 'there's no point in asking you if you saw anything.'

I tell her what I know. The keys, the picture, sending 'Baby Blue' through the radio, the note in her car, the note sent to the Willowwood. She barely so much as flinches the whole time.

'And what are you planning on doing with any of that?'

My blood runs cold. It's what I've been saying to myself this whole time, but hearing someone else say it – hearing Mary Anne say it – is a different beast. Perhaps I've accomplished nothing at all.

One of the officers calls from the diner. 'Mary Anne?'

I don't know what to do. Where to go. For the entirety of their conversation, they're all looking at me, and Mary Anne keeps shaking her head.

She shrugs. 'She didn't see nothin'.'

She doesn't want to say I did it and I don't know why.

I don't know what to do besides go back to the dorm, then hopefully try and find Ellis so I can talk to him. Lenore stops me on the way back, looking flustered, make-up smudged a little under her eyes. 'Oh, I was hoping you'd be here – I figured as much. I heard about the diner, and I thought, well, I suppose that girl will go where the trouble goes.'

She takes a sharp theatrical breath to collect herself.

'A memory has been bothering me and I can't quite shake it. See, something strange happened a couple of days after Roxy went missing, and I didn't mention it when you two were over. Wasn't at the front of my mind, I guess, hadn't linked the events in my head, I'm not sure, but –'

I'm getting impatient. My mind is already frazzled enough without this additional mania. 'What happened?'

'The Sunday night after Roxy vanished, I was out for a walk, to have a smoke – I went through two packs that day, awful anxiety, you know. And I was near the woods when I saw someone come out covered in dirt. Hands, face, everything. I was sort of concealed by a tree, I think, and it was dark, so they didn't know I'd seen them, but I *had*, and I figured it was police duty but I thought it odd they were there alone –'

'Who was?'

'Lee.'

'Who's Lee?'

'Lee Booker.'

I feel the blood drain from my face. 'And what made you remember?'

She leans in close to me, her eyes narrow and searching, then taps her temple with her ringed pointer finger and in barely more than a whisper, she says, '*Déjà vu.*'

CHAPTER 28

The parking lot is empty except for the Sandown County police cruiser hugging the edge of the woods.

I know where he is.

I find the cut in the fence from before. The cut that *he* made.

Follow the ribbons down to the grave and there he is, crouched, folded up and small, like a boy.

A beat passes and he hasn't moved and there's still no bullet in me. I savour every moment there's still no bullet in me.

I don't move either.

The moment of infinite possibility ends.

'Booker,' I say. He doesn't look up at me but he knows I'm there. 'You knew I was up to no good from the start. I didn't come here because I wanted to be a Seasonal. I didn't accidentally stumble upon some opportune chance to solve a mystery.' My voice is wavering. So often I'd imagined a moment like this, but my voice had always been so strong and assured. I need to keep going. 'I came because I wanted to know what happened to Roxy

Raines and that was the only reason, right from the beginning.'

I wait for him to react, to do anything, but he doesn't.

'I write, online. I write about unresolved disappearances for about fifty thousand people. They all know I'm here. If you do anything to . . . to harm me – if I don't come back – they will know where I've been. And if . . . if anything happens to me now, I've instructed someone to post the finished episode where I lay out the theory that I suspect – which isn't flattering to you. It'll get out. You'll lose absolutely everything and everyone will know what happened.'

It's all lies. I have nothing prepared. I've told no one I'm here.

If my words have affected him, he doesn't show it. His expression doesn't change; he doesn't crumble. 'Miss Mona,' he says finally, arms unfolded and palms turned out, as though in submission, 'let me tell you the story.'

PART THREE

Orion Waves

CHAPTER 29

Booker rises and takes a hesitant step towards me, feet crunching against the forest brush, and I take one back as he approaches. 'Don't,' I say.

'Kid, I'm not gonna –'

'I mean it.' He slowly raises his hands to his chest. A bead of sweat runs in between my shoulder blades and I shiver. I can't tell if my bluff has worked perfectly or has not worked at all. It's dark here in the woods, under the canopy of the trees.

'I don't care if a lick of what you just said is true,' he responds. 'I'm not gonna hurt you, kid. I think you know that.'

I strengthen my resolve. I'm very scared. I don't trust him and I can't let him see.

'I need to know. It was an accident,' I say. 'Right?'

Booker doesn't move.

'You killed her by accident. And Archie knew and was in on it somehow, and Mary Anne covered for the both of you, and you shut off the woods so no one would know . . .'

He tries another step and I let him take it, ambling with a sort of heavy, uneven gait, and I feel the need to draw for something with nothing to draw for. Fists against him won't do a thing. 'To this day,' he says, 'all this time later – I still don't understand how it could've happened.'

'You better understand well enough to tell me.'

'You don't have to shoot your daggers at me. You can shoot 'em at me for being a liar and a coward because I'm guilty of that, but it can't be because I'm a killer. I'm not.'

'Then who is? Who did it?'

'Kid –'

'Who?'

'I know about damned near everything and I still don't understand.' He's near enough that I can see his eyes are red-rimmed.

'Make it make sense.'

He registers my confusion, my frustration. I'm so close now and he's speaking in riddles – *Spit it out, spit it out!* – and he says, 'How much do you know about that night, then? From your digging. What did you find?'

I shuffle my feet and sense my hands flare out from my hips, subconsciously making myself bigger. 'I know it was her last performance before she was supposed to leave for Nashville. She and Mary Anne argued. Then you and Archie left with Mary Anne, supposedly to take Mary Anne home, but presumably to follow Roxy.'

Booker settles into the story. 'The most unusual energy that night. Everyone could sense it. Mary Anne and Roxy were going at it outside – no one knows what about, mind

288

you. Then she talks to Archie, all in tears, saying that Roxy had said something *unspeakable*.' Booker collects himself here. 'She whispered whatever it was to Archie, and he was *livid*. I couldn't believe it. I'd never seen him like that in my life.'

'What did Roxy say to her?'

'I tried asking him about it later but he wouldn't say. So Mary Anne wants to go home. Fine. I'm out of it, I've had enough, I go with the both of them. Not to follow her – to take Mary home.

'Archie's got a nasty case of road rage, mad as hell, but I'd never seen him hurt a fly. He was truly set off by this in a way I didn't understand.'

'Then what happened? You followed her. What happened?'

'So we find Roxy near the edge of the woods and she's about to walk in, but as soon as she catches sight of us, she looks like she's seen a ghost. Damn near bolts into the trees.'

He pauses, like I'm supposed to ask something.

'And I will have you know Roxy wasn't scared of *anything*.' He swipes the air with his hands. 'Nothing. Wouldn't run from a bull coming after her. And that night, for whatever reason, she was scared of us.

'Archie gets out, chasing her, Mary's behind telling him to stop, and I don't know what else to do so I follow. We run for – shit, I don't even know how long, and we're running and I don't even know why we're running and Archie's calling "Stop, stop", and then Roxy does. Stops, I mean. But it doesn't look like it's cos she's tired. It's like she just gives up. Right? Turns round.

'Then she gets this really evil look in her eye and says something I will never forget for the rest of my life. She goes, "You want to shoot me, don't you?" I remember that clear as day. Because it was so sudden, such a strange thing to say. "*You want to shoot me, don't you?*"

'She goes right up to him, yelling and screaming, like she's trying to rile up a dog. Finally she pushes him and slaps him hard across the face and – God, it was dark, and we're drunk – all I know is, I thought Mary thought Archie was gonna grab the gun off my hip, so she lunges for it, and Archie's scared by the movement, and Mary Anne's on top of him, and Roxy's not actually runnin' away, she's getting *closer*, and someone pulls the trigger.'

'Someone?' I ask.

'One of 'em.' He spits this, like those words were inevitable, required to exist at this time and this moment and he had to force them out.

'What do you mean?'

'Archie says it's him. An accident. I don't know,' he says finally. 'I don't know.'

'How don't you know?'

'At one point he had a pistol in his hand . . . there was a tussle, and I couldn't see anything, I was trying to get him off her, and then there's a shot. Pierces the night like the end of the world. All I know is it hit Roxy, not Archie. Cos he scrambles up, shaking, convulsing, practically, and he looks me in the eye and says, "We gotta get out of here." '

'So then what?' Silence. My heart thuds so powerfully I'm sure I'm feeling the vibrations of it in my skull.

Booker doesn't speak.

I'm putting it together when it occurs to me. I'm not sure I can even say the words. They're too despicable. They're too cowardly. '*Then what*, Booker?'

'There was so much blood,' he says, barely choking out the words. 'At least, it seemed like there was, but it was dark.'

'You left her there,' I breathe.

'Mona, understand –'

'You *left her there*? How could you?' I say it again, because I can't fathom it, the cowardice, the selfishness. 'How could you?'

'Archie was my friend and I didn't understand how this could've happened. I was looking right at it – at her – and I didn't know. I remember Roxy lying there, all crumpled up all wrong –'

'*You're a cop*. You had a duty to –'

'I was a boy before I was a cop. Barely older than you. I'd barely broken up bar fights – this is a quiet town, kid. And to a twenty-year-old boy from a quiet town, God, any blood like that is a lot of blood.'

'So what happened? You left her there, then –'

'It was Mary's idea to chuck the guitar into the sea.'

'Then Frank found it on Sunday.'

Booker nods, solemnly casting his gaze downward. 'The two days that followed were hell on earth. I stayed in bed all day on Saturday. Tried to convince myself I'd dreamt it. For a while I actually believed that. But then Archie came over wanting to talk it all through and everything came back. I will say one thing, though – Mary always seemed strangely calm about the whole thing. Meanwhile Archie and I were having a really hard time, but she was . . . What I mean is, when she said she was upset, it still never really showed behind her eyes. Y'see? Think some people handle the stress of situations like that differently, you know.'

'Sure,' I say.

'Anyway,' he continues, 'I went back to the woods on Sunday to try and bury her, but I couldn't –' he chokes up here – 'find her. I couldn't find her anywhere. I thought I'd remembered where we'd been but I figured I probably wasn't looking in the right spot . . . Well, I was, because I found the jacket she'd been wearing, all torn up.'

'Only the jacket.'

'I figured, uh, animals, must have got to her. There're all sorts out here: foxes, coyotes. Thought they must have dragged her off. Anyway, I, uh, buried the jacket, built a little gravestone with rocks and twigs and things . . .'

He looks sort of pathetic.

'And then Sunday was the day Frank found the guitar in the bay.'

'But the note, it –'

'That's it.' His eyes have a new fire in them now that I can't place. 'I swear to you, to God, to anyone who's listening – we did not leave that letter in her car. Neither of us put that note in her car. I swear on my life, on my mother, that I didn't do it and I made Archie swear he didn't either.'

'Didn't she ever tell you? It was Mary Anne.'

'Mary? Why would she have –'

'I don't know yet.'

The weather is terrible. Wind whips past and the sky is so much darker than it ought to be at this time of day.

'Why didn't you do anything?' I ask.

'Archie was my friend. Him and Mary were gonna have a life together, and Roxy was troubled, so troubled, and it was Sandown's belief that she was gonna do something like this anyways, and they already decided that that was how they wanted her story to go.'

I felt vaguely like an adult consoling a child. 'Her story? You think that warrants no investigation? What you all decided she was?'

'I swear to you, kid, even if I had wanted to play along, I'd barely been on the force for all of five minutes – think they're gonna listen to me? Not even when we found her guitar and especially not after the note. Folk wanted her gone. Folk knew she did stuff like this. It would have been a waste of time, everyone said. And that note – well, I got to thinking that maybe she *had* left it somehow, but . . . God. No matter any more, I suppose.'

I scoff. 'I suppose.'

'What are you gonna do about all this, then? Huh? Now you know. What are you gonna do? You're smart. I'm sure you've been recording this whole thing. You got your confession.'

I brush my phone in my pocket, microphone side up.

'Send a sick man to prison for something I'm not even sure he did? Worse, humiliate him, because there's no conviction without evidence? I bet he doesn't even remember it better than he remembers this morning. And me? Well, I've lived my life. This was my one get-out-of-jail-free card and now God has come back to remind me how fragile this all is. You win, Miss Mona. Hope it's a good show.'

He's quiet. 'People deserve to know what happened,' I say, maybe more to myself than to him. 'Ellis deserves to know what happened.'

He shrugs. 'You think? I don't know if *you* did. Generally I don't know if folk deserve anything in life. As for Ellis, sure, that kid deserves the world. A different one than what we've made here.'

I recall the heap of podcast equipment on the floor of my dorm. 'Booker, did you know about the podcast before I told you just now?'

He scoffs. 'Well, I figured you were after something.'

'Right.' I don't know what to do now. This is everything. But there's still the question of what Mary Anne knows but won't say. And who broke my equipment. Mary Anne? And if not her, who else has something to keep hidden?

'Well,' he says, with a sort of childish, quiet inflection. 'Best of luck with whatever you decide.'

I take this as an invitation to leave. I don't say anything, maintain eye contact, and I get back on to the bike and turn myself round.

'Hey, kid,' he calls behind me.

I turn to look at him. 'Hm?'

'There's something that's always bothered me about what happened. I don't get it. Not to this day.'

I leave silence for him to continue.

'When Roxy said, "You wanna shoot me, don't you?" she wasn't looking at me or Archie, who were the fellas with the guns,' he says. 'She was looking straight at Mary Anne.'

A crow screams from somewhere inside the woods.

'Even in the dark, I could see it.' He raises his pointer finger parallel to his nose and moves it, slowly, in my direction. 'Her line of sight.'

My tyres scratch against the rock. I nod.

And then the woods are far behind me, like everything else, like last week. All of it might as well be another life and I'm riding into the next.

CHAPTER 30

My entire body is fluttering with adrenaline and there's no outlet for it. My legs move at an alarming and inhuman speed, all of me clenching, my whole being a knowing knot, full of truth.

Everyone I pass looks at me. Either everyone knows now, or I look like a girl with a death wish.

I text Ellis, navigating one-handed.

> **Me:** Where are you?

I'm nearly at the dorms and he hasn't responded.

> **Me:** Urgent, Ellis. Where are you?
>
> **Ellis:** Your dorm.

Something about his reply feels wrong. Worse than the usual feeling of everything being incorrect and manic. What's he doing there?

I suddenly remember something strange. That night when I found the grave in the woods, had that nightmare and panicked. Peyton apologizing. What had Peyton been apologizing for? It happened after our fight. I assumed it was about that. But it wasn't a *fight*, not really, and if either of us had said anything pointedly hurtful then it was me.

So what else was there that warranted an apology?

I toss the bike against the bike rack without bothering to park it properly and head up to the room. I barrel up the stairs and there're kids dotted everywhere who are staring but it doesn't bother me because they have no idea, no, not even the slightest. They couldn't possibly understand. They couldn't possibly understand the cosmic weight of what's happened. Word must have got around that it was me who broke into the diner. But I'm already past that. It already doesn't matter.

I swing open the door to reveal them – Ellis and Peyton, sitting on Peyton's bed. And no, I don't know why they're both here, but I figure whatever their reason is it pales in comparison to what I've learned from Booker, so I say, 'I know what happened.' Ellis doesn't seem to know what to do with his hands. Peyton doesn't move, stares me down, unblinking. This does strike me as an unusual reaction but I keep talking. 'I just talked to Booker. He's the one who buried Roxy's jacket and was with her when it happened. Archie probably pulled the trigger. Roxy is dead. There're still some questions, but –'

'Mona, shut up for a second,' Peyton says. She's balancing a laptop on her lap. 'Have you told Ellis?'

I blink. Glance at Ellis, who's looking at me with an intensity I've rarely seen from him. 'Told Ellis what?'

And then I realize – it's *my* laptop that Peyton has.

'Ellis,' she says, then looks at me. 'Ellis, you have a right to know something. Has Mona told you?'

And I suddenly realize how foolish it was of me not to think it odd that Ellis was here in the first place.

'Tell him, Mona,' Peyton says.

Blood drains from my face.

'Ellis, do you know about the podcast?' Peyton asks.

Ellis looks bewildered.

'Peyton,' I say. 'Come on. I was going to –'

But she's already got it up on the laptop.

And there it is. My voice.

'The year is 1986 and the sleepy island of Sandown Bay is waking up.'

'How did you find this? How did you know?' I say, and I can't think of anything else to do but slam the laptop shut, and she recoils. I can't even deny it. It's too obvious. There is no point.

Ellis hasn't moved beside me.

'How could you do this? You don't care about Ellis at all, do you? You just want to exploit him for your fucking . . . I don't even know what this is – your show? He doesn't know about any of this, does he? Of course he doesn't. Because he'd never be helping you if he did. God, I knew there was something up about you. Is anything true? Is there anything that wasn't a lie?'

'Can I explain?' I look at Ellis, eyes imploring. 'Ellis, please. You need to let me explain.'

'You . . . when did you record this? Months ago? Before we even met?'

'Ellis –'

'You were never gonna do what I asked. I asked you not to but y-y-you were always gonna tell everyone. Were you just . . . you – you were using me, t-t-t-to – sh-sh-sh-shit!'

'Please –'

'What you just said,' he spits. 'About Booker. Roxy being dead. Is any of it even true? Why didn't you want me t-to go with you? I d-didn't see the grave, I only saw the pictures. I haven't b-been there for anything important – have you b-been making all this up for your story? The grave? The Morse code?'

'I wanted you there, for all of it –'

'Did you make it up?'

'No!'

'Liar.'

I want to hit him.

'Ellis, look at me. Look at my hands. My *face*.' I don't remember the last time I checked a mirror; I must look as spent as I feel. I pull down the skin of my cheeks. '*Look at me.*'

'I d-don't believe you. I-in the woods? It's all in the woods? Why can't I see it then, huh? Just wait. I'll figure this out for real. *Liar.*'

Ellis storms out of the room. The slam of the door is so loud it hurts.

The silence left between Peyton and me, I realize when it settles, will stay with me for the rest of my life.

In the end, it's me who breaks it.

'When did you find out about this?' I ask her, realizing the answer halfway through the question. I remember it clearly, now: in the middle of my nightmare, she had apologized; I had never stopped to consider what for. 'My stuff.'

Peyton grips on to her scalp with both hands.

'My stuff. *You* destroyed everything.'

She sighs. 'I only wanted to freak you out enough to get you to stop but you're a maniac who's not scared of anything and I didn't know what to do. I knew you wouldn't listen and Ellis wasn't listening, either. I'll pay you back for whatever I broke – I didn't even know what half of it was, but I couldn't stand the thought of Ellis's life on display, everyone judging him and talking about him . . .'

Then we're quiet. Peyton seems to soften.

'Ellis told me about your sister,' she says. 'Why didn't you tell me? I understand now, I guess. I don't think you *don't* care about Ellis, but your reasons are selfish, and misguided, and –'

'What Ellis told you about my sister was wrong.'

She stares. 'What do you mean?'

'I lied to him about her.'

Peyton scoffs, point proven. 'So she didn't go missing?'

'Oh, she went missing,' I said. 'But the day she disappeared was the best day of my life.' It's melodramatic but I say it for the reaction. 'She didn't do any of the stuff I said she did. She lied and hurt me and treated me like shit.'

Peyton is backing away from me.

'Did Ellis tell you what happened? She got lost in the woods. And you know what? I hope she was out there for weeks. Because maybe that way she would have got what she deserved, and maybe she would have thought about what she'd done and regretted it. And after all that I couldn't even be the good daughter.' I wave my phone at Peyton. 'This will make me the good daughter. I'll have done something worthwhile. More than she ever did. I'll have done something good.'

I'd discovered what had happened to Roxy.

'You don't know what you're saying. You're stressed.' Peyton gently reaches for my arms and I rip her off me.

'I'm still writing this,' I say.

'You can't. These people aren't bad, they're –'

'I don't care.'

'This *one thing* Ellis has asked of you, has asked of *anyone* –'

'It's not his story to keep.'

'What do you mean? Of course it is. It's *his* family.'

I feel possessed by a force outside myself. 'People deserve to know what happened.'

'*Who*, Mona? You're acting like this is the case of the century or that people have been slaving over some mystery or like you're doing people a favour, but no one outside Sandown gives a shit about Roxy Raines and you know it. Who does this help?'

I tell her what I've known about myself all along. 'It's not about helping. It's about truth, and liars –'

'Can you even *hear yourself*?'

'– and people so blinded by cowardice that they can't even face their own truth.'

'You're impossible! What's wrong with you? You aren't entitled to other people's life stories, Mona, not their pain, not their death, it's not yours. Even if you're the one that figures it out.' She stops. 'Was Ellis right? Is any of this true or did you make it all up?'

'I haven't made anything up.' My pen is flying. Finale. Rain lashes the window. 'Not one thing.'

'You've abused his trust *so* completely. Do you know how much he looked up to you? He thought you were a genius.' *I know*, I'd say, if I could manage it. I can't. I can't even stand to listen. 'You should be so ashamed of yourself.'

It almost hurts.

Almost.

We're quiet in the dorm save for the scratching of my pen. I can't even hear Peyton breathe.

Then she asks, 'Why the fuck do you call yourself CAP?'

I don't look back at her. I keep writing. 'They're my sister's initials,' I say. 'Celeste Avery Perry.'

A moment passes. 'You're insane.' Another lick of time, fuzzy with rain. 'You know what, fuck this, I'm not sleeping here in case you try and murder me again,' she mutters under her breath. Then she gets up, duvet wrapped round her shoulders, taking nothing else with her, and leaves, slamming the door with a resounding crash.

I write, and write, and write.

CHAPTER 31

SATURDAY 12 JUNE

I don't remember going to sleep but I must have done, apparently, because a sound riles me awake, and I peel my cheek from the sweating wood of my desk. The curtains are open but there's no sun in the room. Utterly dreamless. I look around and assess – Peyton isn't here.

Visions from yesterday, spectral and thin, like a rapidly dissipating dream.

She's dead, then. Roxy Raines is dead.

The supposed end of a search. Then why isn't it satisfying? Booker laid it all out in technicolour. What's left unresolved? Perhaps the fact that the only other person who this information mattered to now hates my guts.

My phone. That's what woke me up, I realize, and I click it awake to discover a text from Dad.

On my way.

I scramble awake. Not now. We're – I'm – almost finished. I still need to talk to Mary Anne.

I still need to talk to Ellis.

Me:	Now?
Dad:	There are evacuation orders for the entire east coast.

Evacuation orders?

The hurricane.

The night before all comes back to me. Ellis and Mary Anne and Booker and Peyton . . .

Peyton's still not here. I consider whether she'd be with Liam, or at Sylvia's, or if Sylvia even knows what happened. I think for a moment that I might be missing a shift at the diner but then remember everything that's happened. I forget how quickly things can and have fallen apart, how quickly things become ridiculous. Two weeks. I'd set aside a whole summer and it has only taken *two weeks* for everything to fall apart.

But Ellis and I had come so far. We'd discovered so much. Nothing's fallen apart – I've uncovered something. Or rather, I've *built* something.

Then why does this feel like chaos? Why do the answers still seem so far away?

I need to talk to Mary Anne but it's likely that I'm the last person she wants to see right now. I can't even remember what day it is. Sit and look at yourself from the outside and tether yourself to the ground, Mona. It's Saturday. I flip my laptop open and google 'weather' – article upon article upon article. *Hurricane's early. Coming now. Bigger than they thought. Get away from the coast. Urgent weather warning for Sandown County and surrounding areas.*

Me: When will you be here?

Dad: I drove through the night. All flights cancelled. I'll be two hours tops.

I scramble from the room. I'm out of time and I need to talk to Ellis.

A noticeable hush falls over the hallway as I march through. I scan the faces for Peyton. Liam catches me on the way out, having clocked me from the kitchen, and holds my arm gently to keep me there.

'Hey, man, what the *fuck* is –'

'Liam,' I say, and shake him off me, 'even if I wanted to explain it to you I would have literally no idea how to start, and I also don't have the time. I need you to get out of my way.'

Liam blinks at me, particularly dumbfounded. So much urgency for a lost girl going nowhere in particular.

'I'm sorry,' I say. So many apologies still to give out. 'I hope Peyton's all right. Really. I mean it.'

He gives me a sideways look then he steps away without breaking eye contact.

'Thanks,' I say, and slip out of the door, mount a bike and go.

Outside is odd. The sky is the wrong sort of colour, a murky biological green, the glass of a giant terrarium. The air is heavy and cool on my exposed skin, thighs, shoulders. There's resistance to it, like I'm walking underwater, though the resistance might not be from the humidity but my own exhausted muscles. My mouth tastes like bacteria and salt and half-sleep, a vinegarish wash to my throat. The emptiness sloshes around in me. I don't know what my body is burning to propel me forward but if it's not food then I imagine it's bits of myself. My body all at once is hollow and full of me.

I need to talk to Mary Anne. Did she want to get rid of Roxy? Maybe Booker was telling the truth but Archie had been lying – not drunk, not overwhelmed but maybe shot her on purpose. Could Mary Anne and Archie have been working together? But why? Booker didn't even sound convinced of the moment.

Why had Roxy run into the woods?

Finding the answers is like scrambling at quicksand, each so-called breakthough brings another displacement that only sends me deeper in.

Mary Anne had to have known Archie had pulled the trigger. Archie must have told her what happened. So she put the note of intent in Roxy's car so no one would go looking for her, and the letter in Sylvia's mailbox. But Archie told Booker he didn't know about the note. So why would Mary Anne not tell him – unless, of course, he was lying?

It feels vaguely like the end times. Everything washed in a strange and sombre air of quiet.

I stomp up and on to the cobblestones of the Willowwood, where a shadow clocks me through a window – I can't see who – and I push the heavy door open. My body hangs from me comfortably. My heart beats in my chest.

Then I'm striding through the vacant lobby of the Willowwood.

'Get out of here.'

I turn slowly, instinctively lowering my head.

Sylvia's leaning against the doorframe of the kitchen.

'Did Ellis tell you? I'm sorry, but Archie killed your mom,' I say. 'Or it might have been Mary Anne.'

'Get out.'

'I'm sorry. It wasn't supposed to happen like this. But we figured it out! There're still some holes, but isn't that important to you? Aren't you glad? Roxy didn't leave you, she didn't run away or kill herself, she was –'

'I need you to know something. I'm not a pawn in a mystery,' she says. 'I didn't ask to be born in the wake of all this and I didn't ask for any of it to be made public. Please,' she says, 'stop this. The legacy we're leaving is bad enough. Who are these answers for? Because they're not for us.'

'Ellis wanted to know.'

'Ellis is a kid. You're a kid. He doesn't know or understand what he wants and neither do you. And now you're mixed up in something that never concerned you in the first place.' She takes a deep breath. '*You're* just a kid,' she says to herself. 'Listen. We're all getting off the island today. The storm's gonna knock us out, anyway, but if there's anything to come back to, don't. Please go home. Please don't contact Ellis again.'

I don't tell her that I won't have a choice – though I almost say it because I don't want her to think that she's the one who scared me off. 'Please. I really just came to see him. To apologize.'

Sylvia is quiet. 'You thought he was here?'

I blink. 'I . . . yes, I did.'

'He wasn't in his room this morning. I haven't seen him since last night. I thought he was with you.'

My gut drops. 'No. No, I – I haven't seen him since last night, either.'

Sylvia stares at me for a moment longer, then swears under her hitching breath and rushes back into the kitchen.

What had Ellis said yesterday? That I'd made everything up. That he'd see for himself.

I bolt out of the Willowwood.

CHAPTER 32

I text Peyton in case she knows something; she's the only other one who might, who he might have confided in.

She replies almost immediately. Of course she does – it's about Ellis.

> **Me:** Ellis missing. Since yesterday. Have you seen him?
>
> **Peyton:** Oh my god. I haven't. Did you talk to Sylvia?

She calls but I can't talk right now. I need to check first.

> **Peyton:** Mona, what happened? Please please please pick up.

I pedal furiously to the No-Names because there is no fucking time to lose and I see a shape on the ground there, instinctively knowing what it is – Ellis's bike, lying on its side, but no Ellis. *No Ellis.*

My mouth runs dry. Maybe he has *just* gone in? Sometime today? But no – Sylvia hasn't seen him since last night. No one has.

I start towards the south side of the island, nearly killing myself along the way, three separate close run-ins with cars.

Ellis went into the woods. Ellis went into the woods and hasn't come out.

I send my bike clattering to the ground when I arrive at the police station and crash through the front door and shout for Booker.

He comes hurrying out from the back, eyes wide with terror. I must have scared him. Good. I don't remember the last time I was this afraid. He ought to be too. He doesn't look good, face pale and shadowed.

'I just got off the phone with Sylvia,' Booker says, his tone, somehow, firm and measured. 'Don't worry, I know nobody's seen Ellis.'

'No, I found his bike in the parking lot of the No-Names. He's in there.' I know I'm stumbling breathlessly over my words but I can't make myself stop. 'We have to go and find him.'

'Mona – argh, shit,' he says, and kneads his brow. 'What in the hell is he doing in there?'

'I don't know. We had an argument, about Roxy, about everything, and he said he wanted to look for himself, and – I don't know what could have happened. Anything could have happened. He wouldn't stay out there that long unless he was hurt or worse. He gets nervous, he would've turned back. He –'

'All right, relax, I –'

'What? *What?* We need to go *now*! He's in there for sure. I know for a fact he's –'

'Kid, I believe you, and you bet your ass I'm gonna be the first one out there looking for him, but this entire island is Category A,' he says, voice raised now. He settles, blinking, in what seems like some silent apology. I understand. I want to scream too. 'Everyone's gearing up to evacuate. We need to get a party together, we – damn it! Why did he have to pick *now*?' Booker mumbles something into his walkie-talkie.

He asks if Sylvia knows.

'Not that he's in the woods.' How am I even speaking? I can feel my mouth moving and my vocal cords flexing but I don't feel I am compelling any of these things to happen.

'Shit,' Booker says quietly, and frowns. 'Well, I'm stayin' either way.'

I'm silent, my gut twisting at the thought of Ellis lost and alone, hurt and scared, convinced he'll never find his way back out. 'Through the hurricane?'

He shrugs as though the answer's obvious. I have to go with him. I have to go in. But the woods – I don't want to go into the woods. I don't want to go into the . . .

Mary Anne. I need to talk to her.

I give Booker my phone number and ask him to please call me, let me know when they're going to start searching. Booker nods sadly and puts a hand on my shoulder. 'It's all right,' he says. 'It's gonna be OK. We'll get him, we'll get him.'

I have to believe him if I'm going to find the energy to will my body through the door of the police station and straight to The Island Spot.

The diner is empty and vaguely apocalyptic. No usual passers-by or joggers. The glass on the outside reflects the churning yellow of the sky. Round the back, there's still the police tape from my antics, bits of window still scattered on the ground. Something about it makes me feel powerful in a way I haven't before.

I try the front door, which is unlocked, and I am blasted with air conditioning. Mary Anne's there, as I expect, leaning on the bar counter in a defeated sort of way.

I don't know where Archie is.

If she's surprised to see me, she doesn't show it. 'Haven't had enough of me yet?' She sounds older, somehow. Tired.

'If you know where Ellis is,' I say, 'you need to tell me.'

She blinks.

'I'm begging you. I know you don't want to talk about any of this and obviously you have your reasons, but –'

'*Listen*,' she says, with a venom like the day she'd confronted me about my investigations. But this seems different: heavier, I realize, with the weight of real death. 'I'd give my life for that kid. You think you're so smart, picking apart everyone's lives, but if you think I could *ever* lay a hand on Sylvia, on Ellis . . .' She chokes. There's another name she'd wanted to list but she'd stopped herself. 'Then whichever devil you belong to should have sent a better detective.'

On Roxy? I believe her. Her eyes are wet with tears and she's trying not to let me see. She strikes me as a terrible liar so I say what I'd realized in the police station. 'You're Baby Blue.'

Mary Anne says nothing.

'Do you know about the letters? Did you ever see them? She wrote all of them for you.'

A tear leaps from her cheek and bursts against the counter.

I piece it together as I speak. 'You were supposed to go with her to Nashville. Right? And that's what the argument was about. She changed her mind. Or you didn't want to go.'

Her mouth twitches. 'She was so *hurt*,' is all she manages at first. 'Sylvia didn't come from Roxy's indiscretion. That's what they all thought . . .'

'What do you –'

'Peak of your life, everything about to begin, and a stranger rips it all from you for no reason. The pain she . . .'

Silence. 'Does Sylvia know?'

The welling tears burst now, and Mary Anne, taller than me, looks so small and breakable. 'Why'd she wanna know a thing like that?'

'I'm sorry. Why do any of this?' I ask. 'Why leave the notes? Why grab Archie's gun?' She's stopped functioning and this is the final question I can think to ask, and I do, barely feeling my lips move, almost a growl. 'Where is she?'

Time seems to halt for a moment. 'Ellis will be fine,' she says.

Behind us, the door opens accompanied by a chime. I whip round.

It's my dad.

I'm locked on him for a moment but, no, he's ruined everything, and I turn back to Mary Anne. 'What did Roxy say to you? That caused the row the night before she disappeared?'

Mary Anne knows our conversation is over and I swear the corners of her lips turn up with the answer. 'She loved me.'

Hands grip me from behind and I know it's Dad, and I want to keep looking at Mary Anne, can't stand the thought of the moment falling apart, but Dad forces me round and into his chest into the least-wanted hug of my life. And when I turn back, Mary Anne's gone, locked in her office.

Dad pulls me into him, not a hug so much as the preliminary hold of a kidnapping. 'Mona,' he says.

'My friend's missing.'

'What?'

'My friend Ellis is missing. He went into the woods.'

'Well, they better find him.' And I realize now that I am not my father. I don't have to be my sister. I don't have to be any of it.

I need to stay for Ellis. But God, I don't want to go back into the woods.

Dad looks me up and down, seemingly registering my exhaustion. My only other blood. The only one I've taken everything from.

'They're evacuating the entire island,' Dad says, 'and the next boat is in an hour. I'll take you back to the dorm to pack – quickly – and then we're out of here. I booked a hotel for the night; I think we can probably make it to Erie –'

'I think I have to stay.'

Dad raises his eyebrows. 'What?'

'I have to stay.'

'What does that mean?'

I don't speak. Where is my voice?

'I'll pack for you, then. Give me your keys.'

I think of what Lenore had said about Roxy, that even though she'd wanted nothing more than to leave, she was plagued, always, by the feeling of being inexorably bound to her circumstances, to her blood. How in public she was a spitfire but behind closed doors, at the will of her mother, only a girl.

And this I think is why, despite knowing what is right with every fibre of my being, even after everything, I drop the keys, gently, into my dad's outstretched hand. Good daughter.

There's a frenzy at the dorms, everyone with the same idea.

I almost hope Peyton is in the room but she's not. Dad and I don't speak. I don't like him being here. For the obvious reasons – I don't appreciate what he's here to do – but I don't like his shape in a space I'd resolved to make my own. He looks completely out of place, made of different stuff from what I thought I'd accomplished here.

Outside, the sky grows increasingly alien and volatile, ready to burst.

So much has changed. My podcast equipment is gone. Packing takes all of two seconds, the most laborious task involving balling up the first bag into the other. There's barely anything left.

Word gets around – they're putting together a search party for Ellis, and I can't be a part of it.

I'm struck by the unfairness. How could this be the way it ends? Not just the situation, but I'm rattled by a sort of cosmic lack of justice, of how I got every answer I came to find and still feel like I've achieved nothing at all.

Dad left his car on the mainland so we both get into mine.

It's not me who holds the wheel, who puts my foot on the gas, who points myself in the direction of my own failure. It can't be.

I didn't even see Peyton to say goodbye. Didn't get to explain to Booker.

But still, we board the ferry, the line of cars waiting to evacuate the island feeling like a funeral procession. The sea is angry. It's rocking in an ominous sort of way, waves unfamiliar, too high and too aggressive. Soon nothing will be able to cross it. Not me. Not Ellis.

'I can't believe any of this,' Dad says.

No. Me neither. The sky churns grey.

We sit in silence and soon the ferry pulls away from the dock.

There's a terrible weight in my stomach. Infinitely heavy. A black hole. It's not exhaustion. It's guilt. Utter failure.

An overwhelming sense that I'm no longer where I ought to be. I don't feel very much like Mona right now. I don't feel like anything at all.

I've made a terrible mistake.

I'm thinking of Celeste, who I hate more than anything, who made me the person I am, small and terrible. I'm thinking of the mom I didn't have. I'm thinking of Sylvia.

Dad, with only one daughter left to lose.

I am logical and I know there may be no one on this Earth I can trust. I know the woods are fourteen square miles and I am small and that if Ellis is out there, the odds I will find him myself are infinitesimal. According to Peyton, I've never done anything for another human being that didn't benefit me.

I know I'm afraid of heights, for some reason.

And yet it doesn't stop me from flinging open my car door, sprinting to the edge of the ferry, and leaping overboard.

Dad's voice is the loudest behind me, maybe *No!* or *Stop!* or my name, but it doesn't really matter, because by now I'm flying through the air, and I am not Mona when I'm flying through the air for an impossibly long moment. I might be Mona when I hit the arching fronds of the ocean, the stinging contact, the cold, the sinking, the being whipped underneath and held there that threatens this choice to be the last choice I ever make. Maybe nothing tells one who one is like the threat of imminent death, of the girl you stand to lose, and if that's true, then I'm a cougher, I'm a thrasher, I'm a not-yet-spent thing.

Float, I realize. Float, like Ellis taught you.

I'm underwater for what feels like too long, the cold seeping into my very sinews and heaving me further into the dark. But I push and push and then my mouth is up and out, searching for life, for a tomorrow where everyone is home and warm and safe and none of this sick shit ever happened to any of us: that's what the first gulp of air tastes like. The salt slashes my throat but now I've at least got air and, flexing my shoulders, I'm moving against the angry rhythm of the waves towards the pier. I am intentional. I gag and cough a little and then I settle, moving in time, finally, with the ocean, with the brine. I'm breathing. That's all there is. Breathe. But I can't stay in here for long, I realize, or else I'll lock up.

I twist my head to the ferry, moving further away with every oceanic lick. Dad leans over the railing, is making a commotion behind me, but as far as I can tell, nobody chases. The boat doesn't turn round. Of course it doesn't. It can't. There's no time.

There's a hurricane coming.

Nothing can stop me now.

Ellis is something special and I have never been so sure of anything in my life.

I don't care about Roxy any more. I'm throwing away everything, all my notes, everything I came here for. No Celeste. Nothing else matters now. I have to make this right.

I'm going to find my Ellis.

CHAPTER 33

I haul myself up on to solid land, every muscle-bearing part of my body bubbling with snappy adrenaline. Thrill of the chase, maybe, except I'm not sure who is chasing who. I slosh down the street but everything is heavy and wet, even the sky, so I don't get the immediate relief of air on skin. Humidity settles on top of saltwater. This is when I understand a body does have limits because I collapse, stumble down on to my knees, taking long, unsatisfying breaths. My field of vision trembles, littered with stars. Can't move. Can't believe I did that. The ferry is far enough away now that I can't make out anyone on it but I'm sure they're all looking in this direction.

I remember my phone in my pocket and finger around for it; it's busted, obviously, so I rear it behind my head and chuck it into the ocean, and it's swallowed the way I imagine Roxy's guitar was too.

Everyone, I realize, is staring at me, including Peyton, who abandons her suitcase and Liam and place in line for the next ferry and moves to me like a moth to light. I just stand there, palms exposed, like I'm offering myself to her, water cascading from my clothes. I smush a wet tendril of hair from my face and smirk despite myself.

Peyton does too, finally. Rushes beneath the barriers, runs to me and wraps me up close, even though I'm soaking, and my shape imprints itself on to her.

'Did you – did you see –'

Peyton shrieks into my shoulder. 'Yeah, everyone saw, you attention-seeking piece of shit.'

'I'm sorry,' I say.

She grins again, looks like she's about to cry. 'Did you nearly drown and have an epiphany?'

'Yeah. Yeah, I think that might have been it.'

'Well, I'm glad you lived to tell the tale. Otherwise you just would've died a jerk.'

'I shouldn't have done any of this. At least I should have been more gentle. I've been selfish. I hurt you. And Ellis. He's there because of me, I . . .'

Her gaze travels over my body and there's nowhere to hide. She's stiff, arms crossed over her chest; although she's relieved that I'm here and still breathing, she's still upset with me. I don't blame her, given what's happened. 'What are you going to do?' she asks finally, sniffling a bit. 'We wanted to help with the search, so many of us – you should have seen. I was about to lose my mind, but they're making all the Seasonals evacuate – legal shit, I don't know – but it was *cops* and I didn't know what else to do.'

I step back, look up the hill to the north, towards the isthmus, then back at the crowd waiting for the next ferry, a sort of manic disbelief zapping through them. 'I mean, what are they gonna do if we go now?' I say. 'Not let us look for him?'

Peyton turns back. 'Liam,' she calls, 'I'm going with her.'

Liam recoils. 'Well, what? You think you're gonna go be heroes without me?'

A few more Seasonals join our quest and then we're a small, strange army, eight or nine or us, and I'm leading the pack, leaving a trail of saltwater like a slug. I recognize Liam's room-mate, the kid from the Indigo, the butterfly house girl from the first night. No, not a real army. But more legs. More eyes. Anything.

There's so much water clinging to my clothes that I feel like I'm carrying around an extra one of me. The place is deserted and it's creeping me out. The sky is still the wrong sort of colour, and the beam from the lighthouse seems not to cut through but to haze over it, everything yellow and glowing.

We make it to the woods in about fifteen minutes. I'm still sopping wet by the time I find the cluster of police cars at the entrance of the No-Names, most of them mainland police, surrounded by the community. I spot Lenore, Mary Anne, the woman from the florist's; on the whole, a disturbing lack of faces.

Of course. Who's going to look for the cursed boy in a hurricane?

Well, us, that's who. The good guys. I try to tame my anger.

Booker notices me first and looks at me like I'm an idiot or a gift and I can't decide which; maybe it's neither. Takes us all in. 'Christ,' he says. Everyone already there is looking at us now. 'Well, you're here, I guess. Can someone get her a change of clothes, please?'

The single female officer mercifully has a clean T-shirt and shorts in her trunk. I hang the sopping remnants on a branch. My shoes, unable to be replaced now, are still soaking and horribly uncomfortable; the skin in between my toes is pinching.

'Sylvia and I want to thank you guys for staying around. We don't have a lot of time,' Booker says. 'Barely any. In two hours the water will be too choppy to boat out of here and they're saying – they're saying the whole island's gonna flood. Southern half, anyway, around the coast, which is us. We need to make sure everyone is out and safe by then. Including Ellis. But do *not* put yourself in any danger, because then we'll be out there looking for you too. If the rain picks up, if visibility's poor, if you've just got a bad feeling for any reason, then come back to base, out in the open, where people can find you. I'll give you all markers – they're bright pink and reflective and should still be visible while we're in there. Tie 'em to the trees as you go. This is very important so please listen: if for any reason you become separated or disorientated, do not move. Hug a tree, sit there and scream as loudly as you can for as long as you can stand. We'll find you and get you out. It can get confusing in there.'

Before this, the primary goal was to get off the boat and find Ellis. Now I'm reminded that in order to find him I do actually have to go back into the woods – and I'm sick with worry.

'Here're the markers. Everyone gets a flashlight.'

'He can't have gone far,' Sylvia tells us. 'He's probably barely in there and we can go in and pluck him out. How far could he have got? Really? Unless he was, you know, *sprinting*, unless –'

'We're gonna find your boy,' Booker says, and then we're in. 'Be *loud*. Lots of noise. Sound'll travel further than our lights will.' And as if to show us how to yell, he does, and it sounds like thunder. 'Ellis!'

This sets off a chorus like cicadas and Ellis's name is on all of their lips except mine.

The trees loom ahead of me.

It's only half-dark and I can already feel my eyes falling for tricks. My hands are filmed in sweat, my chest scraping my skin seemingly from the inside like barbed wire. I can't breathe through it. Breaths are sharp and unsatisfying.

Booker turns and sees me, doesn't understand, but knows enough to realize I'm unwell. 'You stick with me.'

I know my face isn't showing it but, even after everything I've learned, something about Booker makes me feel safe. I nod.

He stiffens resolutely and screams out, '*Ellis, Ellis!*' Frantic and gut-wrenching – I don't know how his throat isn't bleeding, that's how hard and long and loud the sound strangles out of him. We know Ellis is here somewhere. He has to be. *Ellis, Ellis, Ellis.* Booker and I press on but I'm not even noticing him wrap the tags round the trees; so as far as I know we're lost.

A black dot of fear blooms in the middle of my chest.

We're lost.

Celeste, fumbling through the dark –

Mona, why'd you leave me out here?

'We're lost,' I think I say.

'Kid, we're not lost, don't be –'

Tell and you die.

I think I might puke.

Black oozes from behind my eyes and I don't even see it happen, the spray and bile. When I'm finished, I know it's mostly seawater by the way it stings my gums and hollows out my nose. Booker's hand on my back. 'We gotta get back to base, kid,' he says.

'*No.*' I stand up straight and wipe my mouth with my bare forearm. 'I'm staying.'

He grips my shoulders hard. 'We're gonna find him,' he says.

I want to believe him.

A beat. We walk maybe twenty steps. 'I talked to Mary Anne,' I say.

'That's right. You went running. I saw; you figured something out.'

'She loved her.'

Booker stops. Turns and stares at me. 'Hm?'

'That's what Roxy told Mary Anne that upset her. It was that she loved her.'

Booker considers this. Chuckles to himself. 'Damn.'

'It's just weird that – weird that everyone I talked to said they couldn't stand each other.'

'Funny, isn't it?' he says. 'That sometimes love and hate look damned near the same.'

We go forward for about an hour without finding anything, saying little else beside his name, and then Booker's cradling his walkie-talkie. He speaks into it. 'Probably about two miles in, no dice; you guys got anything?'

The speaker crackles. A man's voice on the other side: 'Nothing.'

'Shit. How're we doing for time?'

'You gotta get back.'

'What, now?'

'This storm is moving in like all hell. Too fast.

'Shit, Chuck,' he says, then hovers his mouth round the receiver, hesitating. 'I've got the kid with me.'

'Get back here.'

'She's fine. She's keeping up.'

'You gotta turn round.'

'Copy. Over.'

Booker looks at me and I realize now what's happening. *We're leaving him.* We're leaving Ellis. He's gonna die. 'No,' I mutter again.

'We gotta go, kid,' and it might be tears in his eyes, it might be the moisture in the air. Doesn't matter. He's telling me to go and of course I want to, but obviously I can't.

'He's gonna die.'

'I've gotta get you home.'

'I'll stay. I'm gonna stay with you.'

'No. Nobody's staying. Not you, not me.'

'He's gonna die! He's gonna die and it's my fucking fault, but it's a little bit yours too!'

Booker tries to wrap me up in big bear arms but I'm running on rage and that's always been fuel I know how to use. One of his hands is too close to my neck and I dig my teeth into it until I taste pennies and run.

Run. One leg in front of the other. My body is a machine and I run on rainwater and everything that's ever hurt me and there is enough of that to run to the other side of this island and back. A root almost trips me up and I stumble but keep on pressing forward. Rain splashes into my eyes. Howling in my ears. Can't see. Running. Black. Rain. My shoulder scrapes against the rough bark of a tree. I've still got my flashlight and I'm shining it but the field of vision is too small and I can't breathe so I stop and back up against a dip in a hill.

Ellis's name becomes mine.

'*Mona!*' Booker screams and it almost hurts. Almost. It doesn't hurt quite as much as the thought of Ellis dying all alone out here. He screams it again and again and again, and once he screams it almost right beside me because he doesn't know I'm here, because if I can't see three feet to either side of me in these woods then neither can he. The trees are too close together and now it's almost dark and he won't find me. I hear him move and again, from maybe twenty feet to my left, he speaks into the walkie-talkie, out of breath and fragmented. 'Ah, uh, I, uh, lost her. I lost the girl.'

'What do you mean?'

'She didn't want to leave Ellis, ran off deeper in; I can't find her anywhere.'

'Christ. Her choice, Booker. Add another casualty if you want but this can't wait for you.'

'I know.' I don't think he's holding the speak button when he curses into the trees so strongly it's loud even over the rain. His voice is broken when he swears into the radio. But he doesn't move. He's not finished. 'Mona, can you hear me? Mona! If you can hear me . . . Christ. I'm sorry, kid. If I had known any of this was gonna happen I would have rotted in jail to keep you kids safe. I never wanted to hurt anybody. And this is what I deserve, I guess. People can hurt you, no problem, and you can take it – or at least I can. I've always been able to. That's not really what hurts somebody, is it? It's knowing that you're responsible for hurting folk that don't deserve it. Or people you care about. And I do care about Ellis. And damn, do you remind me of her. Roxy. And I cared about her too. And there're things about this that feel the same but, oh God, this is worse.

'Please, kid,' he says miserably, 'you gotta come out. It can't be both of you, and you tried. Hell, Mona, you flew off the goddamn ferry to save your friend. You tried. I can't have another one of you slip right through.'

He can.

I don't move.

'Please. No one's gonna come back, kid. I leave and that's it.'

And then it's just us and the blackening sky and the rain, which covers all of me now and patters in my ears. No. This is not the time for me to leave. I don't know what's left for me out there if I go. Another failed venture. A world which has suffered more than it needed to because of my being in it. A world made worse because of me.

'*Mona!*'

A flock of birds, demented, scramble from a tree.

Fifteen slow seconds pass. I count them.

'God,' Booker says. 'Oh God.' I hear the walkie-talkie sizzle back to life. 'Chuck, I'm staying.'

The other end protests – *No, wait, what do you* – and then the walkie-talkie's off.

'Mona, if you ain't coming back, then go to the north end.' My ears perk up. 'Go *north*, Mona. Up the incline. Can you hear me?' North? What does that mean? 'And take these.' I hear something hit the ground, then the sound of his feet sliding against grit, which grows fainter and fainter until he's gone.

And now I'm alone.

CHAPTER 34

I don't know how long I sit, motionless, in the crook of the tree.

As I've moved through life I've become aware of an invisible tether, a cord which fastens one to everyone else, of everyone who has lived and will live and lives. Even when alone I can sense it, the unobserved ticking of the world; a car whooshing past outside, the memory of a conversation I had that day, the news playing faintly from downstairs. Out here, as nothing more than a pest clinging to the body of the No-Names, I'm certain that has been severed. I have never felt so utterly alone, so inconsequential, so like something biological and forgotten.

I think, fleetingly, about my woods theory and hate myself for daring to entertain such a strictly evil hypothesis.

The rain picks up. It is somehow darker than it was before.

And then there's a voice in the dark.

'Mona?'

A voice. Not mine. Not Booker's. 'Ellis?' I ask, spine straightened. 'Where are you?'

But the voice doesn't come again, and a terrible second lurches past where I realize what I've done in letting Booker go away. My chest seizes. My heartbeat rattles my bones.

Why would Booker tell me to go north?

I'm alone. The storm is approaching quickly. All I have is my flashlight, which is nothing, because the beam barely tracks a metre's diameter. I stand slowly and keep my gaze tracked on the ground for any hint of differentiation, some demarcation in the uninterrupted browns and greens, leaves and dirt and moss. The forest floor isn't remotely even – it's a series of steps and ledges and depressions. Difficult even to take two paces in a straight line without needing to adjust my footing, either to avoid a low-hanging branch or roots. I don't even remember where I've come from. I couldn't guess which way Booker went.

I remember that he dropped something. For a panicked second I can't find whatever it was but the plastic reflects the tiny bit of light I still have: he's left his tree ties, and his cellphone.

I pocket them both, then move in the direction I suppose is forward, tying the trees as I go.

How could Ellis have thought I was making all this up? He could have just talked to Booker. He didn't need to come into the woods, not angry, not at night, not with a hurricane approaching. And why wouldn't he have marked his path?

But this is my fault more than anyone's, of course. I was the one who lied to him in the first place.

I know that if I hadn't lied we'd have never found the truth – but knowing it now, I'm still not satisfied, the sensation of the bite but no chew, and Ellis might die for it.

And my whole body's set alight. *No, no, no.* Ellis is not gonna die.

I press forward, my breathing heavy, raindrops sinking on to my tongue from the corners of my parted mouth.

I walk. I'm soaked now for the second time today, through to my bones. I can't believe I miss the heat of the last two weeks, the glare of the sun, the trickle of sweat down my breastbone. I walk. My calves scream, the incline unrelenting. My back aches. I want to curl myself around a tree to stretch my throbbing muscles, but I need to keep going. I walk. There's an enormous difference, I'm learning, between almost pitch-black and pitch-black. I have no peripheral vision, no concept of shapes; I can see nothing more than what's revealed within the glow of my flashlight.

I walk. I'm afraid.

God, I'm afraid. When I cast the spotlight on the thought for any moment too long my whole body revolts so I shove it away. Instead of my utter aloneness there is the crunch of my feet against the ground and how the ground feels solid and how my body is a machine and how I could do this forever. Not what's lurking outside my flashlight's glow. Not what unfeeling torrent has opened above me.

My throat is hoarse from calling his name but this doesn't stop me from calling anyway. I count steps. Five and then 'Ellis!' then ten and 'Ellis!' but I can't even hear myself, and I'm not sure if it's because of the ferocious wail of the storm or I've run out of sound. Branches rear back like whips.

I can barely see.

I found the truth, most of the truth, but Booker was right. What do I even plan to do with it? Everyone else was right. Peyton was right – it's a truth but a bitter and pointless one. My dad was right – I should never have come out here in the first place.

Celeste was right – I'm a worthless piece of shit.

A voice.

'Mona.'

I stop. The trees are looking at me.

'Mona.' Their leaves are all eyes; oh my God, there's a million fucking eyes staring at me in the rain! I can see them blinking at me in the dark and I can't –

'*Come on, Moaning Myrtle. I wanna see what's over the edge . . .*'

'*Please don't . . .*'

There's something moving on my skin.

What is it? Don't know. But there's one and then a million and my whole body is crawling. The forest functions in billions. I'm six in the woods with piss on my shoes and blood on my palms. Celeste. Celeste. Why is Celeste talking to me? Not now, not now –

'*Moaning Myrtle,*' she said. '*Guess what?*'

'*What?*' I look down at small hands. Child's hands.

'*Daddy's busy. I'm gonna take you out hiking.*'

'*Celeste, please.*'

'What's the matter?'

'In the woods? Please, I don't want to go to the woods –'

'Yes. Lots of wood.'

'Please, Celeste. I don't want to go.'

Two go in. One comes out.

I'm back and I'm seventeen and somehow the beam from my flashlight is smaller than it was before. Or is the light just dimmer? Doesn't matter. Can't see. Can't hear. The roar of the rain and the trees and the ocean is unbearable.

Then a scream.

'Mona!'

I whip my shoulders round so fast they jerk from their sockets and the rain is so heavy on my back that I can't even stand up straight and it makes my temples ache but I need to get out so I run.

I run. I can't see. My arms are stretched out in front of me as far as they go and I'm crashing through what's breakable and it feels like there are fingernails or claws or knives from everywhere and soon the flashlight is battered out of my hands.

I stop, don't move a muscle, try to slow my breathing, but the rain is so damn loud that just the noise of it is startling. Fine, here I am, disgusting and punished – I can solve a mystery but I still can't even tell anyone the truth about –

My flashlight's gone. I have no idea in what direction I've run.

I go back towards where I think I came from and there's something oddly shaped moving around, battered by the rain – it's a tag. But it's on the ground, not attached to anything, and a gust of wind sends it careening across the forest floor.

If I hadn't already resigned myself to my fate, this is the moment that I do.

I carry on walking, numb now.

'Ellis.'

I walk.

'Ellis.'

My voice is so quiet he wouldn't be able to hear it if he'd been two feet in front of me, without the thundering rain.

Nothing.

I'm shivering.

I didn't know a person could be this cold and still live.

My feet, pressed against the wet of my shoes, feel like they've been shredded to ribbons, a red siren blaring with each step. I think of trench foot, of the images from history class of the skin of soldiers' feet purple and sloughed. With the adrenaline faded now, here's everything: the terrible weakness of my skin. The glitch of my brain.

The rain doesn't let up. I manage to find a denser patch where the rain isn't quite so severe and I lay my head against the bark of a tree and I sense the passage of time but nothing specific about it. But after a moment or minute or a hour, through the static: the sound of water. Ocean. Waves. Oh God, maybe I walked straight towards the island's perimeter, and if I can get myself to the edge then I can at least get my bearings, stick to the edges and find my way round – but I don't know where the waves are calling from.

The tree.

There's a cluster of branches towards the bottom of the trunk and I haul myself up with the last ounce of strength I have, my arms wobbling against the strain and quivering in the cold. One cluster. Pull myself to my feet and then there's another. I look above me – there's probably another fifteen feet, and beyond that, perceptible through the tessellated branches, is the sky, and God, I wish – I *wish* I could see stars, wouldn't that be something. Then a little higher, there they are. I can see the stars now, poking through the shapes made by the trees, and I'm human again.

Suddenly there's a blinding flash of light. A deafening boom.

Below me, a snap.

Then the fall.

I land on my right arm and scream.

The pain is repulsive, shoots up hard and fast around my jaw and makes my eyes water. Atoms split. My body and I reach a new understanding – if I survive this, I will be indebted to it and never complain about anything again.

I run my fingers up and down my arm, find the tender spot where there's a convexity that wasn't there before, and prod it experimentally; the pain itself seems to cry out. Truth seems awfully small from down here. I throw up on to the forest floor.

There's another crack. The tree in front of me. The leaves shudder, heavy with rain.

A terrible groan.

I try to hurry away, jerk to my left, but there's no friction and my feet are sliding against the forest bed and the tree falls.

For a hellish moment I think my foot is stuck, but I'm able to dig my white-hot heel into the softness of the ground, dig and yank, and the tree doesn't fall on me but the branches claw and dig into the soft skin of my cheeks, and now I'm certain my ankle's trashed too, but I attempt to stand and it supports my weight.

I have to keep going. I spread myself out like an explosion and howl. Every direction. I'm not Mona. I'm a feeling. I'm a black hole. I'm this whole island. I'm the ocean. I'm a liar. I'm a liar. I'm a liar.

Rain lashing my face and eyes and brain.

My arm throbs in time with my heartbeat.

The thought first quickens into my head – *I'm going to die out here*. I hear it so loud at first I think someone else has said it. Then, *I'm going to die* alone *out here. Ellis is going to die alone out here.*

What did Booker say?

North. He said north.

The rain eases off slightly, the edge of it dulled, the howl a whimper. I look up at the sky and that's cleared, too.

It's the eye, I realize. I'm smack in the middle, effectively its pupil. And it's so beautiful – really – I can't believe how beautiful it is out here. I throw my head back as if in prayer to the pinprick stars. And there it is. Orion.

Orion waves,
Orion waves . . .

The belt's right there, framed like a painting.

I move forward in its light for what feels like a long time. I don't think of anything besides warmth.

Soon the clouds are closing back in and the familiar howl of the wind re-emerges. I savour the last bit of moonlight, am clinging on to it for dear life, when I stumble upon a small cave tucked away in a groove in the undergrowth – and I can't believe my luck. I nestle myself into a slimy nook a few paces inside and curl myself into a small, pathetic ball, the wrath of my delirious trembling now seismic.

I swear I hear music. No, unreality, I recognize it. It's in my head.

It's 'Glass Daughter'.

I'm shivering like a blade of grass.

The music disappears as quickly as it had arrived.

The peace is so momentary. I watch as the rain picks up again, and after a moment my sluggish brain realizes what's happening – there's water running into the cave.

I try to scramble upwards but everything hurts and I can't see properly, and my battered feet slip and I fall into a previously unseen crater in the rock. It's impossibly quick, the time it takes for the water to rise to my stomach, then my shoulders, and I can't swim out because the water is moving too fast *and I see her. Traipsing towards the summit.*

Go and take her out, Celeste. I've got work to do. I've got anything else to do.

It doesn't matter what Dad said. It just matters that he wasn't there and Celeste and I were.

She's ahead of me on the trail. Signs. Danger. Unclear paths. Red crosses. What's this park called? I'm eleven. Teeth sharp with braces. Sixth grade? Seventh? Doesn't matter. Moaning Myrtle. Little girl. Daddy's busy, Moaning Myrtle.

'Come here.'

Sky. Sky full of those wispy skeletal half-clouds, and I'm staring, and then suddenly it's hands, hands much bigger than mine, and they're pulling me over to the ravine.

'Celeste! Stop!'

'It'll be fun. I just want to find out what's over the edge, Myrtle.'

Water drips into my lungs and I guzzle it and choke, hands slipping against the slimy rock of the cave, anchoring me. Please, please –

I dig my heels in, sprays of dirt kicked over the edge into oblivion, but the trail's all debris and slippery and there's nothing to grip, nothing to hold. Grunt. Pull. She won't let go.

Celeste and I are at the ledge and my feet look for something, anything, solid ground, because below me is a cliff, impossibly deep. I'm too small. I'm too small to fight and she's got her hands on my shoulders and with the whole world stretched out below me I'm too scared to speak. I want nothing more than to claw or bite her, to taste her blood, but I can't twist round far enough.

'What are you gonna do, Myrtle? What if I dropped you? What would you do?'

I clench. The sky is immeasurable and the world is stretched out before me, yawning like a giant, and my feet find their grip on something sturdy and I wrench, pull, heave myself from her. I summon all of it, every hurt, every hollow of my skin that she both scooped and filled, scooped and filled; she made the girl who could do this, with enough anger to focus like a fire-hot poker and press hard.

'Get off me!' I scream.

There's the scrape of feet against hard undergrowth. An underwhelming scuffle.

no way out

'Fuck you, Celeste, get off me –'

no way out

'Get off me!'

And then she does.

The edge of the ravine crumbles and Celeste goes with it.

It takes forever, it seems, from the short moment where we had both realized she was going to fall, for her to finally slip over the edge.

So unextraordinary. Body limp and heavy crashing against the cliffs, blood spurting from her in bursts like swarms of red flies. She was probably dead after the first connection of bone and cliffside, but the hill was so steep and she just fell and fell and fell and fell until she was out of sight completely, down the merciless curve of the earth. There's her eternity.

She didn't even scream.

I lowered myself, calmly, to the ground.

Pure amnesia. Whatever part of my brain decided which memories should stick said this one would not, and I didn't even know what I sat there thinking of until the old couple, kind faces, found me two hours later.

My sister is gone. I think she left. I don't know my way back. I believed it. My sister is gone and I can't find her. I wasn't lying. I believed it.

The only thing left is her phone that she dropped, that teetered close to the ravine that I had tossed back on to the trail.

'Glass Daughter' twirls from it, quietly –

I realize that I'm drowning (so this is what it feels like).

They can't find her. They look and they look but there are no search parties down there, where she fell; too steep, too thick, too wooded. The rain would've washed away any footprints.

Can't find her.
Left her phone? Why would she leave her phone?
Can't find her.

I know where she is. She's still there.
I know where the fuck she is because I left her there.
my lungs are boiling
Booker says they left her there –
float float ellis taught me to float
Gasp. Gasp. No air just water in my throat and eyes,
and everything is black and Roxy is singing –

eyes stare
oh when a million eyes stare
who is the woman the sister the girl they see there
who is the face on display

not me not mine no no no. they don't see me, someone
else completely – a girl who has not done these things; a
girl who is smart and maybe distant but good, who wants
to create something instead of taking life, but
this whole time she's repenting for the worst thing she
ever did
she wants to be so good, so smart Dad will forget about
the whole thing, but
a liar can't trust anyone not even other liars
she can't let anyone close because if they stare straight
into her eyes

they'll know she's a murderer.

do you get to glance at heaven before the descent? because there it is

Heaven is Ellis and Peyton and me on the boardwalk with nothing better to do, young and alive and full of feeling and time, heaven is Ellis and me bobbing in the inky water, heaven is trust, is trusting the strangers for no good reason, trusting they'll love you, trusting when you open your mouth and your eyes wide like a reckoning that they'll see the black that blooms there but keep on loving you, despite what you carry, and you regret everything.

Clarity arrives, white and beating.

Who was Mary Anne sending messages to?

The woman at the docks, in the dark, sneaking through the dense of the trees. We saw her. Ellis and I. I'd thought it was Celeste.

I bet you want to shoot me, don't you?

The woods do have a name and it's Roxy Raines.

water lungs head smack pain pain pain pain! make it stop   crack

out

CHAPTER 35

My head swims in the dark.

Then, sunshine. Warm and buttery on my face.

The sensations start there. Pleasant heat. Then, air in my lungs. It's incredible. I take one breath to ground myself, then another for fun and then another to clear the black vignette that seems to seep even into my skull and not just the corners of my eyes.

The euphoria of breathing is short-lived; the pain, I remember. There's a knot of barbs tangled at the base of my throat and my mouth is sharp with blood. A crater on the inside of my cheek I can't stop running my tongue over. I try and clutch my right arm, not sure what I'm expecting to find in its place, but where I hope to touch flesh there's something solid; wood, held in place with fabric. Someone's tied a splint round my arm.

I can't get my bearings; my eyes are spinning in and out of focus. But I'm inside, I think. I *think* because I'm in a bed, in a room, but above me is sky – bright, pale blue. A hole has been smashed into the ceiling. It's a cabin, maybe;

small, just one room, a tiny kitchen covered in dark wood, a cot bed that I'm sitting in. One of the walls is loaded with radio equipment that looks like what I found in Mary Anne's office. The place smells like earth and rain and something metallic. I want to sit up and look around but just the thought of it makes my abdomen throb.

And then I remember – Celeste. Celeste. It was me. I knew it, I knew it all along, but I didn't –

A ray of sunlight forces its way through the hole in the ceiling and shines into my eyes; I manage to shield my face with my good arm. I sense movement nearby.

I crane my neck and will my eyes to focus. They land, finally, on the most wonderful thing I've ever seen.

Ellis. Ellis, as alive as the day I scared him out of his skin in the bike shed. Ellis, alive.

He's here, crouching down gently to meet me. 'Hey,' he says.

I try to speak but my throat just gurgles; when the sound finally does come out it's weak and broken. 'Ellis. You're OK.'

Alive, maybe, but he looks exhausted, dirty, with scrapes on his cheeks. He's in clothes I haven't seen before: a thick plaid work shirt and jeans that are baggy but too short. I can't read his face. He looks happy to see me but melancholic and afraid all at once, and I'm thinking I should stay on the defence, that something's not right.

'I am,' he says, smiling.

I hear a male voice nearby say *She's up*, but I can't turn to place it.

'I'm so glad you're OK,' I manage, and then I say it again and again and again. I want to tell him that I don't know what I would have done if he hadn't been.

'Booker says you jumped off the ferry,' he says, smiling a little.

'A girl's gotta do,' I say, so much weaker than I intend. 'I'm so sorry.'

'It's OK. I am too,' he says quietly. 'Mona, um . . . this is crazy. This is really crazy.'

'What is this? What's going on?'

'She's just – she's not how you think she's gonna be, OK?'

Someone else says my name and I hear the stomping of boots, and I feel someone kneel down beside me, and crane my neck, not even sure what I'm expecting, but it's Booker. I blink at him, unbelieving. 'Hey, kid,' he says, looking a state; there are splotches of mud across his cheeks, a croaky, exhausted barb to his voice. 'How do you feel?'

'Yeah. I don't know. Fine, I think.'

'Think you can sit?' he says, managing to prop a hand behind my back to haul me up. Then it's said so quickly that I can't be sure of it: 'Keep your nerve, I'll get us out of here.'

'What?' I say quietly, worried I've misheard him, but he doesn't repeat himself.

'Let's get you up, for now.' He does, and my insides light up with pain.

More footsteps from somewhere else – and they're approaching. And seeing the two of them, side by side, there's no way not to understand.

I was right. She's been here all along.

CHAPTER 36

Roxy Raines.

She's standing there beside Ellis as if it's the most usual thing in the world. Her blonde hair is peppered with grey and waterfalls around her shoulders down to nearly past her hips, thick roots disappearing into wispy, fog-like tendrils. She wears a sort of forest green hiker's jacket and sturdy brown trousers. She still looks how she did in the photos: her eyes bright and charged with knowing.

She was alive this whole time. Not just alive; she'd never left.

What do you say? I pray for someone to speak first so I don't have to.

The first question I pull from my delirious brain is a terrible one, but it's all I can think of. 'How long have you been here?' I could have figured this out for myself, but the answer was too ludicrous for me to believe it came from my own brain. I needed her to say it.

Booker moves beside me. 'Don't worry about that now.'

Roxy smiles.

'How did you – how are we all *here*?' I ask him.

'You took my phone. Didn't think you would but thank God you did. Tracked you to not even that far from here.'

'But you –' I meet Booker's eyes, searching. 'You knew about this place.'

He presses his lips together, casts his gaze downwards. 'I didn't. Not really.'

'Is this why you said to go north?'

He locks tired eyes with mine. 'Mary told me, kid.'

'*What?* Told you what?'

'About the place. Her.'

'When?'

'When she found out that Ellis was missing. Figured he'd end up here, gave me the coordinates. Couldn't believe it. Still can't believe it.'

Ellis sits down beside me, and it's a comfort, but not enough. I want to plead for any sort of answer or explanation. A bolt of fear ripples through me.

Booker fiddles with the wall of radios opposite us, turning the dials, the radios hissing and screaming in reply. 'Hello?' he says into a microphone. 'Anyone copy?'

Then I look at Roxy, propped on the couch, scrutinizing us in a way that seems detached and cold. She doesn't seem real. I get a closer look at her clothes – she's in a full survivalist outfit, thick and shapeless and army green. Despite this, she has a stoic, quiet sort of grace, straight-postured and poised.

But I so badly want to hear her say something. I want to scream, *Say something. Anything.*

'How do you feel?' Roxy says finally. She asks, but it's not really with concern; more the sort of observational question asked to a test subject. And I realize I've never heard her speak, but it's *that* voice. As young as the day she disappeared. Maybe with a new edge. Smirking slightly.

'Not dead.' My stomach flutters with nerves.

She nods to my arm. 'Bet that hurts like a bitch!' I notice now that her knee is rapidly bobbing up and down, enough strength in it that the floor is creaking loudly beneath her with each cycle.

I swallow the little moisture in my dry mouth. 'Not that much, weirdly.'

'I gave you something,' she says. 'For the pain.'

'Thank you.' I glance at Booker to try and understand if what she's just said ought to concern me, but he's busy with the radios. Beside me, Ellis is stiff as death.

Roxy pours herself a drink of something brown from a glass bottle that thuds when it hits the wooden table top. 'We've been chatting while you napped. Ellis says you're a *writer*.' She's speaking oddly – a strange, inhuman inflection, statements that sound like questions, the stress on unusual words.

I glance at Ellis. Her statement feels like an accusation. 'I . . . write about people who've gone missing.'

'A journalist?'

'Yes. Something like that.'

Roxy scoffs, then repeats, 'Something like that.' Mocking me in a pitiful little voice, high-pitched and whiny. '*Something like that.*'

I'm not prepared for how seemingly unhinged she is, and honestly, I'm not sure if I've recovered – or will ever recover – from my night in the woods. Suddenly I'm feeling out of my depth and very afraid. 'It's a . . . podcast. I don't mean to patronize you, but do you know what that –'

'Yes. Generally. A broadcast. Online. Right? Yes? Right?' She won't stop asking until I nod. 'How many people listen?' I notice now a twitch, intermittently jolting across the right side of her face.

'About fifty thousand.'

If she thinks this is a lot, like I expect her to, then she doesn't show it. Instead she acts like she doesn't even hear me, shuffling the items on the coffee table – her drink, a notepad, a walkie talkie – in front of us in a manic, territorial way, the scrape of it searing temples. When she's finished, all the items are sitting in the exact same position as when she'd begun. 'And you had planned to write about me.'

'Yes. I'm sure you can imagine . . . that people found your disappearance strange.'

'My imagination is fine, thank you. Does your programme have a title?'

'*How to Disappear.*'

She reels back, an ill-sounding hack of a laugh spewing from her. 'Gosh. A bit schlocky, isn't it? *How to Disappear*? Do you think these people who have gone missing *strategized* their departures?'

'You did.'

Roxy smiles at me, horribly.

Across the room, there's a crackly voice from one of the radios: 'Holy shit, that Booker?'

Booker breathes in sharply, then cackles like a madman. 'Yes! Hello! You copy?'

'Clear as fucking day. We gotta get you out of there.'

'I have the kids with me. Mona Perry and Ellis O'Hare. They're safe but pretty beat up – they're gonna need attention. Mona especially.'

I prickle. Everything does hurt, but maybe it's worse than I've even had the time to inspect.

'You all right?' the radio voice asks.

'I've never felt better, to tell you the truth.'

'Where in the hell are you?'

'I've got the coordinates.' He sends them by typing something into a panel, and I don't understand how any of it works, I'm just thrilled that it does.

I glance to Roxy, who is silent, shifting her gaze between Ellis and me. I feel sick.

'Christ, you're far north. Think we'd be able to get a chopper out there to you?'

'Wouldn't count on it. Boat'd be better.'

'All right, all right. Stay nearby. Could be out to you in thirty minutes. Conditions clear as day. Fucking miracle. But I gotta be honest, you get those kids ready and keep 'em close – it's a circus out here.'

Ellis and I share a glance.

'Copy. I owe you one. Over.'

Roxy looks at Booker, taking another sip of her drink. 'Really is a *pleasure* to see you again, Lee.'

Booker doesn't seem charmed. Not just that – he speaks to her like he's coaxing her into something, as though he's trying not to provoke a wild animal. 'What happened that night, Rox?' The tenderness of it, the familiarity, astonishes me. As if no time has passed. If I wasn't able to before, I can now, so clearly, imagine Booker as a young man, rowdy at the Indigo. 'Do you know what these kids have been through trying to find out? Hell and back.'

Roxy shifts on the couch, her aura darkening by the second. She slumps back and crosses her arms, almost pouting like a child. 'Oh. I see. That's all you care about, right?'

'Roxy – you destroyed us.' Booker links his fingers. 'All of us. Why did it have to happen like this? And what the hell are you doing here?'

'I don't want to write about you any more,' I pipe up, assuming that's why she isn't speaking. 'If that helps anything.'

Roxy's bemused again. 'Surely not because this is less interesting than you'd hoped?' she says, almost offended.

'No. The opposite. Obviously. But I realize now that it's not my story to tell. I think all of us . . .' I look at Ellis. I really see him now, close up; his face is covered in cuts, his eyes are red-rimmed, his hair's a mess. I think of him, soft, fleecy Ellis, going through what I did and want to cry. So I reach for his hand and link. Even if it meant never getting the answers, I'd happily trade being here for each of us at home in bed, even if that meant not getting the chance to speak to her. 'I think all of us just want to understand.'

Roxy looks around the place, fondly, sadly. It's really been battered by the storm. 'You are the only other living people ever to be here. Hm, isn't that something?'

'What is this place?' I ask.

Roxy settles in. Maybe she will start answering questions. 'If you wanna know, you have to understand Mary Anne. But you must already know some of it because she blabbed to Lee, and she wouldn't have done that unless –'

I'm growing impatient now. 'Please. For Ellis's sake. We just want to understand and go home.' I look at Booker as if to confirm whether or not we're actually in imminent danger.

He nods subtly. *Go ahead. Find out.*

'This,' Roxy gestures around us, 'was part of a plan. From the time we were teenagers, Mary Anne and I. I liked to hike, walk and walk and walk, and I came across this place, abandoned. Old hunting cabin, lousy with ammo cartridges. I decided I'd like to fix it up. And I did, on my own. Me and Mary waxed poetic about coming out here, the two of us. The original plan didn't include arriving and never going back, but that's sure as hell how it worked out for me. I'd spend a lot of time here writing, thinking, and when she was being civilized, we'd make contact through –'

'The radios,' I breathe.

'Yes.'

'That's why you needed money. Beforehand. Because you were fixing this place up.'

'Oh, you know *all* about me, don't you?' She takes another sip from her glass. 'Anyways, yes. Frank knew his stuff about ham radio at the time, so I sought a bit of guidance from him when I was, oh, maybe eighteen,' she says, tripping mischievously over the word 'guidance'. Roxy looks at her radio unit. 'No ping today.'

'From Mary Anne? There won't be. The entire island's been evacuated.'

Roxy laughs, loud and long, none of us sure why; it's long enough for Ellis to shift uncomfortably beside me. 'Always something to say, that one. *Baby Blue*, recently.' She taps her temple. 'That was the panic word.'

'And you don't respond,' I say, doing my best to keep the conversation directed.

'Except, of course, when I found out my mother had died. Of course that was a cause for celebration! And I asked her to forward a message.'

'Why would you do that to her?' Ellis asks, and we all know he's talking about Sylvia. It's a pointed and entirely brave question, given how volatile Roxy has shown herself to be. He's been so quiet and now he's *loud*. In fact, I've never heard his voice sound stronger – he must have been sitting there simmering this whole time. '*How could you?* Since she found out, she can't even hear your name without – and I was trying to prove that you wouldn't just leave. Or run away. *But that's exactly what you did.* And actually, you didn't even run away – you were basically here the whole time.'

Roxy is quiet for a moment. Blinks. 'Are you finished?'

'*Oh*,' Booker groans, 'come on, Roxy, he's –'

'In my home!' Roxy shouts, and the sentence is almost laughable – the cabin has no roof – but nobody is laughing.

A robin perches on the sharp of the wood, chirping. 'That's what! He's in my home and is a child who can't possibly understand, whose feelings I'm not interested in sparing.'

'Is this all because of Mary Anne?' I ask. 'Because she wouldn't come with you?'

She leans forward and, in a theatrical stage whisper, says, 'I was going to be *famous*,' the *famous* dripping with derision. 'Didn't you know? My agent was endlessly optimistic. He had heard about some charming girl off the mainland with a set of pipes and moxie and had travelled over just to hear me sing. He was charismatic enough, with all these highfalutin ideas about how he planned to change me and make me a star. He said I was going to sell a million records. He said I was going to be on TV.' She scoffs, a dark weight to it.

'And what happened?'

'I discovered my own lack of autonomy,' she says in a moment of off-putting, bleaching clarity. 'Which so happened, unfortunately, to coincide with Sylvia's existence.'

Ellis shifts beside me.

Roxy leans forward. 'There is not one scrap of good on this rock,' she says. 'None of it. None of it! No one cares about you, and everyone wants to use you, and everyone treats hurt like a thing that happens to *other* people instead of what will inevitably and invariably happen to *you you you you you*.' And with each *you* another sunbeam seems to sink in the space behind my eyes. I wince.

The sun beats down into the cabin.

Roxy takes another sip of her drink. 'I grew up understanding that Sandown Bay was hell on Earth. An ignorant bubble cut off from the rest of the world, full of regressive people who hide behind tradition. And Mary Anne wanted to leave too. She *said* she did, anyway. And when she went back on her word to stay with Archie, that was when I realized that you can't trust a goddamn person in this entire goddamn bullshit world. Even the ones you think you love. The ones you think love you.

'And once I'd come out here for good, the more and more I considered it, all these wonderful things I'd been promised, I realized that people are horrible everywhere. The entire world is full of Sandown Bays. I decided I didn't want any part of it.'

'Why not just disappear, then? Why the theatrics when Archie and Booker and Mary Anne followed you?'

'Indeed, extraordinary measures must be taken when one cannot keep to one's own fucking business,' she says. 'They'd seen me go in. I needed to give them a reason to think I wasn't going any further in but I sure as hell wasn't going back out, neither.'

Booker leans in. '*You wanna shoot me, don't you?* That's why. You told Mary to make it look like you'd been shot. That's been the question of my life, Rox. Bothered me for three decades. No idea why you said it. Why you said it to her.'

'I'd never loved her more than I did in that moment,' Roxy says quietly. 'How she knew *just* what I wanted,

355

without the words.' Roxy smiles to herself in a way I feel we're not supposed to see.

'Then you told her to leave the note in your car,' I say. 'To make it look like you ran away. Via the radios.'

'Mary was street-smart,' Roxy says, 'and from the sound of it seems like she can run a fine business, but couldn't wield the weapon of *language* to save her life. That woman gave a new meaning to sweet nothings, God, just *nothing nothing nothing*. I didn't think anyone would come looking for me, anyways. Turns out she writes *so* poorly that I might have been better off not asking her to do anything at all. People didn't like me. They knew how I was.' She pauses, turns to Booker. 'But blocking off the entirety of the goddamn woods was a helpful exploit of pure *cowardice* that I had not been expecting.'

'How do you survive out here?' Ellis asks.

'I once had a beautiful garden growing,' she says, floaty and exaggerated, like a damsel. 'Hunted. There's a ravine off to the side where I could get close to the sea and fish.'

It doesn't escape me that she's speaking in the past tense.

'Oh, and pemmican is beautiful stuff, you wouldn't believe. Need to develop a bit of a taste for it, but once you do you're golden. Anyway, I could get to the mainland in about thirty minutes in a dinghy. Stay there for a few days at a time.'

'You mean – you leave the island?'

'How else would I stock up on supplies? I've got another place on the mainland, friends who don't know nothing about nothing.'

'Then why stay here? It would be so easy to just go somewhere else. No one would know you. Maybe they would have when it first happened, but not any more. Why here?'

She leans in close to me, a sort of conspiratorial smirk stretching her lips, and it frightens me. 'Are you familiar with the term *schadenfreude*?'

Booker rolls his head. 'Oh, Jesus, Roxy.'

'Lee,' she says, 'do you remember the *fires*?'

I watch his mouth start to form the words – *What fires?* – but he shifts into a picture of realization.

I remember something Peyton had mentioned. The weekender cabins catching fire. Objects inside mysteriously moving and disappearing.

A ghost in the woods.

'That was you?' he says. 'I swear, everyone's felt under some curse . . .' Sandown's ghost.

Roxy speaks to Ellis and me again, almost pretending Booker isn't there to hear it, and despite everything, the attention is welcome. 'Fine, I'll play the part of Sandown's *wound*,' she says in a low growl, 'but I'll make damn sure it never heals.'

I think back to the woman watching me in the woods, who I thought I was imagining, who I thought was Celeste. That night at the police station, then while I was running in the morning –

'I saw you,' I say.

Roxy smiles at me, a horrible heavy smile. 'I hated every last one of them and it's an understatement to say it's been

357

an unencumbered joy to watch them rot.' She leans back on the sofa.

I think about what Lenore said: how it was the horror of Roxy's life, that she wanted nothing more than to leave but couldn't bring herself to.

'All people will do,' she says, her tone now unsettlingly sing-song, 'is disappoint you and hurt you.'

I'm conscious of Ellis beside me. She should be saying this to him. I've hurt him so thoroughly.

'The sooner you understand this,' she says, 'the better. The only damn person on this planet I can trust is myself. The only way to discover who you are is to be alone. I mean this. People don't *change* in solitude! They become who they're meant to be.'

And this? This is who you're meant to be?

'I'll be honest,' I say finally, trying to put the words together before I have to say them, 'we might have figured out what happened to you – but we had you all wrong. People said that you were angry, jaded, fought against everything that moved. And retrospectively, as someone who's been trying to find you, there's something almost . . . romantic about that. About a talented and enigmatic musician who writes about solitude and then goes missing.'

'Damn right there is.'

'I related to it. And I understood it, because there's a lot I don't like about people either. But now that I'm here looking at you and hearing you talk, I'm thinking, actually, it's just incredibly sad.'

She's silent. My blood runs cold.

358

'Is that really what you planned to do?' I ask. 'Torment everyone until you got bored, thinking that was some kind of purpose; then just lay down here and die?'

'Mmm. Till I heard about the storm,' she says. And it's with such a quiet calm, such submission, that I know what it really means – she'd thought it had come for her. To both serve her and claim her.

We're silent. Then finally Roxy says, 'Come with me. All of you,' and leaves the cabin through the open back door, and Ellis and Booker and I all exchange glances. Observing Booker, I realize, firstly, that he has his gun on him for the first time since I met him, and secondly, that his hand has been hovering just above it.

We're unsure what to do next.

'Stay near me,' Booker mumbles to us.

We follow. Outside is a disaster. Fallen trees, debris, leaves everywhere. I realize the cabin might once have had a deck but it's been smashed to pieces. A large section of roof is destroyed. Stray splinters of wood stick out in all directions. To my right, there's a levelled plot of land absolutely decimated by the storm, which might have been separated into even rows – what were once her farm plots, I assume.

We say nothing for the whole five minutes the walk takes, and I look up at the sky, and the clouds are finally moving further north.

Eventually, the trees part and the whole thing opens up and it's just ocean, cerulean and lapping, the jagged grey peaks of rock near the conclusion of the land bursting forth like fingers.

There's a relatively flat slope to the left, where a railing has been screwed into the ground; at the bottom of the slope, a dinghy, tied to a small dock.

'Why would I ever wanna leave?' Roxy says, a new, tranquil flatness to her tone. 'When I've found everything. No betrayal. No masking. No mistakes. I can go and find my mind on the mainland when I'm stir-crazy, then come straight back here. And I can watch the fires I set burning. All the way down to fucking embers.'

Roxy Raines turns, regards the three of us.

I lock eyes with her, and I think maybe we're sharing a moment of understanding – because I do understand. I understand because I thought the same thing. I understand because I've spent my whole life running from what I've done, and because of that I've never been able to connect with anyone; because of that I've hated everyone; and I thought that same thing, once. Hell, maybe that's why I *came* here – a desire to distance myself from everyone, pretending it was a way to connect, to help.

I can relate to the thought of keeping yourself from hurt. I understand that.

'And you're here to take it all away.'

And that is when Roxy moves towards the edge of the cliff like a bolt of lightning.

I don't know how I do it, but every cell in my body compels me to *leap*, to move, and that is what I do. Roxy tries to throw herself over the cliff edge but I get there first and pull her back. I don't know why I do it. My actions won't kill anyone else.

I can't breathe, I'm almost over the edge myself, I'm falling, I can't –

A shadow appears in the corner of my vision, rapidly approaching, and it's Ellis ploughing into us sideways with a rage I didn't know he had in him. I fall forward but the cliff is on an angle and I'm falling, I'm falling, I'm –

Ellis. Hot tears run down my face. He's got my good arm in his grip and I'm sure my shoulder is out because the pain goes all the way up to my jaw. My fingernails are bent backwards. I kick my feet in the nothing. I feel the drop. I feel it in every pore of my body, every rattling bone. I try to breathe, *Pull me up*, but there's nothing, and I'm looking straight at the sky, and I need to say – I need to tell you this – that I've never seen anything bluer in my life.

'D-d-d-don't look down,' Ellis says and grunts with exertion. Up, up, up, and then I'm scrambling up the side of the cliff like an animal until my belly is flat against the ground and my legs aren't hanging over the edge into the abyss.

Roxy's to our side in a heap. 'I didn't want anyone to come looking. I just wanted to be left the hell alone. It's all ruined. The storm's ruined it. You've ruined it. There's nothing for me here any more.'

Booker hovers over her, gripping her by the shoulders. 'Come back with us, Rox,' he says quietly. It's so intimate I don't even feel like I should be looking. 'Come back with us. You gotta. There's always still time.'

'Nothin' for me,' she says, then rises and without even giving us so much as a parting glance steals off back in the direction of the ruined cabin.

A slight and faraway whirring.

I worry the storm has come back to claim me, but as it gets closer and closer I know what it is: the boat.

'Thank ever-loving Christ,' Booker mutters.

It's a small four-seater speedboat zooming towards us. We start towards the shore.

'What are we going to do?' I ask Booker.

He knows what I'm talking about, gives one last forlorn look in the direction we've just come from, and says, 'I don't know, kid. Don't worry about that now.' Booker leans in, so I can hear him. 'Home. We'll get you home, first.' I don't know how to admit the place he's speaking of doesn't exist.

We traverse the treacherous path down from the top of the cliff face – I can't imagine Roxy doing this – and we're helped into the boat, my stomach tumbling with adrenaline.

Booker says something to the man piloting that I can't hear over the engine.

Once we're in, Ellis hands his phone to me.

'What's this?'

'When we were talking, I recorded all of it.'

I almost want to laugh. 'Ellis, no. I can't believe you did that – no. I'm finished with the podcast.'

'Honestly, I don't even care any more.'

'It's not mine to tell.'

Ellis looks at me.

'You're welcome to. But not me,' I say.

'You're gonna shut the whole thing down?'

'I don't know yet. Honestly, Ellis, something happened in the woods. I remembered. Something bad. From when I

362

was a little girl.' I look at him. 'I need to tell you about it once we're home.'

Ellis nods. I know he doesn't understand yet, but Ellis has confronted enough for now. For now we're safe.

Within moments, we've pulled away from Sandown's boundaries, far enough that the border of the woods stretches out in front of us, rolling past at impossible speed. I try to place where I might have been. I can't believe that was the whole world once. What I thought, choking on black water, would be the finale of my world. It's so seemingly navigable from out here. The grass is bright and silvery with rainwater.

I watch Ellis regard the rolling wood, then the horizon with a sort of wistful, rosy air about him, as though returning from a trip he'd always dreamed of taking. Booker is sat on the lip of the boat, supporting his face with his hand, kneading his brow so hard that thick veins pop on his arm.

I think about Peyton in our dorm, me going on and on about the woods, her sprawled out on her bed, all lovely and angry and parting the sea with her hands.

I'm not a forest, she says.

What are you then?

A big open sky.

CHAPTER 37

I have enough thoughts for a lifetime on the twenty-minute boat ride to the ferry dock on the mainland.

They're not yet characterized by calm reflection, but by manic ticking; my adrenaline, which somehow hasn't depleted totally over the past two feverish weeks, is still kicking its back legs at my chest. I think of Ellis, how his fears about Roxy were not just founded, but obscenely correct; of Roxy and the sheer improbability of her existence, of any of this; of my analysis at the beginning of my time on Sandown, a mystery that simply needed to be coaxed from the island; of Celeste, and what I've done.

I'm also thinking of that night Ellis and I had suspended in the black water, vulnerable little knots of life, wanting and ready to make anything ours.

Is that really what a life could be, after this? Could it always feel like cool black water?

No one speaks. Perhaps we are all too exhausted. Even the man driving the boat politely asks no questions.

On our eventual approach to the small crowd of people gathered beside the slipway, I feel an overwhelming sense of shrinking, as though they're not becoming human but we, too, are becoming ants.

Alongside the people there are official-looking vehicles, two ambulances, a van that reads ELEVEN EYEWITNESS NEWS. I don't understand why, at first, after we've been helped off the boat, they are so interested in Ellis and me, why they tug us away from one another with such speed. Someone drapes a blanket around my shoulders. Booker says something to a uniformed man I don't recognize, who then glances at me.

The succession of people that follows is unreal, somehow, and I don't know where to look. Mercifully Peyton shows up and just says, 'You got him, you got him,' over and over, and I let her, the moment perhaps more for her than me, and at first I'm not sure if this is the right time to tell her – but the face she makes when I finally say into her ear, low and urgent, 'We found her, alive,' confirms it was the right time. I don't think I'll ever see as complicated and wonderful an expression again, disbelief and horror and absolute exhilaration. *I was right, you idiot*, I want to tell her, but that can come later.

Dad, after delivering a panicked reprimand for my jumping off the ferry (which I've, up until now, entirely forgotten about) and an awkward acknowledgement of my myriad injuries that I think he intends to be paternal, says, ominously, that my friend and I are going to be busy. I ask why. 'Well, I think they found your show.'

Dad lets me borrow his phone.

ok, hear me out that Mona girl has to be CAP!!!

They said she was there working for the summer and that the kid is grandson of a musician who went missing . . . all lines up

That's Roxy fucking Raines!!! Holy shit could she be out there? Did CAP find her?

They might find her, but it won't be me who tells them where to look. Even if they knew exactly where she was, or traced the route from the boat, if I had to guess, there won't be anything to find for much longer. I think sadly of time, aware of its passing, seconds trickling down my back.

I look sadly to Dad, thinking of what I'm going to have to do. What are the words? There seems like there should be a different language for confessions. The impossible sun beats down, heavy and accusatory, trembling from a hundred million miles away.

I'm led inside to the covered area where people wait for the ferry and I'm helped down on to a bench. A paramedic shines a little torch into my eyes.

I glance upwards. In the corner of the room, a small mounted television plays the news; I recognize the station as the county's local. They're talking about Ellis and me.

A picture of the two of us flashes on the screen.

I remember this being taken, though I never saw the picture – Peyton took it, the night at the beach.

I lift myself slowly from the bench – I feel the paramedic reach for me – and move towards the static.

Ellis is grinning with his teeth. I'm smirking, lips are pursed tight, eyes directed slightly above the lens of the camera at Peyton. Above the two of us there's the neon glow of the boardwalk, blurry with movement. Just behind the lens, I know, is the ocean. I see her, now. With my stiff hand I run my fingers gently over my own palm, and that is the truth, and then over the notched skin on my lips, and that is the truth. There she is. My heart beats in my name's language, *mo-na, mo-na, mo-na.*

I recognize her so well that my body falls from under me as if it was never there at all.

ACKNOWLEDGEMENTS

Richard Pike, for taking such good care of me and the stories. Sara Jafari, an editor endlessly clever, attentive and encouraging. I can't explain what an honor it is to sit among Penguin's authors; never were there better hands. I'm grateful for contributions by the entire team, notably Stephanie Barrett's careful eye; Alice Todd's incredible cover design; and Alesha Bonser and Harriet Venn's advocacy. Holly Jackson. Bertie Gilbert. Holly Harris. Nathan Singleton. Kathy Zagar. It doesn't escape me how fortunate I am to be surrounded by so many creative and interesting people; stars, stars, stars. Always my parents, for whom my love is sometimes shy but unrelenting.

AUTHOR INTERVIEW

Did anything inspire the story of *The Things We Don't See*?

Generally, I like to start with a theme, a setting and at least the essence of a protagonist and their voice, then leave the rest to sort of unfold (or, more realistically, be pried open) within that framework. I knew I wanted to write about vulnerability, which eventually morphed into an amalgamation of truth and identity and the idea of moving on and remaking ourselves once we get to where we're going. I was also stuck on the idea of a teenage girl with the temperament of a hard-boiled detective, a bit of a nasty but ultimately well-meaning piece of work, willing to go to great and often dubious lengths for what she thinks she wants. Setting-wise, the Sandown in my mind borrows heavily from an island off Ohio's Lake Erie coast called Put-in-Bay; I spent a lot of summer days in my childhood there and always thought it'd be interesting to set a story in a similar sparsely populated visiting-place. That was the initial skeleton.

What is your writing process like? How does your novel-writing process differ from when you write your poetry?

Total anarchy. I outline then ignore the outline, add characters halfway through and often edit non-linearly. It's bad and I can't make it stop. I therefore need great stretches of time where I can focus solely on a book to get anything done. There's definitely a life-consuming element to writing a novel – for months it appears in the shower and on walks and in bed – but I tend to write poems in short bursts. Poetry to me is also a slightly freer intuition-and-aesthetic-based endeavour, while novels are more structure-reliant. Luckily they've each improved the other; I think writing poetry makes me more economical and deliberate in my novels, and writing novels makes me a better storyteller in my poems.

How did you find inhabiting Mona's point of view, and getting into the mind of an unreliable narrator?

Her original skin was easy to slip into given the fact we share a certain less-than-savoury mood involving misplaced cynicism towards most people and things (though Mona has her reasons and I just suck). And though I've not dealt with the same situations as her I did tap into events from adolescence that I feel have affected me in unwelcome ways in adulthood.

It was important to me that Mona be so-called 'unlikable' but engaging, laser-focused but still a girl and still uncertain. Her personhood feels out at sea to her, and she's insecure; it's unclear to her why she is how she is, how much of herself she hides, what she doesn't even realize she's carrying. All of her actions are informed by this discomfort, and a dislike of herself, and the secret that she's actually quite sensitive and terrified of being hurt, down to her finding an odd comfort in Peyton's playfully disparaging sense of humour and creating false versions of Celeste in her head. Fear tells us to turn the unforgiving story into something more bearable, and I liked the idea of the fear extending so far so as to affect both how she tells the story as a narrator and how she tells her own story to herself. I loved writing her.

Do you have a favourite character in this story, and if so who is it?

My very unexciting answer, for reasons above, is Mona, but there's at least a mote of me in all of them – I resonate deeply with Ellis's fear of being misunderstood, for example, and Peyton's occasionally misguided inclination to protect. And naturally I love Roxy. It was a lot of fun to play with a character whose physical absence for most of the story means she's more mythology than person, which forces everyone who once knew her to interact with her memory instead.

What books would you recommend for fans of *The Things We Don't See*?

We Were Liars by E. Lockhart; *A Good Girl's Guide to Murder* and its sequels by Holly Jackson; *Sadie* by Courtney Summers; *Burn Our Bodies Down* by Rory Power.

What would you like readers to take away from this story?

An impossible question! More than anything I just hope they're happy to have read it. If it facilitates within anyone an interrogation of their relationship to their own identity or loss or trauma, or how they view girls with classically 'unlovable' traits, then that is also cool.

Do you have any advice for aspiring authors?

I find it helpful to occasionally (not always, as this tends to be a magic-killer) read books as though I'm performing autopsies on them. Otherwise, don't rush, or underestimate the importance of seeking out new and interesting experiences, and don't take being an observer of the world lightly.

**If you loved *The Things We Don't See*,
try *Lock The Doors* by Vincent Ralph**

Tom's family have moved into a beautiful new house.
But there are strange messages written on the walls
and locks on the bedroom doors . . . on the outside.
Will their dream home become a nightmare?

If you loved *The Things We Don't See,*
check out Savannah Brown's first novel,
The Truth About Keeping Secrets

Sydney's dad is the only psychiatrist for miles around
in their small Ohio town. He is also unexpectedly dead.

Sydney believes the crash was anything but an accident.
And when the threatening texts begin, and June Copeland
– homecoming queen and golden child – appears at
his funeral out of nowhere, she's sure of it.

Soon it becomes clear that secrets can't go away, and the
truth might bring everything crashing down . . .

**'HEARTBREAKING, HILARIOUS, SCARY,
MYSTERIOUS, ENDEARING, PROVOKING AND TENSE.'**
Holly Jackson, author of *A Good Girl's Guide to Murder*